THE PIONEER

THE PIONEER

BRIDGET TYLER

An Imprint of HarperCollins Publishers

HarperTeen is an imprint of HarperCollins Publishers.

The Pioneer
Copyright © 2019 by Temple Hill Publishing LLC
All rights reserved. Printed in the United States of America.
No part of this book may be used or reproduced in any manner whatsoever without
written permission except in the case of brief quotations embodied in critical articles
and reviews. For information address HarperCollins Children's Books, a division of
HarperCollins Publishers, 195 Broadway, New York, NY 10007.
www.epicreads.com

ISBN 978-0-06-265806-7

Typography by Jenna Stempel-Lobell
19 20 21 22 23 PC/LSCH 10 9 8 7 6 5 4 3 2 1
❖
First Edition

For my parents, who taught me to build worlds

THE
PIONEER

PROLOGUE

My earliest memory is riding on my mother's shoulders late at night. Dad was walking ahead of us with Teddy and Beth. We must have been in one of the depopulated zones, because it was dark enough to see the stars in the sky. That was the first time I'd ever seen them.

I held on to Mom's hands and leaned back to soak in the starlight. It was so beautiful it made my stomach ache, but in a good way.

"Our home is out there, Joanna," Mom whispered. "A brand-new planet orbiting one of those stars. All we have to do is find it."

My mom never lies to us. It took twelve years of searching, but we found it. *We found it.* Just thinking the words makes me smile. In forty-eight hours our ship, the

International Space Agency ship *Pioneer*, will leave Earth. Seventy-two hours after that we'll leave this solar system, possibly forever. The next time I tether into this chair, we'll be orbiting our new world.

Shuttles don't get official names, but Dad dubbed ours the *Wagon*. Get it? Pioneer? Wagon? My dad is kind of a dork.

As the *Pioneer*'s cadet pilot, I'm in charge of shuttle runs. There are a lot of shuttle runs. The *Pioneer* is way too big to land—it was built in space and it's going to stay there.

I must have made the trip from ISA Mission Control up to the *Pioneer* and back three dozen times in the last week, ferrying people and cargo up to the ship. I'll have to do the same thing in reverse when we get to our new home. But I don't mind. I'm always happy when I'm flying.

This is my last run before we leave Earth, and the *Wagon* is mostly empty. My sister, Beth, is the only other person in the passenger cabin, and she's totally lost in whatever she's working on. Teddy and Miguel are messing around in the cargo hold. I could make them come strap in, but we're all going to be in insulated deep sleep for the next eight months. They might as well blow off steam while they can.

Beth and Teddy remember a time before we were pioneers. I don't. My parents were already running the Galactic Frontier Project when I was born. Dad is the GFP's primary investigator (that's science for "boss"), and Mom is pilot commander of the *Pioneer*. She'll also be planetary governor until the population is big enough to hold elections.

Being raised to pioneer human life on new worlds was not a leisurely childhood. Some Project kids resent that, which is fair. But I've never wanted to be anything other than a pioneer. Most little kids draw their families standing in front of a house. I didn't. My family portraits featured five crayon stick figures labeled Mom, Dad, Beth, Teddy, and Joanna, holding hands in front of a wobbly spaceship on a different world. The only thing that changed from picture to picture was what new and bizarre ecosystem I'd invented for our future home.

Luckily, our new planet is nothing like the ones I dreamed up as a kid. Its official name is Tau Ceti e because it's the fifth planet from a g-type star called Tau Ceti. Creative, the International Science Foundation is not. But despite its less than poetic name, Tau is kind of perfect. Scratch that. It isn't "kind of" anything. Tau *is* perfect. It has tons of biodiversity, a gentle yellow sun, a twenty-two-hour day, a 225-day year, and plenty of oxygen and water. And, most important, there's no intelligent life. Nobody thought we'd find an uninhabited world so like Earth.

"Computer," I say. "Can you bring up a three-sixty of the Diamond Range on Tau Ceti e?"

"Certainly, Joanna," the computer's crisply artificial voice replies. The cabin explodes into a thousand shades of green as a panorama of our new world covers the walls, ceiling, and floor. If not for the rows of high-backed white passenger seats, it would look like Beth and I were sitting in a lush valley instead of a space shuttle.

The ISA Rangers who did the preliminary survey of Tau described it as "verdant." If the rest of the planet is anything like these recordings, that's an epic understatement.

My sister's voice hooks me out of my daydream. "I'm trying to focus, you know."

Beth came straight from her doctoral thesis defense. She's still all dressed up, but she's been dissecting her long French braid as she works, so her muddy-red hair is a hurricane. Beth's advisers at MIT didn't think she could finish before we left. She ignored them, of course. Beth has more than her fair share of the Watson family cockiness. But she just completed a PhD in biological engineering at nineteen, so I guess she's earned it.

"How can you be working?" I fire back, without changing the display. "Today of all days?"

"How can you be so emotionally compromised by a transition we've been anticipating since before you were born?" She punctuates the question with a single raised eyebrow.

"I am not emotionally compromised! I'm excited." I throw my arms wide to take in the panoramic image of our new world. "Aren't you excited?"

"Of course," Beth says. "But our long-term food supply depends on my Stage Three genetic calculations being right. So can we just—" She gestures to the wall screens, rather than finishing the sentence.

My flex buzzes gently on my wrist. It's an alert from the navigation app.

"We're approaching the *Pioneer* anyway," I say. I call to the computer, "Switch to exterior cameras, please."

"Certainly, Joanna," it replies. The wall screens flicker from the rich tapestry of green to the view from the *Wagon*'s exterior cameras.

As always, the black glitter of space fills my stomach with butterflies. Near-Earth orbit is crowded with stations, ships, and space junk, but it's still beautiful. Below us, dawn looks like an ultraviolet rainbow sliding the dark back across the planet.

The *Pioneer* is in orbit just beyond that bright line, basking in sunlight. Deep bellied and trailing long space-time stabilizer fins, she looks like a luminescent space whale. The silver flecks of her satellites cling to her back like bubbles running over her skin.

"This is just as distracting," Beth mutters as she goes back to scribbling on her flex tablet. "And totally unnecessary to complete docking maneuvers."

"Yup," I say. "But it's cool."

I unwrap my flex and shake the velvety sheet of touch screen until it snaps stiff into tablet form. I press one edge firmly against the arm of my seat. It bonds with the ergofoam and stays upright, leaving my hands free to work. I tap the nav app icon, and a control panel blooms across the screen.

My grandfather taught me to fly in his antique Cessna. The cockpit was full of levers and handles and gauges you had to keep track of all at the same time. Modern spacecraft don't have any of that. Just apps you use to give the computer instructions. That's why Grandpa taught Teddy and me to fly his ancient airplane first. He says flying and programming a computer to fly for you are two different things. That's why I like three-sixty mode. It's the closest I can get to the cockpit of the Cessna.

I wish Grandpa was coming with us. Mom asked, but he wouldn't even consider it. I'll miss him, but I understand. Fixing Earth up is pretty much his life's work. Grandpa retired from the ISA to run the Earth Restoration Project. He and his team developed a set of nanoscopic scrubbers that filter carbon out of the air. They deployed them into the upper atmosphere thirty years ago, and it worked. Planetary temperatures are back into normal ranges, and the reforestation of the Amazon is almost complete. The ERP is going to launch a nanofiltration system into the oceans next year. We should be able to start breeding programs to reverse the twenty-first century extinctions by 2120. But I should say *they*, not *we*. Earth isn't my world anymore.

"Almost home!" Teddy calls as he climbs through the hatch from the cargo hold. We'll all have to shave our hair off before we go into insulated deep sleep for the trip, so he hasn't bothered to cut his floppy, red-brown hair in a while. He's wearing a gray ISA flight suit too, but his isn't zipped all the way up, so you can see the classic NASA logo on his T-shirt underneath. My big brother is a sucker for nostalgic space program crap.

"If by 'almost' you mean seven months, twenty-eight days, and thirteen hours," Beth snarks, giving up on work and folding her flex around her wrist. "Give or take roughly fifteen minutes for docking maneuvers."

"Twelve minutes and thirty-two seconds." My brain supplies the number automatically. I may not be able to do high-level math in my head, but I'm kind of obsessed with the *Pioneer*. I've memorized every detail of her specs. It's almost as good as getting to fly her myself.

"Nerd," Teddy says cheerfully as he drops into the seat next to mine and taps the tether controls on his utility harness. The black straps that run over his shoulders extend a fine webbing of nanocarbon filaments that bond with the seat.

"No. Pilot," I fire back as I request docking clearance from the *Pioneer*. "A pilot who fully qualified for solo suborbital, orbital, and open-space flight before my fifteenth birthday, thank you very much."

"Which is almost a year younger than you qualified, isn't it, bro?" Miguel Silva points out, swinging his med kit up onto the deck before hauling himself through the hatch after Teddy. The top half of Miguel's flight suit is tied around his waist, and his thin black undershirt does beautiful things for his shoulders.

Miguel grew up in Mexico City, but he spent his summers in the little beach town where his grandparents live. His grandmother taught him to surf as soon as he could swim, and it shows. Don't get me wrong, Miguel is almost as much of a brother to me as Teddy. But that doesn't mean a girl can't admire what a lifetime of surfing does to a guy's physique. He drags his shaggy, rainbow-dyed hair back into a ponytail and throws Teddy a playful smirk. "Kind of embarrassing, getting one-upped by little sis like that."

"Joanna was sixteen months younger," Beth corrects. "He failed the first time, which was embarrassing for us all."

Teddy shoots her a good-natured glare. She *tsks*. "The occasional challenge to your ego is healthy, Theodore."

"Some people don't feel the need to compete with their siblings," Teddy grumbles.

"You're right," I say. "But none of them are members of the Watson family."

Teddy bursts out laughing. My face splits into a grin. I can't help it. What is it about making your big brother laugh? It always feels like a tiny victory.

"You're cleared, *Wagon*," my mother's voice flows over the comms. "Welcome aboard."

"Enough funny business, Watsons," Miguel says, carefully stowing his med kit under his seat before tethering in.

"You heard the lady. Let's get our dock on. I gotta put these civvies on ice before they go bad."

Since Tau is so similar to Earth, almost two-thirds of our Exploration and Pioneering Team are civilians. There are almost two hundred of us now, including fourteen kids. The other E&P team is restricted to ISA officers and engineers. Their planet, Proxima Centauri b, needs a *lot* of terraforming. It won't be safe for civilians for a while. Not like Tau.

Everyone except the *Pioneer*'s crew went into insulated deep sleep back on Earth and won't come out until we're on our new planet. We're carrying the last group of civilians in deep-sleep crates. Miguel is with us in case a crate malfunctions. He's seventeen, like Teddy, but he just finished medical school. Project kids complete training in our fields of choice as quickly as we're able. The less unskilled dead weight an E&P Team has to support, the better.

"Don't have to ask me twice." I swirl my fingers across the navigation app to put the *Wagon* into a lazy spin, matching the *Pioneer*'s rotation. I know this shuttle well enough now that she moves like an extension of my own body. Docking is like dancing—a harmony of metal and electricity that makes my heart thump in time with the gentle roar of the engines. There's barely a shimmy as our docking clamps connect with the *Pioneer*.

This must be the fiftieth time I've successfully docked the *Wagon* on my own. You'd think it would get old.

It doesn't.

"You know, you used to make that same face when Dad bought us ice cream," Teddy says, smacking the control panel on his harness to release his tether. The web of black nanotubules slithers back into his shoulder straps, and he bounds out of his seat.

I toss him a narrow glare as I untether. To my surprise, the look on his face is mushy rather than mocking. He catches me looking and covers the sentimental expression with an eyebrow quirk and grin. "Nerd."

"No," I repeat, heading for the rear airlock. "Pilot."

I swipe my hand across the door to bring up the lock screen and enter my code. The seal releases with a hiss of pressurized air. The others file into the cubical white chamber, and Teddy seals the door behind us before I open the other side and step into the *Pioneer*'s loading bay. That's the whole point of an airlock, to keep pressurized vessels like the *Pioneer* and the *Wagon* from losing too much atmosphere when people pass from one to the other.

The air on the *Pioneer* is different than it is on the *Wagon*. It's softer and warmer thanks to the huge algae tanks that surround the engine's electromagnetic core, absorbing radiation and giving off humid, oxygenated air. Every breath sings with the vibration of the engines. You can't really hear it so much as you can feel it. Like the ship is a bell that's just stopped ringing.

If not for the warm air, I'd think I just stepped into

space. The loading bay wall screens have been set to a huge three-sixty panorama of the view from the ship's exterior cameras. Earth rolls under my feet, brown and blue and gray. The moon glitters with artificial light overhead, and beyond it the stars beckon.

Leela Divekar and Chris Howard are sprawled on the floor at the center of the bay, looking down at Earth. They're both in uniform—Leela is a Marine Corps cadet and Chris is a cadet engineer. Leela's long, black hair is loose, falling around her head in thick waves. She's been my best friend since her family moved from Pune to Frontier Project HQ in Australia, when we were both five. Chris's flight suit is a little too short. Again. He just turned eleven and he keeps hitting these crazy overnight growth spurts. Chris is like a little brother to Beth, Teddy, and me. His mom, Chief Engineer Penny Howard, is my mother's best friend. They grew up together in base housing at the Langley Research Center.

"About time," Leela says, yanking her hair back into its usual ponytail as she rolls to her feet. Between her dance classes and the martial arts belts Leela's been stacking up since we were kids, she moves like flowing water. "We've been waiting to help you unload for like an hour." Her dark eyes are red rimmed. She's been crying, but she wouldn't want me to notice.

"'Cause you'd rather be inventorying freeze-dried beans and rice?" I say.

"Yes."

"You're a terrible liar, Divekar," Teddy says as he seals the airlock behind us. "Always have been."

"I'll take that as a compliment, thank you," she fires back.

He grins. "You should. Honesty is hot."

He crosses the bay in a few long strides to kiss her. With tongue.

"Gross," I say. They've been dating for almost a year, and I'm okay with it. I guess. But she's my best friend and he's my big brother. It's not something I need to watch.

"Whatever," Chris mutters. "I have to get back to engineering. Mom has a deadly to-do list for me." He enjoys Leela and Teddy's public displays of affection even less than I do. Chris has had a hopeless crush on Leela since forever. It's not that Chris isn't cute. He is, or at least, he's going to be. But he hasn't even hit puberty yet.

"This is mega-awesome," Miguel says, drinking in the view of the stars around us.

"Chris set it up," Leela says, coming up for air. "Isn't it cool?"

Chris flushes a deep plum. Poor kid. "It's just a live three-sixty. No big deal."

"Yes, it is," Leela says. "It's a big deal to me." She gazes down at Earth. "You think we'll ever see it again?" There's longing in her voice, but I don't think it's the blue marble haloed in space junk and satellites she's been crying over.

Everyone I love is on this ship, except Grandpa. But that isn't true for Leela. I got half the flight time I needed for my clearance taking Leela back to India to visit her cousins and grandparents. I can only imagine what it must be like for her, thinking she might not see them again.

Teddy wraps an arm around her waist, pulling her close. "You will. If you want to, you will."

"It's not like it's going anywhere," I say, staring down into the blue globe. It's beautiful. It's home. I can't wait to leave it. "And there's a whole universe out there just waiting for us."

Chris makes a face. "Are Watsons even allowed to have doubts?"

"Nah," Leela says. "It's in the Project bylaws."

"What is there to doubt?" Beth says. "This is who we are."

"That's right. And this new world is going to be ours," Teddy says. "Not a hand-me-down that's held together with solar paneling and wishful thinking."

Everyone gets quiet then.

The moment shimmers around us. Endless and fleeting. Soaring. The six of us, standing together, surrounded by the infinite stars. Our home already behind us. The great wide unknown stretching in front of us.

REET! REET! REET!

A shipwide alert shreds the quiet like claws through flesh.

"Is this a drill?" Leela shouts over the alarm.

Fear snaps across the back of my neck as the wall screens burn white and then drop to black. "I don't think so."

The ship rears and bucks under us. Leela yanks Teddy and Miguel safely down to the deck, but Beth loses her balance, stumbling into Chris. I smack the autoconnect button on my utility harness as I throw myself forward, looping one arm around her waist and grabbing Chris's hand as his feet fly out from under him. My tether lines snap out, automatically bonding with the nearest airlock as another hard jolt rattles the ship. My harness bites into my shoulders and my waist, but the tether line keeps all three of us from being thrown across the bay.

Between one heartbeat and the next it's over. The ship is abruptly steady, and the reboot sequence snaps up on each panel of the wall and floor screens.

"Everyone okay?" Miguel says, breaking the stunned silence.

"I don't think so," Chris groans. His deep brown skin is tinged with gray.

"I think his shoulder is dislocated," Beth says, carefully helping Chris ease into a seated position.

While Miguel works on Chris, Teddy pulls off his flex and starts texting.

"What happened?" Leela asks.

"No replies yet," he says.

The words tie my stomach in knots. The computer

should have a status update by now. Repair assignments should be going out.

Something is really wrong.

"We should report to stations," Leela says. I'm about to agree when my flex flashes and buzzes with an incoming message.

"It's Mom." Relief hits me so hard that my hands shake as I unfold my flex and hold it up so the others can see. "Can't be anything terrible if she's got time to call."

Mom appears on-screen. Her eyes are grim, and blood is dripping from her left ear.

Suddenly I'm not relieved anymore.

"Is the *Wagon* intact?" she asks without preamble.

"It should be," I say. "But Mom—"

"Good," she says. "You're abandoning ship."

"What?" Teddy says. "No, Mom, we're here. We can help!"

"Yes," she says. "You can. There are twenty-five civilians in inso crates that haven't been hooked into the system yet. Load them onto the *Wagon* with the forty-two you brought up, and then abandon ship."

"It's that bad?" My voice is so fragile I can hardly hear it over my pounding heart.

She nods. "We got hit by a massive solar flare. The early-warning systems missed it, so the shields were off-line, and the electromagnetic radiation fried the computers. Now the engines are melting down, and the core's auto-eject system is completely nonfunctional."

Clammy dread soaks my skin. "What about the manual override?"

"There's a hull breach blocking our access to the engine room." She grits her teeth. "No more questions, Jo. You've got less than twelve minutes before core breach. Get moving."

"What about you?"

"We can't get to the escape pods, either," Mom says. She swallows hard. "I love you. Now go!"

Her image disappears. I stare at my blank flex, uncomprehending. The air feels as though it has turned to ergofoam in my lungs. Forcing it in and out feels more like vomiting than breathing.

"Joanna." Beth's sharp tone tells me that it isn't the first time she's said my name.

"Yeah?" I feel like I'm moving underwater as I turn to look up at my sister.

Her gaze grabs mine and holds on, reeling me back from the abyss of should-have-beens. "We don't have much time. You need to get the *Wagon* ready for departure."

"She's right," Miguel says, swiping at the tears running down his face. "The rest of you, help me load those inso crates."

"No way!" Leela protests. "We have to try—"

"We have to save as many people as we can," Beth says. "Which is not the same as trying to save everyone, given the circumstances."

"She's right," I say, hating every word. "We need to be well clear when the engines blow."

"Screw that," Leela snaps. She turns to me, pleading. "We can't just give up. There has to be a way. You know every centimeter of this ship, Joanna. Think!"

I can hardly find the strength to shake my head. My body feels like it's wilting. The *Pioneer* is going to die. My parents are going to die. All of our parents are going to die. And there's nothing I can do about it.

Or maybe there is.

"Wait!" The word punches past my teeth. "I think . . . I think . . ." I can't even complete the thought, my brain is working so furiously. I jab at my flex to pull up the maps app and swipe through to a schematic of the *Pioneer's* maintenance tubes with shaking hands.

"What is she doing?" Chris says.

"Just chill a sec," Teddy says. I can hear the thin threads of hope weaving through his voice. It steadies my hands as I scan the map. I have this ship memorized, from the hull strength all the way down to the suction settings on the vacuum toilets. But I need to *know* that I'm right before I tell them.

Because if I'm right . . .

"We can save the ship."

"Joanna—" Beth starts to say, but I cut her off.

"There's an access hatch to maintenance tube thirty-two right there," I say, pointing across the bay. "We can take thirty-two to fifteen to ten, which should get us to the corridor just outside the engine room. Then we can release the manual override clamps, eject the engine core, and—"

"We can save the ship," Teddy says, staring at the map. I can almost see his brain spinning up to match mine. "It won't take all of us. Miguel, you still need to get those crates on the *Wagon* and get the civvies out of here, just in case we screw this up."

"Copy that," Miguel says, already heading for the door. "But don't screw up."

"You're all being ridiculous," Beth says, talking over him. "If a plan this simplistic would work, Mom would have thought of it."

"Not necessarily," I say. "She probably hasn't looked at the maintenance tube layout since she signed off on the final design plans. That was years ago. I've been poring over the *Pioneer*'s schematics for months. We can do this."

"No, you can't," Beth insists, every word accelerating. "The odds of teenage cadets being able to save a spaceship when senior command staff cannot are astronomically low. And my whole family will be dead when you fail, which is the only plausible outcome."

"You're right, sis," Teddy says. I open my mouth to argue, but he keeps talking. "The odds aren't great. But if there's a chance, we have to take it. That's who we are."

My older siblings stare at each other for a long moment. Then Beth nods. "I'll help Miguel with the insulated-sleep crates. Please . . ." She trails off, searching for the right word. "Just be improbable, okay?" She spins and half runs out of the bay before either of us can reply.

Chris follows her. Teddy turns to Leela.

"You need to go prep the *Wagon*."

"What? No," Leela snaps. "I'm with you."

"You're cleared for space flight," Teddy says. "They can't evacuate the civilians without you."

"But if you're going to eject the core, then—"

Teddy takes her shoulders, turning her so she has no choice but to look him in the eye. "Lee-lu," he says, "I need you to make sure they're safe. I need *you* to be safe." Then he kisses her. Hard and gentle all at once. "Please?"

She stares up at him for a long breath. Then she shoves him away and marches to the airlock where the *Wagon* is docked. The look on Teddy's face as he watches her go is electric and strange. Unreadable. Like his emotions are suddenly speaking a language I don't understand. Finally, he turns back to me.

"Come on, sis."

The maintenance tubes are narrow, so we have to crawl through them. Tube ten is so cold that it tears at the skin of my palms. We must be close to the hull breach. I pull the sleeves of my uniform down over my hands and keep going. It's just a little farther.

The tube dead-ends in a hatch. I pop the seal so fast that I almost fall into the corridor beyond. The smoke billowing from the engine room gives the air a sharp, poisonous tang. I fumble for the flex-breather I keep stashed in my utility harness as Teddy crawls out of the hatch behind me. "You carrying O_2?" I say.

"Always," he says, pulling out his own breather and fitting its translucent membrane over his nose and mouth as we head for the engine room.

Inside, flames are chewing on the walls and the ceiling. The smoke is so thick I can taste it even through my O_2 mask. The *Pioneer*'s fire-suppression system must be busted, which is lucky. If it were online, it would have sealed this section and vented the oxygen.

There are nine emergency override switches that have to be thrown in order to release the massive carbon-alloy claws that hold our electromagnetic engine cores in place. They are evenly spaced along the walls at knee level and covered with panels marked **EMERGENCY ONLY**. Five of them are on the other side of the fire.

"You handle this side," Teddy says, darting between the flames before I can argue.

I drop to my knees beside the nearest manual release. I flip open the panel and grab the flat red handle inside. It pulls out easily enough, but it takes all my strength to twist it to the **UNLOCKED** position.

I stay on my hands and knees and crawl to the next panel. The smoke is a little thinner down here, but it still rasps over my skin like steel wool. I feel raw all over by the time I finish releasing all four switches. "Done!"

"Get out of here," Teddy calls. "I'm right behind you."

Between the smoke and the tears streaming from my burning eyes, I can hardly see. I trip over the lip of the door and go sprawling into the hallway. As I scramble to my feet, a new, deeper alert blooms from the engine room.

Terror rips through me.

"Teddy!" His name shrieks through the chemical desert of my throat. But it's too late. The engine room doors slide shut between us.

"Fire-suppression system activated," the computer says. "Venting atmosphere now."

I pound helplessly on the blank touch-screen surface of the sealed door. I think I'm screaming. My throat is so raw, I can't tell. I don't care.

Then my flex buzzes. I have an incoming call.

I rip my flex from my wrist and shake it out. Teddy's soot-smudged face appears on my screen.

"Well," he says. "That was poorly timed." He's trying to be funny, but I can hear the fear crackling in his voice. It's been a while since I thought my big brother was invincible, but the fact that Teddy's afraid still freaks me out. "How long until the doors unseal?"

I check. "Four minutes, twelve seconds."

He throws a look over his shoulder toward something I can't see. Probably a status readout on the engines. "Whole ship will be space dust by then."

Panic sinks its teeth into my neck, but I shake it off. There's no time to freak out now. I have to think. I have to—

"Override!" I say, pressing my flex to the wall screen next to the engine room doors. It sticks there as I pull up the *Pioneer*'s main menu on the wall screen beside it. As I work, I say, "If fire suppression is back online, the crew must have managed to reboot the computer. I should be able to get into system controls. I can override the door seals from there."

"Then what are we standing around for?" Teddy says, shooting me an adrenaline-charged grin.

My fingers fly over the wall screen, pulling up window after window. This is going to work. I'm going to save Teddy, then we're going to save the ship. "I can do this. We're going to make it. You believe me, right?"

He grins. "Always."

Reality abruptly slices through my optimism. "No. No, no, no, no—"

"What's wrong?" Teddy says.

I smack the wall screen in frustration. "If I unseal the doors before the section repressurizes, the core will rip free and take the engine room and most of this corridor with it."

"Damn it!"

We're both quiet for a moment. Searching for options we don't have. Then he says, "Do it."

"What? No," I say. "You'd die. And right after that, I'd

get sucked out into space, suffocate, and die."

"Yeah," Teddy says. "But everyone else would live."

"There has to be another way!"

"No, there doesn't," he says. His voice is thin but he sounds so sure. Steady, despite the fear I can see in his eyes. "We can do this, Jo."

"We can save them." I whisper the words. A whisper is all that can slide through the jagged chunk of terror lodged in my throat.

"We can save you, too," Teddy says, brightening with the thought. "It takes twelve seconds for the hull to seal over a breach. Tether in. With your breather, you can survive a hard vacuum for that long."

"Teddy—"

"Tell me you can do this, Jo. Tell me you're going to be okay."

I'm not going to be okay. Even if I live through this, I'm not going to be okay. Teddy will be dead. That will never, ever be okay.

I force my shaking fingers to press the autoconnect button on my utility harness. The line snakes out and bonds with the nearest contact point, behind me.

"I'll be okay," I say. I almost sound like I mean it.

"Are you ready?" he says.

"No."

That makes him laugh. "Neither am I," he says. "I love you."

My throat feels like it has rusted shut. I have to force each word free. "I love you, too," I say. Then I press my fingers to the wall screen and initiate the override.

It happens so fast, it's like I don't see the engine room tearing away. The *Pioneer* just spits me out into the shining dark. I spin and tumble, falling in all directions at once. Then my tether snaps tight and all of my ribs break at the same time. I feel it, but it doesn't hurt. Nothing hurts. Does that mean I'm dying? I'm not sure it matters anymore. My tether starts to retract. I *feel* my heart breaking, like my grief is imploding in my chest. Teddy is out there somewhere. Dying. Maybe already dead. And now he's going to be alone.

The infinity around me starts to collapse. The brilliant black is replaced by a dull, close darkness. The *Pioneer*'s hull is sealing itself. I'm safe. Or maybe I'm dying, and that's my brain, shutting down. Either way, I'm gone.

ONE

I lurch upright in my inso crate and throw up all over the deck.

The environmental controls in the deep-sleep center circulate air faster than in the rest of the ship. The soft, artificial breeze feels good on my hypersensitive skin.

Mom is crouched next to my crate. She rubs my back as I cough up more of the opalescent gray gel. "That's right, Jo," she says. "Get it all out."

Inso gel tastes foul and looks worse, but it's better than getting deep-fried by the space-time bubble that the *Pioneer*'s engines generate around the ship in order to move faster than the speed of light. I scrub the sticky stuff from my eyes, blinking until the world slides into focus.

Mom and I are alone in here. The wall screens are set

to a soothing, artificial-sunset glow. Since insulated-sleep crates look more like freight than medical equipment, the sleep center is an odd combination of a hospital ward, a cargo pod, and the fancy saunas we visited on vacation in Iceland when I was twelve. The Watson family isn't big on time off, but Dad forced Mom to take a few days on our way home from an equipment test in the IntGov Arctic Wilderness Preserve. The valleys that were left behind when the polar ice melted are just about as remote and uninhabited as you can get on Earth.

When I can breathe without choking on goo, Mom hands me a bag of water. I take a big gulp and swish until my mouth tastes less like rotten candy. Then I spit the water out into the drain at the bottom of my crate and take another drink. I'm so dehydrated, I can feel the slippery chill of the liquid tracing down my esophagus and into my stomach.

"Better?" Mom asks. Her hair curls in a dark halo around her face. Her eyes are chocolate brown, with flecks of amber lingering at their edges. All three of us kids inherited them. I wonder if she sees Teddy's ghost when she looks into my eyes, the way I see him in hers?

The thought burns. I slather it with sarcasm to dull the ache.

"Are we there yet?"

A snicker sneaks through Mom's exhaustion. "Almost. We're in orbit."

That takes me by surprise.

"Aren't civilians revived planetside?" I say as I climb out of my crate. The heated ergofoam deck has the resilient give of flesh under my bare feet. It's meant to be comfortable, but it just makes the air feel colder.

"Technically," Mom says, steadying me as my muscles remember how standing upright works. "But I wanted the whole family to be together the first time we land on Tau. I thought you'd want that too."

Of course I want that. But I can't have it. Neither of us can. Teddy is dead. Our *whole* family is never going to be together again. Just thinking about it makes me feel as though my throat is swelling shut. It's like I'm having an allergic reaction to reality.

"Would you like me to stay for your physical?" Mom asks. She sounds so unsure of herself. I hate that. My mother doesn't do hesitant. At least, she didn't before the accident. Now she acts like I'm made of glass and the wrong word will shatter me.

"I'll report to medical after I hit the showers," I say.

"Before," Mom says.

"Seriously?" I wave a hand at myself, indicating my attire or lack thereof. I'm wearing a one-piece bathing suit. My head is shaved. Insulating gel is drying on my bare scalp and my bare legs like crusted snot.

"Your heartbeat is being maintained by a flock of nanomachines floating in your blood," she says. "Nanomachines that have been running without maintenance for the last eight months while you were in inso. So yes, I'm very serious."

"Fine," I say, trying not to sound as surly about the idea as I feel. It's not like she's wrong. I never fully recovered from the accident. Ironically, it wasn't being tossed into space without a suit that caused permanent damage. It was getting saved. I felt my heart burst when my tether retracted and yanked me back into the ship. At the time I thought it was, I don't know, emotional or something. It made sense to me that losing Teddy would feel like being torn apart on the inside. But it turns out that's just what being torn apart on the inside feels like.

ISA medical spent almost six months trying to find a way to fix me well enough to return to active duty. They failed. So, for the rest of my life, my blood pressure will be monitored and maintained by little machines about the same size as my blood cells, called pacers. They work just fine under normal circumstances, but they can't handle really high speeds, or big altitude changes, or basically any-thing else that happens on a regular basis when you're a pilot. Blacking out every time the ship turns too fast is no big deal if you're a passenger, but it could be fatal for every-one if you're in the pilot seat. That's why I'm a civilian now.

"Do you want me to come with you to medical?" Mom asks.

Yes. I want Mom to hold my hand and tell me I have

beautiful bones, like she used to do when I was little and I was scared of the body scanner. But I say:

"Not particularly."

"Fine," she says. Her voice is chilly and still, like deep water has drowned the irritation and concern that were there a few seconds ago.

She leaves. I feel like an asshole. I should just talk to her. But I can't. I've tried before. Putting these feelings into words is like picking up shards of broken glass with my bare hands. It accomplishes nothing and leaves me shredded. Besides, it's not like she's been exactly forthcoming with her own emotional damage.

After the accident, everyone else drove me nuts, talking about how I was a hero. Mom couldn't even look at me. The day after Teddy's memorial service, she signed on to test the ISA's newest superluminal engine and disappeared into space for ten months.

Dad pretty much disappeared too. He came home at night sometimes. But sometimes he slept in his lab for weeks on end.

It took fourteen months to rebuild the *Pioneer* and confirm a new launch window. I spent most of that time in rehab and physical therapy. Alone. Except when I was in the hospital cafeteria bullying Beth into eating. She got scary thin for a while, because she was living on coffee. Mom and Dad were too busy burying their grief in work to notice.

Screw this.

I'm taking a shower before my physical. If my heart fails in the shower after surviving eight months of deep sleep, then I won't have to bother figuring out what I'm supposed to do with my life now that I can't fly.

The wall screens in the locker room are usually switched to mirror mode, but when I walk in, the walls and part of the floor are covered in chemical equations, DNA sequences, and strategic genomic algorithms.

Oh goodie.

"Beth?" I call.

"What?"

The word swats at me like an irate house cat. I find my sister working a tangle of equations on the wall screen at the end of the first row of lockers. She is dripping wet, bald, and naked.

"Beth. Towel."

"Why?" she asks without looking up.

"You're naked." I grab a towel and toss it at her. She ducks and keeps working.

"I'm also in a locker room," she says. "Nudity is perfectly acceptable."

I don't bother to argue. There's no point. Beth doesn't give a crap what other people think of her. I open the supply cupboards and collect a uniform, boots, and utility harness in her size. I pile them on the bench next to her. "Just get dressed, okay? Mom'll blame me if you're late for launch."

"That would be irrational," Beth says, "and unlikely,

since you have forfeited your place in the command structure on this ship."

"Gee, thanks for reminding me," I say as I shuck off my swimsuit and try not to stomp on my way to the shower room.

I swear, we used to be able to talk to each other. I guess our relationship is just another thing that doesn't make sense without Teddy.

I choose a shower stall at random. The last person in here set it to a three-sixty that makes it look like I'm taking a shower in a rainforest. This was shot somewhere in the New Amazon, I think. The trees are big, but nothing like the stuff in the old documentaries that Beth was obsessed with when we were kids. I'm supposed to be doing an ecological survey of a forest just like this one with Grandpa right now. That was the plan. Dad wasn't a big fan of the idea of me staying behind on Earth, but at least he understood why I didn't want to be a part of the GFP anymore. Mom didn't. She came back from her superluminal test flight and informed me I was back in the Project, and we were leaving Earth in four months. And I'm still seventeen, so what I want doesn't matter.

Actually, "want" is the wrong word. I *want* to be a part of the Project. I *want* to be there the first time the *Wagon* touches down on our new planet. But I don't want to be a passenger. I want to be Joanna Watson, cadet pilot. And I'm not her anymore.

I seem to be the only one who realizes this. The academy would have let me finish my degree and officially be a member of the *Pioneer*'s crew, but only because I'm a "hero." I didn't want that. The only crew position I'm even close to qualified for would be in the *Pioneer*'s dedicated marine squadron, but I don't want to be a marine.

I have no idea what I *do* want to be and there was no time for me to train in a new field before we left anyway. That means I'm listed as "Accompanying Family: Minor" on the manifest. The next oldest AFM is seven years old. It's embarrassing.

My scalp tingles as I scrub in the follicle stimulator. You have to shave your head for insulated sleep because it's impossible to get inso-gel out of hair. We learned that the hard way after our first test run of the system, when I was nine. Thankfully, we have stims. They're great, as long as you don't spill any on your feet. I learned that the hard way too. Teddy called me "hobbit" for a year.

I let my hair grow to the middle of my back. It isn't practical, but I grew my hair out after I left the Academy. This is what I look like now. That's just the way it is.

I turn off the water and step out of the shower.

I can hear someone moving around in the rows of lockers, but it isn't Beth. She's gone, and so are her clothes. She cleared the wall screens and left them in standby mode, so the rows of black lockers stand in stark relief against the pale gray of the screens.

I wrap myself in the towel and go looking for my locker. They're assigned in alphabetical order by last name, so I find mine in the last row, next to the shower room. A gray ISA flight suit is hanging next to the duffel bag full of personal effects I stowed when I went into insulated sleep.

"Subtle, Mom," I mutter to myself as I pull on the jeans and T-shirt I wore to the sleep center on Earth the day I went into inso. The jeans will go into the recyclers eventually. We don't do laundry. It's way more energy efficient to 3D-print clothes, then recycle them when they're dirty. But I'm not recycling this shirt. Not ever. Teddy gave it to me on my fifteenth birthday. It has the early-twenty-first-century NASA logo screen printed across the chest. I distinctly remember opening the package, rolling my eyes, and saying, *Gee, thanks, bro. You sure this isn't for you?* I don't think I wore it once before he died. I've been wearing it a lot since then.

I jam my feet into my elderly high-top sneakers and then I strip the utility harness from the flight suit and strap it on over Teddy's shirt. Civilians don't usually wear harnesses, but civilians aren't usually out of their crates in orbit, either. There's a flex stowed in the harness pockets. I wrap it around my wrist. The ISA gets faster processors and cooler apps than civvy flexible tablets. Waste not, want not.

I switch the wall screens back to mirror mode and braid my hair. The slippery brown strands slide through my fingers, and when I finally capture them all, the braid comes out lopsided and lumpy. I give up and bend over to finger comb it out so I can start over.

"Bold fashion statement," Leela says behind me. If I'd known she was the other person in here, I wouldn't have bothered to mess with my hair. I would have just left.

Leela is another thing I lost in the accident. Theoretically, we're still friends. But in practice we can barely manage small talk without one of us pissing the other one off.

It's sort of my fault. Leela took my place as Mom's cadet pilot after I was medically discharged from the ISA a year ago. You'd think the fact that Leela is my best friend would make it easier to watch her take over the job I trained for my whole life, but I think it makes it worse. Being jealous of Leela seems to be like breathing these days. It just happens, whether I want it to or not.

I try not to be a jerk about it, but I've never been great at hiding my feelings. Especially since the general level of jerkitude is mutual. Leela's never actually *said* that she's mad at me. It just wafts off her, like a perfume that I can't smell but is giving me a headache anyway. I think she blames me for Teddy's death. Which isn't fair, but I blame me too, so I get it.

I can't decide if her wordless aura of accusation is better or worse than all the people who smile extra brightly and ask me how I'm doing just a little too loudly, like they think my heart condition also makes me kind of deaf.

Leela has already trimmed her wavy black hair into a

pixie cut with thick fringe that somehow manages to be both practical and stylish. Compared to her, I look like a little kid playing dress-up with my utility harness strapped on over my jeans and T-shirt.

"Mom was kind enough to passive-aggressively leave a uniform in my locker," I say, trying to act like I'm not feeling outclassed and intimidated, which I totally am. "I figure, waste not, want not."

"You could just put the uniform on," Leela says, tousling her hair and examining the effect in the mirror. "Not like there are a plethora of career options out here."

"Not like wearing the uniform is gonna change that," I say. "Considering."

I swear, I didn't mean that to sound bitter. It just came out that way.

"Considering what?" Leela says before I get the chance to course correct. "That anything less than cadet pilot is beneath you?"

Heat flushes up the back of my neck and prickles under my new hair. I don't know if the flare of emotion that follows is anger or embarrassment, and I don't stop to figure it out.

"That's not what I meant!" I protest. "You always—"

"What? What do I always?"

I open my mouth. Then I close it again. I don't know what to say. If I knew the words to make things better between us, I would have said them already.

A countdown clock fades up on the mirrored wall screen in front of us: **DEPARTURE IN T – 00:23:00.**

I'm late for preflight.

The thought is a reflex, whispering from a universe that doesn't exist anymore. I'm not late for preflight. Leela is late for preflight. It's her job now.

"You should go," I say, quietly.

"Whatever," Leela says, but her voice is still jagged with hurt feelings. She turns and marches off. I don't stop her.

I need to get to the medical center and get Leela's dad, our chief medical officer, to check me out, if I want to be on the *Wagon* when it leaves. I give up on braiding my slippery new hair and scrape it back into a ponytail. Then I grab the duffel from my locker and leave.

Most of the crew must already be on the *Wagon*. The corridors are empty, and the wall screens are all in standby mode. It makes the ship feel like a maze of white punctuated by the occasional matte black rectangle of a sliding door. I don't even realize that I'm almost to the engine room until I come around a corner and see the memorial wall.

A picture of Teddy and me when we were kids has been blown up to almost life size and displayed on the wall screen across from the engine room doors. The words **IN GRATEFUL MEMORY** run under the image in a plain black font.

I was eight when this picture was taken. Teddy was ten. It was our first trip into space. We're wearing little

ISA flight suits that Mom had made special for us. Beth refused to wear hers. She didn't think it was appropriate for a civilian twelve-year-old to be in uniform. Teddy loved it. He loved everything about space. He was going to design spaceships when he grew up. But instead of growing up, he became a hero.

I'm sure this memorial makes the other survivors feel better. It makes me feel empty. Sometimes I think both of the kids in that picture died here, and I'm just a ghost lingering where I shouldn't be.

Melodramatic much, Jo? I scold myself. But that doesn't make the feeling go away.

"Dear lord, woman." Miguel's bright voice bounces up the corridor ahead of him. "You have a taste for danger."

"Huh?"

He closes the distance between us in a few bounds, his med kit and the waterproof neoprene dry bag he uses for his surf gear bouncing on his shoulders. "You know how pissed the commander was when she turned up in medical and Doc told her you hadn't been there yet?"

I wince. "I can guess." I didn't think Mom would actually check on me, not with everything going on today.

"Thankfully," Miguel says, pulling a test tube with a hot-pink membrane stretched over one end from a pocket on his utility harness, "I am a smooth mofo, and I convinced our fearless leader that I could track you down and test your little pacer dudes on the fly."

"You can do that?" I say, relieved.

"Yup," he says. He wiggles the test tube and raises both eyebrows, like he's already laughing at his own bad joke. "But first, I need to do as the vampires do."

I hold out my arm. He presses the membrane-covered end of the tube to the inside of my elbow and says, "Brace yourself."

Pain licks me with an icy tongue as a needle dips through the membrane and my skin, and into the vein. Blood rushes into the tube. "Righteous," Miguel says, tapping the vial twice. There's a quick bloom of warmth as the needle retracts, leaving a tiny patch of adhesive behind it to seal the skin. He shakes the vial, bopping his head to the beat.

"Why are you hanging around this morbid junk?" he says, tossing a nod to the memorial wall.

Guess I'm not the only one who has mixed feelings about this thing.

"I didn't mean to," I say. "I was on my way to medical. Then I saw this and . . ."

Miguel rolls his eyes sympathetically. "People aren't trying to be weird," he says, pressing the membrane side of the vial to the flex on his wrist. It bonds, sticking in place. "They just don't get it. It was a different sort of day for them than it was for us."

"Understatement," I say.

"Nah," Miguel says as he taps into his flex to start the

analysis of my blood. "Just the truth minus all the drama."

Miguel has a way of taking complicated stuff and making it simple. Kind of the opposite of what my brain does.

"What am I doing out here, Miguel?"

He raises a dubious eyebrow. "Exploring? Pioneering? Building a new home for humanity? Unless I seriously missed a memo."

"You guys are pioneers," I say. The words pour out faster with each passing sentence. I couldn't stop them if I tried. "I can't fly and I'm not trained in anything else that's useful. I'm just . . . baggage. Dead weight."

Miguel's face twists into an expression that manages to be confused, sympathetic, and mildly offended at the same time. "No, you're not. You're Jo." He looks up at the memorial wall again and shakes his head. "Ted would be super bummed to miss this. But he'd be psyched that we made it. Especially you. You survived throwing yourself out of a spaceship, dude. Badass." His flex vibrates. He looks down at it, then grins big as he pops the test tube free. "And thanks to these little guys, you'll survive to do more stupidly awesome stuff on our new home."

"I'm cleared?"

"Yup!" He tucks the vial of my blood into his medical kit. "Now we better haul ass or they're gonna leave without us."

The airlock to the *Wagon* is open when we get to the loading bay. Leela is standing next to it, looking annoyed.

"Finally," she snaps. "You realize you two are the last in, right?"

"Gotta make an entrance," Miguel says, cheerfully ignoring her irritation.

"Come on," she mutters, waving us through the airlock.

The *Wagon*'s passenger cabin is full of pioneers, laughing and talking. Happy, excited conversations weave through each other like a school of fish darting through the chilly, dry air. Mom has the wall screens set to a three-sixty of the shuttle's exterior cameras, so it feels like we're floating over the vivid green globe of our new planet.

"Okay, people," Mom calls out as Leela seals the airlock. "Settle."

The swirling current of voices rises as everyone hustles to tether into a seat.

"Come on, guys," Chris says, popping out of the crowd. He grabs my hand and tows me toward the last row of chairs. Beth is already there, scribbling on the flex that's spread out on her lap. "The faster we strap in, the faster we get there!"

Chris has only stimmed his hair a couple of centimeters, so his tight curls hug his scalp. He's thirteen now, and taller than me, though he hasn't gained any weight to go with the new heights. He still looks like a little kid, just one who's been stretched like taffy.

"The commander is letting Leela be lead pilot for descent," Chris says. "Isn't that cool?"

It is. And I want it to be me so badly, I'm afraid I'm going to scream. Or burst into tears, right here in the middle of everyone. I manage a half smile for Chris. I'm sure it isn't convincing, but he's so busy watching Leela do last-minute checks with Mom that he doesn't notice.

Leela disengages the docking clamps and we swing down and away from the *Pioneer*. Piloting is mostly aim and gravity, when you're working this close to a planet. If you point the ship in the right direction, the planet's gravitational pull will reel you in like a fish on a line. Tau's gravity well isn't quite as strong as Earth's—Leela will have to compensate for that in her atmospheric entry trajectory.

It was over two years ago when I did the math for this flight, but I think I still have the calculations memorized. I did them so many times. I wanted to have it perfect, so I could prove to Mom that I was ready to pilot the *Wagon*'s first descent.

Now we're finally here, and I'm just a passenger watching Leela do it.

I should have stayed home with Grandpa.

I shake my head hard, like I can hurl the thought free. Miguel is right. Teddy would kick my ass if he knew I was missing this because I'm moping.

I look away from Leela and focus on the planet turning below us as we drop toward it in a slowly descending spiral. Tau has three continents, one of which is huge and looks kind of like someone smooshed Australia into one side of

Africa and Europe into the other. That's where we're going to land—specifically, on an empty swath of brown-green prairie land that stretches inland from the mountains on its western coast.

Turbulence slams me back against my seat as hot-pink flames lick their way up the shields. We're crossing into the atmosphere.

Leela's entry vector is a little bit off, which perversely makes me feel better. That, in turn, makes me feel like a jerk. What kind of person is *glad* when the pilot of the freaking spaceship that they're flying in makes a mistake?

The shaking stops abruptly. The flames clear, and the wall screens reveal a panoramic view of the planet below. It's all color and light from here, because we're still a thousand meters up. And dropping. I feel my body pressing slightly upward against my harness as we accelerate toward the ground.

Sparkling whiteness blooms across my field of vision. We're losing altitude too fast—my pacers can't keep up with the change in atmospheric pressure. I pass out.

For a few head-spinning moments, I am nowhere and nothing as the pacers in my blood struggle against the shifting atmospheric pressure, and my brain gasps for oxygen. When the world fades up and I regain consciousness, we've already landed.

The wall screens are a riot of color and light. This is what sunrise looks like on our new home.

The cabin buzzes with voices as the others untether from their seats and gather their things. Everyone is excited. I am too, I realize, tapping my harness to release my tether. The tight, tingly feeling is so unfamiliar, I almost don't recognize it.

I grab Beth's hand and tug her along as I follow Mom to the airlock. Dad comes to stand beside us as Mom pulls up the lock screen, then turns to face the crowd.

"My friends! We have come to the edge of humanity's newest frontier." She unseals the airlock doors behind her. "I can think of only one thing to say."

Brilliant sunshine floods in as the airlock swings open and the landing ramp unfolds, smacking down into chunky, silver-brown soil. I expect Mom to start walking down the ramp. Instead, she looks to me and makes a *go ahead* gesture.

She wants me to go first.

Adrenaline surges over me. This is *the* moment. The moment we've been working toward my whole life. The moment Teddy died for. The moment we truly become pioneers.

Miguel nudges me. "Dude. You're killing the mood."

I walk through the airlock and step out into the sunlight. My heart is pounding so hard, it's overwhelming my pacers. I can hear the blood thudding against my eardrums, and hot white sparks are dancing in the corners of my vision.

I reach the bottom of the ramp.

Mom calls out, "This is one small step for a young woman . . ."

My sneaker presses into the soft soil of Tau Ceti e.

"And one giant leap for humankind!"

I can hear the roar of cheers behind me. But I don't look back.

I turn my face up to the cloud-speckled sunlight and breathe in air that smells like salt and pine sap and something I don't have a name for yet. I am standing on a new world. Our world. And just for this moment, nothing else matters.

We're finally here.

TWO

There were so many little things about Earth that my mind took for granted, like white noise my brain just edited out. It's not like that here. Everything is new. I notice every color, every smell, and every sound. Even the breeze feels different. Like it's dancing across the back of my neck. If I had a comparative analysis of air currents on Earth and air currents on Tau Ceti e, I could figure out why. But I don't want to know. Not yet. I just want to feel it.

The sky here is a brighter, greener blue than the sky back on Earth. The color is hard to describe. It's sort of like turquoise, but not really. I don't think that shade of blue exists on Earth. The sun is rising over the prairie, but the twin moons are still visible, hanging low over the western horizon. They have low orbits compared to Earth's moon.

It makes them look huge in the sky. They're close enough that you can see the pits and craters etched across their fat, silver bellies.

The Diamond Range is even more beautiful than I expected. The mountains sparkle in the early-morning sunshine like someone tossed glitter across green velvet. Ribbons of gray and blue twist down through the hills and wind together into a river that runs just to the south of us. The trees that cluster on its banks are tall and delicate. Their long branches are dusted with tiny flowers in neon colors so bright they hardly look real. In contrast, the tough, springy prairie grass is such a dull green it's almost gray. It grows in low clumps that end in pink-tinged yellow seedpods.

The *Wagon* looks starkly out of place here, looming over the prairie with its wings folded back and the sun casting dark rainbows across its iridescent black skin. I guess that makes sense. It *is* out of place, like the spaceships that are always attacking Earth in the twentieth-century movies Dad loves. Only it's *our* ship. We're the aliens here.

"Idle hands ruin plans, kiddo." My father's voice pulls my soaring thoughts back into the present. "Save the wool-gathering for another day."

Dad is living his lifelong dream right now, and it shows. He has his favorite wide-brimmed, dorky dad hat pulled low over his red-brown hair and a goofy, too-happy-to-hold-it-in grin on his face.

"We *just* landed. Can't we . . . I don't know, take a second to deal with this?" I say, gesturing to the world around us.

"We'll have a lifetime to 'deal with this,'" Dad says. "We're pioneers. Not tourists. And we've only got eight hours to unload the *Wagon* before the next launch window."

The *Wagon* isn't nearly as delicate as old-school, rocket-propelled spacecraft used to be—you can fly her in pretty much any atmospheric conditions. But you waste a lot of fuel if you don't work with the pull of gravity, so you want to sort of spiral around the planet to get into orbit. That's why we schedule our launches at the times in Tau's rotation that will give us the shortest possible path from here to the *Pioneer* in orbit. Scratch that. *We* don't schedule launches, Mom and Leela do.

"Is Leela taking it up?"

I didn't mean to let the bitter taste in my mouth flavor my words, but it does. Sympathy floods Dad's face. "I'm so sorry it isn't you, Joey."

Dad has no poker face. I can see him aching for me.

I open my mouth to tell him that it's no big deal and I'm fine. Then I realize that I'm going to cry if I actually try to say anything. I hate this feeling, like I'm being held hostage by my own sadness. I shrug, hoping it comes off as casual, but I inherited Dad's total lack of chill. Everything I think and feel shows up in my face.

He pulls me in for a hug. I don't mean to, but I hug him

back. I lean my head on Dad's shoulder, and for a few seconds it feels like it used to, when I was small and he could fix every problem. Sadly, I'm old enough to know better now. I push him away. "Idle hands ruin plans, remember?"

His favorite made-up cliché lures a smile to his lips. "That's right, baby girl," he says. "And we have a whole lot of plans. A *whole* lot of plans."

We part ways and I go looking for Chief Penny.

As head of engineering, Chris's mom is in charge of the duty roster. Chief Penny puts me on unloading duty. The *Wagon*'s hold is packed with huge crates of raw plastic and four disassembled industrial-size 3D printers.

We unload the printer components first, so the engineering team can start assembling them. The 3D printers are the only equipment we brought from Earth. We'll use them to make everything else we need—including our cabins. We have a lot of printing to do if we want to have a place to sleep tonight.

While the engineers assemble the 3Ds, the rest of us use the *Wagon*'s hover carts to unload the crates of raw. A hover cart looks sort of like a really uncomfortable black mattress that floats a meter off the ground. They're standard equipment for shuttles like the *Wagon*.

Even with a hover cart, unloading the big crates of raw is hard work. Five hours later, I'm sweaty and sunburned, and I have epic blisters on my palms and the backs of my heels, where my sneakers are slowly rubbing the skin away.

I'm halfway down the ramp, pulling a huge load of raw, when there's a loud, metallic coughing sound and my hover cart sags to the left.

"Crap!"

The cart's field generator is dying. I swear, fighting to control my cart. These crates are heavy enough to crush me. I'm not strong enough to push this cart back up the ramp, and I won't have time to jump free if I let go and it slides down. I'm screwed.

There's another sharp, metallic cough, and then the hover cart dies altogether.

I brace myself for impact, but nothing happens. The cart doesn't move a centimeter.

I lean around the loaded hover cart, which isn't hovering anymore. A marine I don't know well is holding up the other end. He smirks like this is the best joke he's heard all day. "Shall we?"

"If you insist."

He snorts a laugh as we wrestle the busted hover cart to the bottom of the ramp. I lean against the crates of raw to catch my breath. He isn't even winded.

"The word you're looking for is thank you," the marine says.

"That's two words."

"Touché," he says, chuckling the word. "But you must admit, I saved your butt."

It takes me a second to remember his name. Lim. Private

Jay Lim. He's one of the new recruits they brought in to replace the four marines who were killed in the accident on the *Pioneer*. He looks like he's about my age, maybe a year or two older. He's Korean, but he must have grown up somewhere in the So Cal Metro, judging by his blunt California accent. He'd be hot if he didn't look so pleased with himself.

I really should say thank you. He might have saved my life. But I just can't give him the satisfaction. "Nah. I'm stronger than I look."

"Mutant superpowers?" he says.

I shrug, like *for all you know*. He grins. Damn it. He's enjoying this.

Lim pulls a bag of water from the cargo pocket in his pants and takes a swig. "That how you ended up on fetch-and-carry duty?" He offers me the water. I accept. "You'd think they could find a better gig for the daughter of the commander and the PI."

"I'm a pioneer," I say, taking a swig and handing it back. "Not a princess."

"From what I hear, you're kind of a hotshot," he says. "Did they really give you the Medal of Honor at fifteen?"

"Yeah," I say, working really hard to keep my voice casual. "But I don't fly anymore."

"Cool."

"That's it?" I say. Disinterest is not the usual reaction to that statement. My heart condition isn't public knowledge, so people get all surprised and curious when they find out the ISA's junior hero quit. "You're not going to ask why?"

"Do you want me to?"

Yes.

I bite down on the word before it charges out of my mouth. What is wrong with me today? I didn't even want to tell the ISA counselors about the accident. I certainly don't want to discuss the worst day of my life with this guy.

Do I?

"Jo!" Chris calls, jogging down the ramp from the *Wagon* behind us. "What did you do to your cart?"

Just like that, the weirdly intimate moment evaporates. Chris and Lim help me haul the busted hover cart out of the way, and then we all get back to work.

The sun is hanging low over the mountains by the time we're done. I snag a bag of water and collapse in the tall grass to watch the light show. The jagged peaks of the Diamond Range were pretty during the day, but now they're dazzling. They look like huge prisms buried in the prairie, shattering the dusky light into rainbows full of colors I've never seen before.

"Howdy, squirt," Chief Penny says, settling cross-legged beside me. A little smile slips over her face as she takes in the spectacular evening light. "Not half bad, is it?"

The chief is shorter than I am, but you'd never describe her as petite. She has too many muscles. She has dark-brown skin, like Chris, and there's a little gray woven through her black curls.

Most people recycle their utility harnesses every day, along with their uniforms, but Chief Penny doesn't. The straps of her harness are lined with Eagle Scout achievement badges. She always says that she and Mom learned more about running a spaceship in the Scouts than they did in the academy.

"It's . . ." I don't have the words for how strange and perfect this place is.

She nods in agreement with my speechlessness. "Indeed."

We sit there quietly for a while, breathing in the evening air.

"Chief!" Sergeant Kaeden Nolan calls. "We're ready for liftoff."

"You're going back up?" I ask, trying not to sound disappointed. Of course Chief Penny has to go up. She'll have days of work to do, putting the *Pioneer* into standby mode so it can stay in orbit uncrewed after we bring the rest of the E&P team down in their inso crates.

"An engineer can't leave her ship for too long," she says, bouncing to her feet and holding a hand out to me. I take it and let her pull me up.

"Safe flight," I say, fighting to smother the sparks of jealousy in my head.

The chief sees right through me. She tugs at the end of my ponytail. "New world. New start. Who knows what you'll turn out to be?"

With that, she jogs to the *Wagon*.

The others are already on board, so the ramp folds up into the *Wagon* as Chief Penny seals the airlock behind her. The engines are already firing. Dad waves everyone else back to a safe distance. The others linger to watch the launch, but I keep walking. If I watch, I'll just keep wishing I was on the *Wagon* with them. And I don't want to wish that I'm somewhere else. For once, I want to be glad to be where I am.

I walk until I reach the river, then turn toward the mountains and keep going, weaving through the neon-flowered trees. The air smells like peppermint. The long, flexible branches of the trees float out to brush my hair and shoulders as I pass below them. If I didn't know better, I'd think they were dancing on the wind. But, according to the survey report, these trees are carnivorous hybrid plants that photosynthesize like normal plants but also eat the tiny, bright-winged insect analogs that flit through the branches around me. Kind of like Venus flytraps and pitcher plants back on Earth, but a lot prettier. Their taxonomy classification is *Chorulux fidus*, but the ISA Rangers refer to them as fido trees in the survey report. I guess the nuzzling branches must have reminded one of them of a childhood pet.

There are a lot of hybrid plants on Tau. Something about the intensity of the light from this sun and the mineral-poor soil. I wasn't paying that much attention when Beth explained it to me. But whatever the reasons, these trees are perfectly adapted to their environment.

I used to feel that way. I don't even remember when I decided I wanted to be a pilot commander like Mom when I grew up. I've just always known what my future was going to be. *Knew.* I should use the past tense. Now I have no idea. But as I walk through the brilliant trees, it doesn't matter so much. I'm here. I'm finally here.

"We made it."

I feel kind of dumb, whispering the words out loud. But the words feel good, too. Painful and pleasant at the same time, like stretching after you've been sitting too long.

Right before he died, Teddy made me promise him that I'd be okay. For the first time since I made it, that promise doesn't feel hollow. This feels like a place where I could be okay. Maybe even better than okay.

This planet is nothing like I imagined it would be. It has blue sky and green plants and water and air, just like Earth. I assumed it wouldn't be that different. But it is. I can't even put it into words. The words for this place don't exist yet. They'll grow up as we explore Tau. Who knows what they'll be? There's so much possibility here. This can be the home Teddy imagined. The home he died for. I'm sure of it.

The neon-flowered trees are starting to thin out and mingle with another type of tree. Except, if I'm remembering the survey report right, these aren't actually trees—

they're plants the size of trees. I forget what they're called. They look like a cross between the fleshy, teardrop-leaved jade plant my dad used to have in his office and the orchids that Leela's grandmother keeps in her sunroom, except they're twice my height, and the leaves are so broad I could use one for an umbrella—an excessively large umbrella. The flowers—I think those are flowers—are a slightly paler shade of green than the towering stalks and huge leaves. Their petals form deep cups the size of my head that furl out into ruffled edges, like gathered lace. Bright-green vines crawl over the ground between them.

The grove is like a tiny world all my own, built of green and quiet and shade. I'm tempted to find an orchid to sit under and stay awhile, but I keep moving.

The river's tumbling babble gets louder as I walk. I must be coming to the edge of the grove. Ahead, I catch a glimpse of something unexpected through the leaves. A dull, artificial whiteness that doesn't belong here.

That can't be what I think it is.

I walk a few more meters. The orchid trees are getting farther apart. Clumps of knee-high, stiff grass are starting to catch at my jeans. And I can definitely see the gray-white domes of standard-issue ISA cabins up ahead.

I must be mistaken. The only ISA cabins on Tau are behind me, at our base camp.

I push my way through the underbrush anyway. When I emerge from the orchid grove, goose bumps prickle up the back of my neck. A tiny settlement is tucked between the grove and a wide bend in the river. Eight squat geodesic domes constructed of octagonal panels of flex-screen canvas, clustered around a four-meter-square plot of weeds that probably used to be a garden. They're just like our cabins will be, but old—halfway to being ruins. And so is the compact spaceship that stands over them.

The ship's long-nosed body and arched glider wings make it look like a robotic crane hovering over the surface of a lake. I'm still too far away to read the words stamped on its side in red, but that silhouette is unmistakable. It's an ISA scout ship. There are only six of them, and the only one with red markings is the *Vulcan*. It belongs to the ISA Ranger team that discovered Tau Ceti e.

It should have left with them five years ago.

My heart gives a single bone-rattling thud before shooting ahead into an all-out race. For a moment, I'm afraid my pacers were damaged in the trip after all. But my heart is pounding in perfect, adrenaline-fueled rhythm. This is just fear, not an equipment malfunction.

When they submitted their survey report on Tau, the ISA Rangers also filed a continuing mission plan. I read it. Back then, I read everything that came in from all of the Ranger teams.

The *Vulcan*'s team was planning to stay on Tau five more weeks and finish up in-depth studies of a few particularly interesting plant and animal species. Then they moved on, or at least they were supposed to. Their mission plan said they were going to the Wolf 1061 system next to survey Wolf c and Wolf d, both of which are potentially habitable. Wolf 1061 is almost fourteen light-years from Earth and seven light-years from here. They should still be there. But they aren't. They're here.

That makes no sense at all.

Why would the Rangers have stayed on Tau for five years? Did the *Vulcan* suffer some malfunction they couldn't repair? No. If that were true, we'd have known they were stuck here. They'd have been waiting for us when we landed.

Unless they're dead.

I seriously consider turning back for about twelve seconds. Then I keep walking.

The sun is sinking into the Diamond Range, deepening the shadows and filling the blue dusk with fragmented light that shifts and dances around me as I cross the abandoned settlement. A thick layer of silver-gray dust coats everything. The same vines that grew at the feet of the orchid trees drape clusters of shiny green leaves over the domed roofs of the cabins and weave through the seams in their walls. The solar pavement that runs between the cabins crackles under my feet. That popping crumble should sound familiar. Solar paving is everywhere in the metros back home, and a lot of it is worse for wear like this. But Tau is all moist soil and rustling leaves. Here, the synthetic crunch is jarring. Alien.

I reach the far end of the settlement and wade through tall grass to where the *Vulcan* is perched. One of her struts is starting to buckle, making the ship look like it's not steady on its feet. As I get closer, I can see why. Her skin looks like it's rusting. That should be impossible. Carbon composite doesn't rust. But the green-blue crust that's crawling up the landing struts and over the *Vulcan's* hull is unmistakably decay. Tau Ceti e is eating the *Vulcan* alive.

I circle the ship to its rear airlock. The hatch doesn't respond when I try to swipe up the lock screen, but it looks like it isn't sealed. I dig my fingers into the seam between the hatch and the ship and pull. After a few seconds, the hatch swings open, exhaling a blast of stale air.

The landing ramp doesn't extend, so I have to pull myself up and crawl into the ship. It's dark inside. As I switch my flex to flashlight mode, my arm brushes the corridor wall. To my surprise, the wall screens on either side of me power up. The white-and-gray ISA logo screen appears on both walls. Interesting. The ship's solar collectors must still be working.

"Computer," I say, experimentally. "Log in to primary server, please."

The *Vulcan's* computer crackles like it's clearing its throat before replying, "I'm sorry, the requested function is password protected."

The ship's server is password protected? That's weird.

Whatever. I'm sure Mom will be able to unlock it with

her command codes. I should text her and tell her what I've found. But if I do that, she and Dad are going to send me back to camp and I'll never find out what happened here.

Taking five more minutes to look around won't hurt. The *Vulcan* isn't going anywhere. It hasn't gone anywhere in a long time.

I wander the quiet corridors. The silver-gray Tau dust has snuck in here through the cracks in the unsealed air-lock hatch. It gives the pale glow of the wall screens a dull sparkle, like the whole ship is coated in opalescent glitter. Other than the dust, the ship is empty. There are no personal items anywhere. That makes me feel a little better. Whatever happened that made the ISA Rangers abandon this ship, it wasn't a surprise. They packed their things and stowed everything away before they went.

I find the command office. The plaque on the door reads **DR. LUCILLE BROWN, COLONEL**.

Dr. Brown is a legend. Before she took command of the *Vulcan*, she wrote the book on extraterrestrial pioneering. Well, books—plural—actually. She wrote half of my textbooks at the academy.

Her office is empty, just like the rest of the ship. There's nothing on the shelves and nothing on her workstation. I run my hands through the film of dust on the wall by the door, expecting the locked-out ISA logo screen to appear. Instead, the whole office erupts in pictures. A photo collage layered with images of the same four people—two men and two women. This must be the Ranger team.

Most of these pictures were taken here on Tau Ceti e. The images are casual but vivid. Working. Playing baseball. Swimming. Rock climbing. It makes me feel like I know these people even though I only recognize one of them. I've seen Dr. Brown's picture before in her books. She's a sturdy, middle-aged white woman with long, gray-blond hair that always seems to be in a braid. She grins at me from the largest picture in the collage. In the photo, she's wading in a lake that shimmers spring green. Her arms are wrapped around a handsome man with short black hair and olive skin.

They look happy. I really hope they aren't dead.

"Joanna?" Beth's voice pops the bubble of silence so abruptly that my heart slams into overdrive again. What is she doing out here? Of all the people who might have noticed that I was gone, Beth seems the most unlikely.

I take a deep breath, letting my pounding heart settle again before I call back: "In here!"

I unwrap my flex and press it against the wall screen to download Dr. Brown's pictures as a tangle of voices and footsteps bounces through the empty ship toward me. Beth obviously isn't alone.

"Fancy running into you here," Private Lim says, flashing his usual entertained-by-life grin as he precedes my sister into the office. What the hell? Beth and Private Lim have never exchanged a single word, as far as I know. Why would she bring him with her?

"Private Lim saw you leaving camp," Beth announces before I get the chance to ask. "He suggested that I should find you before the particle shield comes online, so that you wouldn't get stuck outside."

"The shield pylons aren't even scheduled for construction until next week," I say. "There are no large predators on this continent, remember? Nothing to shield against."

"The commander tweaked the schedule," Private Lim says. "Surprise!"

Unease prickles over my scalp. Getting the shield online in a single day must have taken most of our construction crew. Why would Mom suddenly decide to prioritize the particle shield over building cabins to sleep in tonight?

"You could have just texted," I say, trying to sound un-freaked out as I pull my flex off the wall and fold it around my wrist again.

"No, I couldn't," Beth says. "The cell tower isn't up yet, remember? Nor is the camp's hot spot."

Embarrassment churns with horror in the pit of my stomach. I can't believe I did something so stupid. I was too busy being emotional about our first day on a new world to remember that it's our *first* day on a *new* world. That means no cell towers. No wireless networks. With the particle shield up, I would have been stranded out here.

The particle shield looks kind of like an enormous soap

bubble blown around the camp, but nothing bigger than an oxygen molecule can get through it. I would have been screwed if Beth and Lim hadn't come after me.

Just when I think I can't get more embarrassed, Chris throws himself through the open office door and startles me so badly that I shriek. Lim finds this deeply amusing, of course. Chris doesn't notice that he nearly gave me a heart attack.

"Guess what?" he says, talking at light speed. "Their 3D printers are all gone, and so are the recyclers. So is all the stuff in the cabins. They didn't leave anything behind." He takes a breath and notices the pictures layered across the wall screens. His eyes get even wider. "Except this, I guess. Weird."

"Did you bring the whole camp?" I snap at Beth, my heart still pounding.

"No," she says, dryly ignoring the rhetorical nature of the question, "only Chris and Private Lim."

"Nice to see you too, Joey," Chris says. I can hear the hurt feelings under his fake casual tone. Chris has always been sensitive about being left out, since he's younger than the rest of us. Why does it seem like words just charge out of my mouth these days without checking with my brain?

"Not to be the voice of reason," Lim says, interrupting my internal guilt trip. "But as much as I enjoy a good ghost town, it might be time to head back to base."

"That's what I was planning to do," I say. "Before the

crowd showed up." I was trying for haughty, but I'm pretty sure that came out defensive and whiny instead. I need to stop talking, before I embarrass myself even more.

I push past Lim and Beth and head back into the corridor. The others follow me out of the *Vulcan*. As Lim drags the unresponsive airlock hatch closed again behind us, Beth looks around thoughtfully. "How odd that we weren't notified that Dr. Brown and her team perished on the planet."

"You think the ISA knows?" I say. "The last time I checked the fleet's in-service map, the *Vulcan* was listed as scouting in the Wolf 1061 system."

"That has to be a cover," Lim says, leading the way back through the abandoned camp. "You really think the ISA just misplaced a ship by half a dozen light-years?"

"I guess you're right," I say. I don't want to believe it, but it's the only logical conclusion. "At the very least, the ISA would have noticed that the *Vulcan's* crew hasn't made contact in years."

"Five years and roughly seven months," Beth supplies. "The survey report was received in December of 2112."

"No way," Chris insists. "If the ISA knew the *Vulcan* was here, the commander would have told us. She always says that everyone on the team deserves to know why and how she makes her decisions."

"Theoretically," Beth says. "But that doesn't mean we're always going to get what we deserve. I agree with Private Lim. It's unlikely that the ISA is simply mistaken about the location of the *Vulcan* and her crew. And even if that is the case, Mom is aware of this installation. If she didn't know before we arrived, our satellites would have alerted her upon their first scan of the continent."

"Why keep it secret then?" Chris says.

The question balloons through the deep-blue evening air as we cross into the orchid grove. Nobody offers an answer. I don't know about Private Lim or Beth, but I keep my mouth shut because all the answers I can think of are terrifying. Especially after Mom went out of her way to get the particle shield up.

Mom doesn't think we're safe here, even though the survey report says there's nothing dangerous on this continent. That means we can't trust the survey report. Or the ISA. It might even mean that we can't trust my mom. Something really bad happened here, and she's keeping it secret even though she's afraid that it's going to happen to us.

The massive, delicate cups of the giant orchids are dyed black with shadows in the last of the daylight. They loom over us, turning the soothing oasis of the grove forbidding and strange.

I hear something. The sound is so quiet that I can't describe it. But it's not the wind. Something is moving out there, in the trees. Something big.

Fear skitters over my skin with clammy feet.

I stop and look behind us.

"Hello?" I call into the shadows.

The whisper of movement evaporates at the sound of my voice.

"You see something?" Lim asks.

I hold a *not now* hand up.

"Dr. Brown?" I call out again. But the quiet doesn't respond.

"We have twelve minutes to get back to base," Beth calls over her shoulder. She's a few meters ahead with Chris. "Then we'll be stuck outside the shield until someone realizes we're gone."

She's right. But I can't shake the feeling that the dense shadows behind us are alive. We aren't alone out here. I'm sure of it.

"Even if she's out there, there's no use hanging around if she doesn't want to chat, Hotshot," Lim says, quietly.

I nod again and start walking. I can still feel the unseen eyes on the back of my neck. Is it Dr. Brown? Or is it the thing that happened to Dr. Brown?

THREE

"Why didn't you tell us what happened to the Rangers?" I thrust the question ahead of myself as I storm into the tent Mom is using as an office.

"Because I don't know what happened to them," Mom says without looking up from the cluster of apps she has open on the touch screen canvas wall. She has the whole tent set to exterior cameras, so it looks like we're still outside and her apps are hovering in midair. She drops a note of *don't push your luck* into her voice as she adds, "I also don't know why my seventeen-year-old daughter would wander off without telling anyone she was leaving camp."

"What, are you tracking my flex now?"

"No," Mom says, offering me an elaborately disappointed look. "I made an educated guess based on your question, which you could not possibly have known to ask unless you took an unauthorized bush walk and stumbled on the *Vulcan*. We're on an uninhabited planet with no cell towers or satellite hot spots. I have no way of keeping track of you. Nor should I have to, since you've been training for this mission your whole life and you know better."

Embarrassment cracks my outrage. I also should have known better than to pick a fight with my mom. She always finds a way to be right.

"I forgot about the comms," I admit.

Mom's jaw actually drops, like I've stunned her with the depths of my stupidity. "You need to read the survey report again," she says, "at least twice. If you're not going to stay on base, then you need to know what's out there."

The sticky heat of humiliation evaporates in an electric prickle of excitement. *If you're not going to stay on base.* She said that like I can just choose to come and go whenever I want. Does she really mean that? I'm tempted to ask, but I decide to keep my mouth shut and not give her the chance to change her mind. I was planning to read the survey report again anyway. It'd be dumb to wander around on this planet *knowing* I'm not prepared.

A fresh question dumps cold water on my excitement. "Will reading the survey report actually prepare me for Tau? Or are there a bunch of other secrets that the ISA is keeping from us?"

The question takes Mom by surprise. She studies me

for what feels like a long time. Then she says, "As far as I know, the report is accurate. However, it is not complete."

"What do you mean, not complete?" I ask. The words feel slippery in my mouth. I couldn't hold on to them if I wanted to. "What's missing? Is something wrong with this planet? Are we going to have to abort the mission and go home? Was this all for nothing?"

Mom smiles gingerly, like the expression kind of hurts. "You mean, did Teddy die for nothing?"

I don't trust myself to speak without crying, so I just nod.

"I can't tell you much, but I can tell you this. Whatever happens here, our . . ." She trails off, like she can't bear to say the words out loud. Then she braces herself and starts again. "Whatever happens here, Teddy's death wasn't in vain. In fact, it means more than you could ever guess."

Her voice is shaking, just a little bit. Unshed tears shine in her eyes. I see pride there. And pain. I understand how she feels. That's a startling thought. I haven't felt like Mom and I understood each other for a long time.

Mom huffs a sigh, exhaling the emotional moment so she can move on. "I wish I could explain everything to you, Jo."

"Why can't you?"

"It's classified," Mom says. "Most Secret. Technically, I am not even allowed to acknowledge that the report is incomplete, but you asked me a direct question, and I don't lie to my people." She looks me in the eye. "I also don't lie to my children. I never have, and I don't plan to start."

"But I'm going to have to lie, aren't I?" I say, my stomach twisting into a knot as I realize what *classified* means in this situation. "The abandoned base must be part of the classified stuff."

"Yes, it is," Mom says. She doesn't make any excuses, or try to make me feel better about this. "You're not a cadet anymore, so I can't order you to keep this secret. But there will be consequences for me, and for this team, if you decide to share what you've learned. I hope you'll take that into account as you decide what to do next."

. . . as you decide what to do next.

She's seriously going to leave it up to me whether I keep a secret this huge? I didn't think she trusted me that much. I didn't think she trusted me at all.

Mom ignores my stunned expression and turns back to the wall screen to close her apps. "Now, I'm hungry, and after your hike I'm sure you are too. Shall we see if Dr. Kao has some dinner left?"

I follow Mom to the temporary mess hall that Dr. Kao set up at the center of what will be our base camp. Keeping the abandoned base and the *Vulcan* secret feels wrong, but so does telling everyone classified information Mom asked me to keep private. I used to always feel so sure about things. Then the accident happened, and nothing feels like it's just right or wrong anymore. I hate that. But I guess if neither of my choices feels right, I might as well do what Mom asked me to do.

It only takes Mom seven days to initiate Stage Two of the E&P plan. I find that kind of alarming. The whole point of Stage One was to give us time to independently confirm the ISA Ranger team's findings before we start building stuff. Given the circumstances, I thought Mom would want to be really thorough about Stage One surveys so we can be sure we're safe here.

I seem to be the only one who's surprised that she's in a hurry. I guess Tau is so perfect that nobody sees the point in being cautious. Dad assures me that he's going to finish confirming the Rangers' findings himself while the rest of us get started on construction. That makes me wonder if he knows the truth about the Rangers and he's completing Stage One alone so that nobody else finds out. I hate this. Even when I was totally pissed off with my parents, after the accident, I trusted them. Now, I don't think I do.

After that, the days fly by in a blur of construction duty, sweat, and exhaustion. Our settlement is getting bigger as fast as the 3D printers can fabricate materials.

First, we build four hot spots, one at each corner of the plot of land we plan to transform into our base camp. The wireless network won't reach more than a few meters past the particle shield, but it's a start. Next we build the hospital—a triple dome with ten scanner beds and a full nanosurgical suite. After that comes the water treatment plant and communal bathrooms. Eventually, we'll run pipes up to the rest of the settlement and have running water in all the buildings, but that's pretty far down the to-do list.

We spend most of the second week constructing the mess hall and the Ground Control Center, which houses Mom's office and all the other ISA administration stuff. Sort of like a city hall, except we don't have a city yet. Lab space comes next, because scientists would rather sleep on the floor next to their electron microscopes than worry about little things like beds or privacy.

On Tau Day thirty-three, Dad prints up a sign that reads: **PIONEER'S LANDING**. He hangs it above the main entrance to Ground Control. Beth points out that the name is factually inaccurate, since the *Pioneer* will never actually land here. But it sticks. By the end of our second month, everyone is referring to the settlement as "the Landing."

That was weeks ago. There are a ton of labs finished now, and we're starting on private dwellings. Doc has started the process of waking civilians from inso so there are more hands to help. There are also more mouths to feed. We've been here for a little over four Earth-standard months, which is a little over half a Tau year since this planet takes only 225 days to orbit its sun. I think I've spent at least a third of that time doing dishes or stirring pots of beans and rice in the kitchens with Dr. Kao.

Dr. Mohan Kao worked on the International Space Station for five years before he joined the Project. He likes zero-g because he's paraplegic, and in space he doesn't need a chair. But he couldn't resist the opportunity to see a new planet. Dr. Kao calls himself our cook, but he's a actually a psychiatrist who specializes in nutrition. He's responsible for making sure we all stay sane. It's a pretty gnarly job, considering how far we are from home. I'm fully aware that I keep ending up on kitchen patrol because he's keeping an eye on my mental health. It's annoying just on principle, but I don't really mind hanging out with Dr. Kao. He's easy to talk to, and he never acts like he wants to fix me.

KP duty also gives me a good excuse to avoid eating meals with my friends. Miguel and Leela and Chris have been hanging out with Jay Lim a lot. Most nights they eat together by the fire pits. Beth joins them sometimes too. It'd be weird if I just avoided them for no reason, but KP is the perfect excuse not to hang out.

When I do sit with them, I end up fixating on all the terrifying secrets we know that Miguel and Leela don't. It elevates my arctic awkwardness with Leela from uncomfortable to unbearable.

They're all too polite to notice that I'm avoiding them. Chris isn't. He keeps bugging me to sit with them. Tonight, I gave in. It did not go well. I've never been so glad to have dish duty in my life.

When Jay comes into the mess hall after dinner, I have to fight the urge to hide until he leaves. I wait for him to say something about how weird Leela and I were at dinner as

I scrub out the bean pots and the rice cooker. He doesn't.

I tie off the bags of compost and recycling. I load them onto a float cart.

Jay just sits there, reading.

I should just take this stuff to the recycling center and go to bed.

"I'm sorry," I blurt out.

"For what?" he says without looking up from his flex.

"For earlier. Leela. Me." I shrug. "We're just . . ." I don't know what we are, actually. But Jay seems to get what I'm saying.

He nods as he folds his flex and wraps it around his wrist. "You two are dealing with some heavy stuff after the accident."

"Good to know we're a hot topic," I say, trying hard not to sound as irate as I feel. It's not exactly surprising that rumors move at the speed of light on a planet with only 197 people on it, but it's still annoying.

"Nah," he says. "Chris said something to me, but he wasn't gossiping or anything. Just sad. Poor kid. Feels like his family got ripped apart."

It did.

The words are on the tip of my tongue, but I bite them back. I don't want to talk about it. With anyone. Especially not a hot guy I hardly know.

Jay doesn't press the issue. He just goes back to his book.

Avid reader was not on the list of hobbies I might have guessed for a guy with so many muscles, but I guess that whole books-and-covers thing is a cliché for a reason.

I want to know what kind of stuff he reads, but I don't want to encourage him by asking. It's pretty obvious that he doesn't come to the mess to read because of the cafeteria-style benches or the instant coffee. He sits in here to read because I'm here. He doesn't make a big deal about it. He doesn't say anything unless I talk to him first. He's just there.

I can't decide how that makes me feel. I mean, he is hot and he's only nine months older than I am. He's also smart, or at least well read. And I'm getting kind of used to talking to him every day. But my life is complicated enough without adding in romantic melodrama. Besides, I can't seem to have even a short conversation with the guy without embarrassing myself in some way. I'm sure my awkwardness will convince him that I'm a bad idea eventually.

I wipe down the counters one more time and then I grab the handle of the float cart with the recycling and head for the door.

"Need a hand?" Jay says. He always offers. I always say . . .

"Nope. Thanks, though."

The recycling plant is a little ways upriver from the Landing proper. I like the solitude of walking out there in the silver light of the moons.

Beth insisted that we construct the recycling plant

without clearing any of the fido trees that grow around it, so their neon-flowered branches drape the recycling center's domes and twine through the doorframes. The trees reach out to me with their feeler branches as I pull the doors open, tangling their tendrils in my hair.

I gently swat them away. "I know, I know, you love the taste of bean juice in the evening."

Another branch wafts out to nuzzle my face with a cluster of flowers. That makes me smile. Beth assures me that it's an instinctive response to movement and the trees are just checking to see if I'm edible. I don't care. It's cute.

I dump the dishes into the recycler and take my time walking back. The second moon is rising, and the Landing glows in the silver-tinged darkness. It's really starting to look like a place now. The streets are paved with solar tiles, and the garden plots in front of each cabin are tilled and waiting for Beth to finish prepping Stage Three.

Stage Three of the E&P plan is terraforming. There isn't much to do on Tau. The atmosphere is already perfect, but the soil is missing some important stuff that we need for growing Earth crops. Part of Beth's doctoral thesis was developing a genetically tailored bacteria that will produce the additional nutrients that Earth plants need without messing anything up for the native species. Basically, we're giving the planet a big dose of probiotics to help it digest Earth stuff, just like we'd give a person who was having stomach problems. Once we've got enough treated soil to go around, every single one of these cabins will have its own garden.

I fall asleep the second I stretch out in the tent Beth and I share. My flex wakes me just before dawn. I go to the mess hall and get the oatmeal started, then run down to the bathrooms to get a shower before the breakfast rush.

The early-morning air is chilly when I turn off the spray of hot water, so I hurry to get dressed. The locker room has stacks of freshly 3D printed uniforms and civilian clothes, plus a couple of drying racks for stuff people care enough about to actually wash instead of just recycling.

My jeans are clean and dry. I pull them on and slip into a long-sleeved thermal, then add my NASA T-shirt. My sneakers are falling apart, so I toss them in the recycling bin and snag a pair of ergofoam-soled hiking boots. I should probably recycle these jeans too, but it feels good to look like a normal girl every once in a while.

After Dr. Kao and I serve breakfast, I wolf down a bowl of oatmeal and report to Sergeant Nolan for a work assignment. He took over ground crew organization from Chief Penny after Tau Day One. She's got too much else on her plate. Sarge puts me on construction again. My first assignment is in the greenhouse. It's built on the same frame as a normal double cabin, but with plexiglass touch-screen panels instead of the usual canvas ones. This morning I'm assembling long tables for the lab at the back of the twin domes. The rest of the space is filled with planting boxes that already contain rows of corn and wheat seedlings, waiting for Stage Three soil. Once the tables are finished, I help Beth move the pair of incubators she's using to cultivate the Stage Three bacteria onto them. The plastic boxes lined with heated ergofoam aren't heavy, but they're delicate. Each one contains five petri dishes of Stage Three.

Once I'm finished in the greenhouse, I move on to the school. This is where Leela's mom will teach the little kids. Most of the other Project children were born during the ten years we spent preparing to leave Earth, so they're a lot younger than us. I envy them. I spent my whole childhood daydreaming about growing up on another planet. They actually get to do it.

The school is almost finished. It just needs doors and windows. The window panels are octagonal, just like the regular wall-screen panels. They're easy to pop into place. The door is not, but I manage to set it on its hinges without drawing any blood, which is a first. I'm getting the hang of this construction thing. I'm not sure how I feel about that.

I don't feel like a useless freeloader anymore, which is good. But every time I hear the deep whine of the *Wagon* preparing for liftoff while I'm in the middle of welding a seam or laying floor tiles, I get so . . . I don't know. Jealous seems too petty and small to really describe the feeling, but I guess that's what it is. I don't want to be stuck here on the ground, covered in dust and carbon caulking and sweat.

I want to fly.

But all the wanting in the world isn't going to fix my

heart or make my pacers less fragile. I should be grateful to those stupid little machines. They're keeping me alive. But I'm not. I hate them for not being what I need them to be.

I step into the schoolhouse and pull the completed door closed behind me. I set the windows to opaque, which should eliminate all the light in the cabin. It doesn't. I can see two slender glimmers still tracing through the ceiling. I mark the weak spots and turn the lights back on as I pull my handheld laser welder out of my utility harness. I turn the power to the lowest setting before I switch it on.

This welder is small, but it's really powerful. The chief made me do a whole day of training with her before she'd let me carry one. If I turned this thing all the way up, I could melt a hole in the cabin wall, and maybe the one next door, too.

Next, I connect the cabin to the *Pioneer*'s data network. A work-in-progress bar appears on each of the walls, the ceiling, and the floor.

I open the windows and the door while I wait. The cross breeze dances over my sweaty skin. Just when I'm starting to enjoy it, a blast of hot air washes the delicate eddies away with a swollen roar. The *Wagon* is taking off again.

Jealousy takes my good mood and twists it inside out. Suddenly, I'm hot, sticky, and bored, and the stupid, swirling breeze is so weak, it can't be bothered to cool me off properly. I just want to get this over with.

"Initializing educator program," the computer says. The animated panda avatar of our educational software bounces over the walls. I press my palm against the bear. It rolls onto its back.

"Hello, Joanna Watson!" it says, recognizing my bio-print. "Are you ready to learn today?"

"No," I say. "Initiate satellite connection."

The panda cocks its animated head to one side like it's concerned. "I detect negative tones in your vocal modulation, Joanna," it says. "Is something bothering you?"

"Just you," I say. "Initiate your satellite connection, please."

The panda looks sad. "That hurt my feelings, Joanna. Is there another way to ask that might make me feel better about helping you?"

Wow, the new empathy subroutines in this thing are incredibly annoying. I already feel like a petty, envious jerk. The last thing I need is a guilt trip from an avatar with no actual emotions. I pull up a window and open the program override. That way I can test the system without this stupid bear pouting at me.

The panda stares at me with big, hurt eyes as I enter my override code.

I just can't do it.

I cancel and close the window. "I'm sorry, educator," I say, approximating a patient tone of voice. "Nothing is bothering me. Would you mind initiating the school's satellite connection? Please?"

"Of course, Joanna!" The panda bounces, excited. "I'd be happy to! One moment!"

Stupid bear.

"I am now linked to Pioneer One, Pioneer Two, Pioneer Three, Pioneer Four, Vulcan One, and Vulcan Two," the educator announces.

That's interesting.

"You're connected to the *Vulcan's* satellite network?"

"I am programmed to connect to all available International Space Agency satellites, Joanna. I can access them for educational purposes."

"Right," I say. My brain is spinning so fast, it feels like it's trying to create artificial gravity on the inside of my skull. The *Vulcan's* computers were password protected, but I wonder if Dr. Brown, or whoever locked the *Vulcan* down, bothered to do the same thing to the satellites.

"Is there any surface navigation data stored in Vulcan One or Vulcan Two?" I ask the educator.

"Would you like to see surface navigation data for this continent?" the educator says. "Or for the southern continent?"

"This one," I say, trying not to get excited. In her book on surveying, Dr. Brown made a big deal about saving navigational data. Assuming she takes her own advice, the *Vulcan's* satellites should be able to tell me the ISA Ranger team's last destination.

A satellite map of the continent appears on the wall screen in front of me. It's crisscrossed with jagged green GPS routes. I can see Pioneer's Landing in the lower right-hand quadrant of the map, and the *Vulcan*, about a kilometer upriver. As you would expect, that's where most of the routes begin and end.

"Educator, can you tell me which of these routes is the most recent?"

A green line that jags from the *Vulcan* into the mountains turns red. "This route was recorded seven January 2113, Earth standard time, Joanna," the educator says.

That's two weeks after the date on the Rangers' survey report. Whatever happened to the Rangers, it started on that trip. It must have.

"Watson!" Sarge's voice booms through the thin walls of the schoolhouse. "You taking a nap in there?"

"No sir!" I call back, pulling off my flex and pressing it to the wall.

"Then get a move on!"

"Educator, please transfer this map to my flex."

"My pleasure, Joanna!" My flex glows briefly. The panda crows, "Transfer complete!"

As I wrap my flex around my wrist again and make for the door, the educator calls after me, "Have a lovely day, Joanna!"

By the time Sarge excuses the construction team, I've decided to steal a flyer and see what's out there.

There are so many reasons I shouldn't do it, even if I were medically fit to fly, which I'm not. But I'm going to do it anyway. If I keep the flyer slow and steady, it'll give my pacers time to handle the altitude changes. I'll be fine. Or I'll crash into a cliff.

Whatever. This is a terrible plan, from start to finish. I know that. I know I should just give the coordinates to Mom. But she wouldn't tell me what she found out there. She couldn't. If I hand this over, I'll never know what happened to the Rangers and neither will the rest of the team. Not unless it happens to us, too.

Something on this planet almost certainly killed a team of the ISA's best scouts. How are we supposed to be ready to deal with it if we don't know what it is? And if we're not ready, will we survive?

The Engineering Department set up shop at the eastern edge of the Landing. They're working out of an open-sided tent built over the 3D printers. Eventually they will have a proper 3D shop and a hangar for the flyers and jeeps. But at the moment both of our flyers are parked in the meadow outside the tent.

Flyers are Vertical Takeoff and Landing vehicles, so the long, spindly rotors that bristle from the ends of their narrow wings rotate once they're off the ground to become propellers, then tilt up again when you land. That way you don't need a runway. They're bigger than Grandpa's Cessna—big enough to hold ten people and cargo—but they're really easy to fly. The autopilot can handle almost everything. If I do pass out, the flyer can probably get me home on its own.

I climb into the closest one and settle into the pilot seat. I feel energized and also vaguely nauseous, like I just drank one of the huge, caffeinated frappes that Beth loves. The little voice in my head reminding me that this is a stupid idea gets quieter as I bring up the navigation app from the wall screen. It feels so right to be back in the pilot seat. Like the ghost of the girl I was just slipped under my skin.

"Computer, switch to exterior cameras, please," I say.

A three-sixty of the meadow and the 3D shop tent flickers onto the wall screens around me just in time for my sister's voice to fill the audio feed.

"My electron microscope needs to be moved to the top of the queue, Chris. This shouldn't even be a debate."

Crap. What is Beth doing out here? I don't see her in the meadow. She must be in the 3D shop with Chris. Just my luck. If Beth catches me, she'll tell Mom. I'll end up locked in the mess hall with Dr. Kao twenty-two hours a day like a little kid who can't be trusted on her own.

I scramble out of the flyer. I'm just closing the rear hatch when Beth, Chris, and Jay emerge from the 3D shop.

"—to the commander, if I have to," Jay is saying. "I'm acting on her orders. Security at the Landing is priority one."

"By all means," Beth snaps. "Let's consult my mother.

A secure food supply is just as important to our safety as weaponry, and I can*not* properly evaluate the Stage Three bacteria's engagement with our soil samples without electrophoresis—"

Chris takes me as a perfect opportunity to ignore both of them.

"Hey, Joey," he says. "What are you doing out here? I thought you were on construction duty."

Before I can come up with a reasonable lie, Jay says, "Looks to me like Hotshot is stealing a flyer."

How the hell did he know that?

I'm about to protest when Beth says, "Jo has no reason to steal a flyer. She is physically incapable of safely piloting an aerial vehicle."

"And thankfully, you're always here to remind me of that," I mutter. "Just in case I forget that pesky heart condition."

"There's no need for sarcasm, Joanna," Beth says.

"It's more of a want than a need thing."

Jay bursts out laughing. "You're a hoot, Hotshot, you know that?"

I try not to glare at him, but I totally fail.

Jay chuckles again. "Don't worry, I won't rat you out. Assuming you tell me why you're trying to steal the birdie. Too much curiosity gives me a headache."

"It's about the Rangers, isn't it?" Chris says, bubbling with excitement. "You found something out. You must have. What else could be worth sneaking off for?"

Damn it. Sometimes being surrounded by people who've known you your whole life just isn't fair.

"Maybe," I say. I pull off my flex and hand it to Chris. As he scans the GPS data, I give them the short version of the story.

"It would be a quick trip," Jay says, leaning over Chris's shoulder to study the Rangers' GPS route. "And unlike Hotshot, I'm cleared to fly."

"Mom went up to the *Pioneer* again to double-check the automatic systems. There's some kind of glitch in the superluminal transponder," Chris says. "And Dad's leading a foraging team on the eastern coast. Nobody'll notice I'm gone."

Beth sighs. "There's no need to be sneaky. Dr. Howard gave me clearance to recruit people for short-range foraging expeditions in his absence, so if we take some cuttings while we're out, then we won't even be breaking the rules."

"Classy," Jay says. "I'm in."

"No," I say. "You're definitely not coming with me. None of you are. It's too risky."

Chris arcs a dubious eyebrow. "For us, but not for you?"

"Yes," I snap. "My idea. My risk. Not yours."

"Too bad," Jay says. "'Cause if you go, we go. Or nobody goes."

His smile is both pleasant and implacable. He means it.

"It's your call, Hotshot."

FOUR

It's good to be off the ground, even if I'm not at the controls. Soaring over the rolling green prairie makes me feel, I don't know, giddy, I guess. It's hard to sit still. I want to untether from my seat and press my face against the wall screens so I can watch Tau flow past us.

Cliffs of cloudy crystal rear up out of the prairie as we head west into the Diamond Range. The gleaming, translucent peaks crash and swell over deep ravines and canyons drenched in shades of green.

I can feel my lungs working harder as we climb into the mountains, like I'm running instead of strapped into a seat. My pacers are struggling with the altitude change. I brace myself for the sparkly mist of oxygen deprivation to cloud my vision, but it never comes. I'm glad. I don't want to miss this.

The Rangers' last coordinates lead us to a narrow ravine cut deep into the glittering cliffs. It's tiny, smaller than Pioneer's Landing will be when we're finished with construction. My head swims as the flyer descends. By the time I catch my breath, Jay has opened the rear hatch and lowered the ramp. I untether myself and follow the others out.

The air has a chilly bite. It smells like cedar and sugared pears. There are no signs of the Rangers. No abandoned flyer. No ruined cabins. Just trees. Clusters of skinny, white-barked trees with crowns of feathery, blue-tinged fronds scatter across the ravine floor and cling to the steep, translucent cliffs. They look like a geneticist got drunk and crossed a palm tree with a parrot. The parrot palm clusters tower over low-slung trees with massive, gnarled trunks and meaty, circular leaves the size of my hand. I recognize them from the survey report's species index. They're carnivorous plants, like the fido trees by the Landing.

Beth is in heaven. She spends an hour collecting samples while Jay and I search for any sign of the Rangers. Chris is "helping" her by walking the river looking for shore and aquatic species. I think it's just an excuse to go wading. I don't blame him. The river is shallow and just fast moving enough that it dances around his knees.

"Looks like fun," Jay says, stopping beside me to watch Chris splash.

"It does," I say as I start walking upriver again. "Kind of against protocol, but this whole outing is . . ."

"Rebellious?" Jay says, finishing my thought.

"That's one way to put it," I say.

"Those rules about not disrupting the native ecosystem always struck me as wishful thinking anyway," he says. "You can't become a part of something without changing it. Whether you want to or not."

I don't say anything for a while. I just walk and watch the dappled sunlight spin as the corkscrew breeze plays with the trees. He's contradicting the thesis we've been working toward my whole life—that it's possible for humans to live on other planets without environmental impact. I want to argue with him, but my brain keeps going back to the jarring pop and crumble of the brittle solar tiles in the Rangers' dead settlement. That noise belongs at Langley, outside Grandpa's office on base, not here. But it's a part of this place now, because we are. We've already changed Tau. I hope that turns out to be a good thing.

We've almost reached the end of the ravine. Water runs down the ragged cliffs, tumbling into the river. Jay reaches out to let the gentle waterfall flow over his fingers.

"Careful," I say, gingerly poking at the spikes of crystal that jag through the running water. They're hard and crazy sharp. They feel more like metal than the crystals you'd find on Earth. "Come on, let's check out the other side of the river," I say, wading into the shallows.

Jay pulls a stun gun from his belt and clips it to his shoulder harness before following me in.

"Gotta keep these things dry," he says, catching what must be a weird look on my face.

"Right," I say, like it's no big deal. But it totally is. Why is he armed? Stun guns aren't lethal, of course, but weapons aren't standard equipment, even for the squad. I remember Mom and Dad arguing about whether to even include them in the 3D printer's gear catalogue. Mom thought we should leave guns behind on Earth. Dad thought that was naive. Guess he won.

"You think you're going to need that?" I say, gesturing to his stun gun as we slosh through the water.

"I hope not," Jay says. "But the commander ordered the whole squad to carry at all times." He hesitates a second, like he's deciding whether to say something. Then he adds, "She's got the perimeter patrols at the Landing wearing body armor and carrying rifles."

My stomach clenches at the thought.

"No way," I say. "Mom hates guns."

"Maybe so," Jay says. "But she gave the order. All patrols have been fully armed since Tau Day Four."

That's so out of character for Mom that I have to resist the impulse to argue with him. There's no reason to think Jay is lying. But Mom didn't want to bring guns here at all, and now she's arming our patrols. I think that might be more terrifying than all the other secrets put together.

My wet jeans cling to my skin, and my feet squish inside my boots as we climb out of the thigh-high water. The banks of the river are covered in patches of tiny, purple-leaved plants that are so closely packed together they feel squishy underfoot, like the ergofoam deck tiles on the

Pioneer. The trees on this side of the river are bigger and farther apart. Unlike the fido trees, they have sprawling, thick branches that would make them look a lot like the ancient oak trees on my grandfather's farm back on Earth, if not for their fan-shaped leaves, which roll in on themselves when we brush past them like oblong tongues licking at the air.

The trees are so far apart on this side of the river that you can see all the way to the other end of the ravine. There's no sign of anything remotely human.

"Maybe this isn't the last place they went," Jay says. "Maybe their GPS broke down or something while they were out here, and the return trip just wasn't tracked."

"I guess," I say. I stop and twist back, turning to take in the tiny valley. The blue-and-green-leaved trees. The vibrant plants clustering over the ground between them. The tumbling river and the dull sparkle of the veined cliffs. It's untouched. Pristine. "If they were here, it sure doesn't look like they stayed long."

My flex buzzes against my wrist. "Excuse me, Joanna," the computerized voice says. "I'm picking up a transmission."

"There shouldn't be any comms out here," Jay says, startled.

"There aren't," I say. Then, to my flex, "Locate the source of the transmission, please."

"The transmission originates from an automated beacon seven meters due southeast," the flex replies. The compass app pops up automatically, displaying a three-dimensional image of an old-fashioned compass with a flashing white light indicating the direction. I pivot until it turns green and start walking.

"It must be a passive RFID alert," I say. "ISA flexes are set to scan for them at all times." I duck under a spray of low-hanging branches, snag my jeans on a bush bristling with yellow thorns, and half stumble into the little clearing.

Three oblong piles of rock lie at its center.

Graves.

I'm stunned. I don't know how long I stand there, staring. Long enough that Jay puts a gentle hand on my shoulder to get my attention.

"I'm going to go find Beth and the kid," he says. "You okay here on your own?"

I nod. "I'll scan the tags."

"Good call," he says, disappearing through the trees.

I crouch next to the graves and shake out my flex to scan them. It finds three passive RFID tags buried in the tidily arranged stones. The graves belong to Dr. Rylan Pasha, Dr. Amahle Obasi, and Dr. Vitor Sousa. There's no other information in the tags, other than a request to leave the bodies in place if they're discovered.

"Whoa," Chris says as he and Beth follow Jay into the clearing. "Mystery solved, I guess."

"Three of the Rangers are here," I say. "Dr. Brown isn't. She must be the one who buried them."

"I wonder if she's still alive," Chris says. The thought of Dr. Brown standing over these graves makes me sick to my stomach. I can imagine how lonely that must have felt. I wish I couldn't.

"According to the burial markers, these graves are five Earth-standard years old," Beth says, unfolding her flex to scan the tags herself. "It's unlikely Dr. Brown survived alone here for that period of time."

I hope not.

How terrible is that, to hope that someone died? But the thought of being utterly alone for years on end is worse.

"We should erect a particle shield around this area," Beth says. "Until it can be examined further."

"There should be a portable shield in the flyer's supply kit," Jay says.

"I'll get it," I say, starting back toward the flyer before they can argue. I need to be alone for a minute.

I don't know why I'm so freaked. I knew the Rangers had to be dead, but seeing the stone cairns made me feel tight and weird. Those graves might answer the question of why the Rangers didn't leave Tau, but they raise a dozen more. What happened to them? Is Dr. Brown still alive? If she isn't, what happened to her? Why did she abandon their ship and their settlement? And why are parts of the survey report classified? What did the Rangers find here that ISA decided to keep secret from everyone, including us?

I'm so busy sorting out my questions and secrets that I'm not looking where I'm going. I trip over a gnarled surface root from one of the hybrid trees and go sprawling face-first into the dirt.

Damn it.

I roll onto my back and sit up.

My wet jeans are coated in sparkly gray dust, and my hands are bleeding. Fabulous. Now I'll have to go to medical and get checked for unknown Tau bacteria and whatever else might be in the gravel that's embedded in my palms. Maybe Miguel can do it, so I can avoid a lecture from Doc. Miguel has been up on the *Pioneer* for a while, putting the insulated-sleep system in standby mode, but I think Leela's bringing him down with her this trip.

I stand up.

The ground crumbles into dust under my feet.

My brain stutters. For half a second, I'm falling out of the *Pioneer* again, tumbling through the endless void of space. Memory sears my skin with the frozen fire of solar radiation.

Then I hit the ground.

The impact snaps me out of my panicked flashback. I'm lying on something soft and damp in what seems to be a cave. It isn't deep—I can see the cave ceiling less than three meters above me. I can't see much else. The shaft of light that tumbles through the hole I just punched in the ground only makes the shadows deeper.

The tree's massive taproot has grown right through the center of the cave. It stretches down into the cave floor in a massive tangle of hairy tendrils that almost look as though they're glowing. No, wait. They *are* glowing. Their pale-pink light is barely bright enough to be seen with the daylight pouring in from above, but it's there.

I sit up cautiously, and the mushy thing I'm sitting on squishes wetly under my weight. What is that? Do I want to know? Mysteriously moist things found in caves are almost guaranteed to be gross.

I switch my flex to flashlight mode. White light blooms from my wrist. I brace myself and look down. I'm sitting on what's left of an ISA sleeping bag. It's just like the one on my cot at the Landing, but shredded and gray-blue with what looks like mold.

Yuck. I scramble to my feet and dust myself off. Then I play the light from my flex over the sleeping bag. Where the crusty blue stuff has been knocked loose, I can see the original fabric is red. *Vulcan* colors.

I look around, holding up my wrist to pan the light over the rest of the cave. Except it isn't just a cave. It's a campsite. Or what's left of one. There's a makeshift fire pit in the middle of the floor and a tiny combo 3D printer/recycler in the far corner. The kind they stash in the emergency kits on flyers just in case you get stuck somewhere for a few days and you need to print basic tools. Twists of cable run up from the little 3D to the ceiling, where shattered fragments of solar paneling dangle like holiday garlands around the hole left by my fall. There must have been solar panels up there that got covered in dirt. They were probably too brittle to hold my weight.

"Joey!"

"Joanna!"

"Hotshot, talk to me!"

"I'm okay," I call up to my friends. "Just be careful. The ground isn't stable around the roots of this tree."

Jay swings himself over the lip of the hole and drops into the cave. He looks around and whistles appreciatively. "Gotta hand it to you, Hotshot. You have a talent for stumbling on mysterious stuff."

"Falling," I say. "In this case."

Jay bursts out laughing like that was a way funnier joke as Chris lowers himself through the hole. He moves more cautiously, dangling for a moment before he drops.

"Crazy," he says, flipping his flex to flashlight mode. "These tree roots are huge! You could build a house in there."

"These trees are *Chorulux neon*, so named for their bioluminescent root systems," Beth says as she leans over the edge of the hole to drive a climbing anchor into the rock. "According to the survey report, the glow attracts subterranean invertebrates, which the tree then dissolves and consumes."

Chris takes a big step back from the roots.

Beth rolls her eyes. "You've got two hundred and six too many bones for *Chorulux neon*'s taste, Chris." She activates her tether. The line snaps out and bonds with her anchor.

As she rappels into the cave, I notice something in the ashes of the fire pit. It's a crumpled flexible tablet. I smooth it out. It's probably long dead, but I swipe a finger over the fire-scarred surface just in case.

To my surprise, the screen flickers to life. The wallpaper is set to that same picture of Dr. Brown and Dr. Pasha in the lake. It must be her personal flex. It has a ton of games and books and music stored on it, as well as three folders full of files labeled Backup, Pictures, and Maps.

I open the Maps folder and tap on a file labeled Diamond Range. A topographical map of the mountains flows over the singed screen. It's way more detailed than the map in the survey report. We already knew the Rangers were planning to stay on Tau a few extra weeks to do more research. I guess part of that research involved an additional survey of these mountains.

Dr. Brown has the flex set to link the geotags on her pictures to locations on the map. Dozens of images pop up for almost every named location. The picture of Dr. Brown and Dr. Pasha is linked to a lake the Rangers named Reflections. It's about one hundred klicks south of here. They named a bunch of other landmarks too—rivers, mountains, valleys. Even this tiny ravine has a name. *Jannah*. I don't recognize the word, so I access the flex's dictionary and discover it's a name for paradise in some of the Islamic traditions. The Rangers must have really loved it here. No wonder Dr. Brown chose this place to bury her friends.

I'm so absorbed that I don't notice Chris coming to look over my shoulder. "Wonder why they bothered to build hot spots out here," he says, pointing to a scatter of bright-green plus signs on the map that indicate wireless network hubs. "Wouldn't it be easier to just carry sat phones while they were out surveying?"

"Judging by how closely they've mapped the area, the Ranger team spent a lot of time up here. It would have been practical to establish a few permanent campsites near points of interest, so that they didn't have to return to the *Vulcan* every night," Beth points out without looking up from the sample of glowing root she's collecting.

"Makes sense to me," Jay says.

"We should check them out," Chris says eagerly. "There might be stuff there that'd tell us more about what happened to the Rangers."

"I'm sure the commander will send teams to recon those sites," Jay says.

"You're going to show the commander this map?" Chris says. "How are you going to explain where we found it without getting us in trouble?"

"We have to tell her the truth," I say. "She needs to know what's out here."

"We're going to be on KP forever," he moans.

"Probably," Jay agrees. "But hey, kitchen patrol means we get first dibs on the grub."

Does nothing put this guy in a bad mood? You'd think

constant cheerfulness would be annoying, but there's something about his unflappable good humor that makes the idea of sharing KP duty with him palatable. I think I might even be looking forward to it.

Thankfully, Chris's flex bleats a reminder alert before I have time for too much self-examination.

"Time for your vitamins?" Jay teases.

Chris rolls his eyes. "I set that to alert me when the *Wagon* was scheduled to depart the *Pioneer*. If we head back now, we have just enough time to get back to the Landing before my mom makes it dirtside."

"Clever," I say.

"Not that it makes any difference now," he grumbles.

"Into every life, a little KP duty must fall," Jay says. With that, he jumps up and hooks his hands over the lip of the cave entrance, then hauls himself out with no visible effort.

"Showoff."

"What is that saying about pots and kettles that Dad likes?" Beth says, tapping her harness again. Her tether flashes out, autoconnecting to her climbing spike.

Beth rappels up the side of the cave and pulls herself up and out. I make Chris go next. He tethers in and then retracts the line at full speed, hooting with joy as it swoops him off his feet and tosses him out into the sunlight.

The sun is getting low in the sky by the time I climb out of the cave. On Earth, this canyon would be drenched in shadows, but that isn't how dusk works in the Diamond

Range. The light catches in the prismatic cliffs, bending and bouncing through the ravine. It's blindingly bright, like the sun is melting all over us.

Beth and Chris are already walking toward the flyer, but Jay is just standing there soaking in the riot of light.

"This planet is something else, isn't it?" he says, as I retract my tether and retrieve Beth's anchor spike. There's something about the awestruck reverence in his voice that makes little nervous butterflies dance in my stomach. His joy in this place is so unfiltered that sharing it feels intimate, somehow.

An impossibly loud snap blasts through the mountain air, followed by a flat boom.

"What the hell was that?" Jay says.

"Oh no," Chris shouts, ripping his flex off his arm. "No, no, no." He shakes his flex into tablet form and holds it up over his head. "Telescopic tracking mode," he snaps. "Seek and lock on to flying objects."

Abruptly, my brain places the sound. I've heard it before, during the first year of flight training. It's the sound of an out-of-control shuttle falling through the atmosphere. There's only one shuttle on this planet.

The *Wagon* is crashing.

FIVE

"Object located," Chris's flex intones. An image rises on its screen. Even magnified, the *Wagon* is just a glimmer of silver in the brilliant blue. Chris double taps to triangulate its location and track its course. A bright-yellow line streams out behind it on the screen as the flex records the shuttle's descent into the uneven horizon of the mountains. The *Wagon* disappears behind a high plateau, putting it out of view just before it actually crashes.

Chris drops to the ground, cross-legged, his fingers flashing across his flex as he calculates the *Wagon*'s likely trajectory from the point where we lost visual contact. After a few seconds, he says, "Got it. They went down within five square kilometers of these coordinates."

"I'm sure the Landing is already tracking their emergency beacon," Jay says.

"Will it work in these mountains?" I say.

"We should report Chris's findings," Beth says. "In case it does not."

"We can't," Chris says. "No long-range comms yet, remember?"

"Isn't there a sat phone in the flyer's supply kit?" I say numbly. I can't believe this is happening.

He shakes his head. "There is no supply kit. I tried to tell you, but you walked off too fast. We haven't printed any of the usual gear for the flyers yet. The commander ordered us to build a dozen assault rifles and body armor for the whole squad first. We had to postpone everything else until they were done."

"The *Wagon*, however, has a full kit on board, including a satellite phone," Beth says. "I'm sure the survivors will call their location in to the Landing immediately."

"But we can get to them faster than anyone at the Landing," Chris says, shoving to his feet. "We have to go."

"We may not be able to help them," Beth says. "We don't even have a med kit."

"There were fourteen people on the shuttle!" Chris's voice cracks on the words. "Mom, and Leela, and Miguel, and Dr. Lovejoy, and Lieutenant Gibbons and—"

"It wouldn't hurt anything to go start triage," Jay says, gently cutting off Chris's list of the probably dead.

"Yes!" Chris says, "They might be injured or, or, or . . ." He trails off, scrubbing away hot, anxious tears. "Please, you guys."

Jay throws me a questioning look. "What do you think?"

Dread and grief squeeze my chest. Why didn't I just finish building the school and spend my night off sleeping, like a normal person? I don't want to be here. I don't want to do this. But our friends are out there. They might be dead already, but they might not be. They might need our help. We can't just give up because I'm afraid to add to my store of nightmares.

"I think we have to try."

It feels like it takes forever to get back to the flyer and power up. Once we're in the air, Jay programs in the fastest possible route to Chris's coordinates, but the flight computer has to stay well under the flyer's maximum speed because of the jagged mountain terrain.

We could go faster on manual. I could, at least. But Jay isn't me. He hasn't put the flyer in manual once the whole time we've been out here.

"Do you think Mom's okay?" Chris asks very quietly. He sounds so young. He *is* so young. It's easy to forget that he's only thirteen, since he started at the academy the year after I did. Chris is brilliant, but he's still the little kid who needed Teddy to check his tent for spiders every night when we were doing equipment tests in the New Amazon. That was only three years ago, even though it feels like another lifetime in another universe.

"I'm sure they're fine," I say, trying to sound like I mean

it. "Leela's a good pilot, and there are all sorts of emergency backup systems."

"I guess," he says, but he doesn't believe me. I don't blame him.

Abruptly, the flyer dives, shooting under a pair of enormous crystal spikes that slash across each other like the mountains are fighting a duel. The maneuver drops us into a deep, narrow box canyon. We shoot forward between spiky, crystalline cliffs that hug the banks of a black-blue river. It's like flying up the center of a geode. The cliff walls are so close, it looks like I could reach out and touch them.

"Jay . . . ," I start to say, but I don't have to finish the thought.

"Computer, manual control, please," he says, planting his hands on the nav app.

He starts to drag his fingers upward to move us out of this canyon.

"Stop!" The word snaps out of my mouth of its own accord. It takes me a few precious seconds to figure out what I'm reacting to. Then I see it. The canyon is narrowing above us. Ragged spikes of crystal jig-jag overhead like closing teeth. We're trapped.

"Damn," Jay mutters, jerking the flyer lower to keep from hitting the sides of the canyon.

"We're going to have to turn back," I say.

"How?" he counters, swinging the flyer wide around a bend. "There's no room to—"

"Look out!" Chris shouts, pointing at the forward screen, while a huge chunk of crystal fills the canyon ahead of us. It's twice the size of the flyer, and there's no way around it.

Jay slams his hands flat on the piloting app and shoves downward. I snatch at the scream that explodes in my chest as the flyer hurtles under the boulder with centimeters to spare.

Sparks explode through my vision. The engines scream and water sprays around us as the flyer's belly brushes the surface of the river. Jay manages to keep us airborne. Barely. I can hear him swearing through the roar of blood pounding in my ears.

Ahead, the canyon is getting wider. I suck in big breaths, fighting to stay conscious. The river drops away below us, tumbling down a set of steep cliffs as we shoot out into the open air of a wide, green valley. It's enormous, compared to Jannah. The towering cliffs look like huge crystal wings thrown wide from a rushing waterfall spine. A forest of the thick-bodied *Chorulux neon* trees we saw around the Rangers' graveyard grows at the base of the waterfall. The trees thin out after about a klick and fade away into thick, black-green grass that fills the rest of the valley so completely, it looks like deep water.

What's left of the *Wagon* is scattered across the green expanse. In an emergency landing, the *Wagon* is designed to break apart into individual pods, each with its own parachute to help slow descent. The cargo pod is sitting on its side, its bright-orange rescue chute flung out behind it. It detached like it was supposed to. The engines didn't. The huge cones of the fuselage are sprawled across the shattered remains of the *Wagon's* passenger section. The orange fabric of the pod's rescue chute is melted all over them like neon cheese.

Jay circles the wreckage until he finds a safe place to land. I reach back and swipe up the flyer's lock screen to open the rear doors. The ramp unfolds as I untether from my seat.

I go to the top of the ramp and look out over the wreckage and the valley beyond. It's absolutely still in the dying sunlight. Nothing's moving out there. There's only one thing that could explain the intense quiet.

They're all dead.

I think I might be sick. I want to scream. But I can't make this moment worse than it already is for Chris.

"Mom!" He shouts, pushing past me and starting down the ramp. "Mom?!"

The only reply is his own voice echoing off the cliffs.

"Maybe we should head back to base after all," Jay says as he and Beth join me at the top of the ramp. "Get help." *And make sure Chris doesn't have to find his mother's pulverized body.* It's a nice thought, but . . .

"Too late now," I say, watching Chris plunge through the field.

We follow him out into the waist-high grass. The stalks

are thin and flexible, but dense. Moving through them is more like wading than walking. A soft white haze diffuses the light and makes the air taste like steel wool and rotten lemons. That's rocket fuel. The engines must have caught fire after the crash. If there are any survivors out here, they're lucky the fire went out. If the core had exploded, this whole valley would be charred.

"Am I the only one who's got a bad feeling about this?" Jay says quietly.

Before I can answer, I trip over something soft.

Not something. Someone. As I scramble to my hands and knees, the person I just tripped over moans my name. My stomach flips inside out. I know who it is, even before I see her face.

"Chief!" The scream rips through my throat before I can snatch it back. Jay is already on his knees, helping me ease Chief Penny over onto her back. She groans again. It's a deep, wrenching sound that vibrates with pain. Her abdomen is soaked in blood, and her intestines are spilling out, onto the grass.

"Mom!" Chris shouts, barreling toward us.

"Careful!" I say, catching him against my chest before he stumbles and falls on Chief Penny. I try to turn his head into my shoulder so he doesn't have to see, but he pushes me away.

"No," Chris says, scrubbing at his eyes like he can wash away the sight. "Mama! No!"

Chief Penny groans again, her wordless agony striking a terrible counterpart to Chris's denial.

"We need to get her to the flyer," Jay says, rapidly tapping commands into his flex as he pulls it off his wrist and drapes it over the chief's neck to track her heartbeat and blood oxygen levels. It pulses red. That means there isn't enough oxygen in her blood.

"I don't think we can move her," I say. "Not like this." My brain feels like it's frozen solid, and I have to chisel out each thought individually.

"I have a small first-aid kit in my sampling box," Beth says, crouching next to Chris. "It's in the flyer."

"I'll get it," Jay says, and sprints off.

"You're going to be okay, Mom," Chris says, easing Chief Penny's head into his lap. "We're going to help you. You're going to be okay."

My eyes find Beth's. She doesn't think Chief Penny is going to be okay either. But she says, "We're going to do everything we can."

Beth pulls out a thin plastic sample bag as I peel Chief Penny's harness back from her wounded abdomen. Her Scout badges are shredded in bloody tatters.

"First, we need to seal the belly wound," Beth says, kneeling beside Chief Penny and pressing her sample bag over the gash. She's being gentle, but the chief groans again at the touch, like her pain is overflowing and spilling out of her. Chris gasps, clutching her hand as tears pour down his face. I suck back a sob. He doesn't need to see my heart breaking for him.

"GET OUT OF THE GRASS!"

That's Leela's voice! My heart leaps as I snap to my feet and spin to find Leela and Miguel standing on top of the cargo pod. They're alive!

"Get down here!" I shout up to them. "Bring a stretcher if you've got one. The chief is hurt!"

"RUN!" Leela screams back. "RUN! NOW!"

With that, they disappear through the emergency hatch on top of the cargo pod.

What the hell?

I spin, scanning the valley around us. I can see Jay slogging back from the flyer, clutching Beth's first-aid kit, but there's nothing else out there. Just a whole lot of grass swirling like it's being whipped by a restless wind.

Oh crap. There's no wind.

"We need to go," I say, grabbing Beth's arm and pulling her to her feet.

"What about Mom?" Chris says. "We can't just leave her!"

My eyes dart to the chief. Blood and sickly, greenish bile is seeping around Beth's makeshift bandage, and I can hear the rattling rasp of her breath. If we move her, she's going to die. If we stay here, we're probably going to die too.

I can't make this decision. I won't.

I think I have to.

"Joanna," Beth says, pointing behind me. I turn and see a tidal wave of grass rolling right toward us. A totally inappropriate blast of relief rushes through me. I don't have to decide whether or not to abandon the chief. There's no time to run.

That's when I remember the laser welder in the pocket of my utility harness. I rip the palm-size welder free with shaking hands and crank it up to high. Then I aim just ahead of the approaching swarm, and hit the power button.

A narrow beam of white light explodes from my hand, slicing through the grass. There's a deafening shriek, and whatever was charging at us veers away.

I stand there a moment, breathing hard. What was that? It was huge, but I felt like I could barely see it.

"Joanna!" Beth calls. "Nine o'clock."

I spin and fire the welder at another charging blur of motion. Then another, and another, and another. The laser is getting hot, but I yank my thermal down over my hand and keep firing.

Between shots, I look for Jay. I don't see him. I hope he made it back to the flyer. We won't. It's too far. The cargo pod is closer—less than twenty meters away. But that might as well be twenty light-years. We're surrounded. The welder's laser hurts them, but it doesn't stop them. They're coming at us from all directions.

The cargo pod's emergency hatch flies open again and a pair of hover carts zooms out. Leela and Miguel are riding them, using packing straps threaded through the handles to steer. Their tiny engines scream under the strain as they hurtle toward us, skimming just above the grass.

"Get the chief," I shout to Beth. "I'll cover you!"

"Take her feet, Chris," Beth says, hooking her hands under Chief Penny's armpits as Leela swings her cart around us and slams to a stop. Miguel is seconds behind her.

The chief moans as Beth struggles to lift her limp form.

"You're hurting her!" Chris cries.

"We have to get her out of here, Chris!" I shout. "She'll die if we don't!"

That snaps him out of it. He grabs his mom's ankles and helps Beth heave her out of the grass. The chief screams, deep and shrill and terrible.

The grass goes still.

I spin, scanning for the creatures. They're all around us. They must be. Why can't I see them?

"Mom?" Chris's voice is tiny in the sudden silence.

I turn to look. The chief's head lolls back as Beth struggles to help Miguel haul her onto his hover cart. Her eyes are open and staring.

She's gone.

"No!" Chris's piercing sob breaks the weird death spell. Suddenly, the grass boils with movement. The nearly invisible creatures are charging at us from all directions. Too many for me to hold off.

"Beth, help!" I shout as I grab Chris and half drag him

to Miguel's cart. Beth hooks an arm around his waist, and together we push Chris up behind Miguel. Beth scrambles onto Leela's cart, leaving the chief's body in the grass. We can't help her now.

Beth reaches out a hand to pull me up, but I don't take it. We're never going to make it back to the cargo pod. Not together. The carts aren't fast enough.

We need a diversion.

I look up at Leela. "Go. Now!"

I don't wait for them to argue. I turn and run in the opposite direction, screaming at the top of my lungs and flailing my arms against the grass. The ground heaves as the creatures charge after me. I fight to run faster, but the grass pulls at me with sticky fingers, like it's trying to drag me back into the roaring green.

There's nowhere to hide. The flyer and the wreckage of the *Wagon* are behind me. In front of me, there's nothing but grass and cliffs and trees.

The trees! I can make it to the little forest at the base of the waterfall. If I can climb one of those huge trees and get out of reach, I might be okay.

My lungs are burning. White sparks are dancing at the corners of my vision. My legs feel like they're going to tear free of my body. But my mind is strangely calm. It's funny. I figured out a long time ago that Teddy knew we were probably going to die trying to save the *Pioneer*. But when I suggested my crazy plan, he didn't even hesitate. I always wondered how he did that. Now I know. In the moment, there isn't any debate. If you can save the people you love, you do.

I don't slow down as I hurl myself at a massive tree trunk. I catch the lowest branch and plant my feet against its smooth gray bark. My arms feel like limp noodles, but I force my elbows to bend, pulling me up. My head swims and my muscles scream in protest. I ignore them. I'm almost there. Just a few more centimeters, and I can rest.

There. I made it. I think I'm safe.

I'm wrong.

Without warning, a fist-size rock slams into my stomach, knocking me out of the tree. Air explodes out of my lungs as I hit the ground.

I roll to my hands and knees, fighting for breath.

Thick, gnarled fingers wrap around my neck and hoist me upright. A second huge hand clamps my left arm to my side as it hauls me backward, the toes of my boots scraping over the ground. The hand on my arm is twice the size of mine. It has five fingers, including an opposable thumb and pinkie. It's green. Then fades to a pink-tan that's the same color as my skin. No wonder I couldn't see the predators. They're chameleons.

Why do I care? This thing is about to kill me. It doesn't matter what its hands look like.

Then I realize what my frantic brain is trying to make me see. The creature is holding my left arm, but my right is dangling free. And my laser welder is tucked into the waist-band of my jeans.

This is going to suck.

I pull the welding torch out, twist my arm to jam it into my attacker, and hit the power button. The edge of the laser beam slices ice hot across my left shoulder. The creature shrieks so loudly that I can't hear myself screaming.

It drops me. I stumble away, gasping for air. It feels like I am trying to walk on the deck of Grandpa's boat in a storm. The ground seems to rise, then falls away under my feet. I think I'm in shock.

I stumble back again, inadvertently turning a dizzy half circle that brings me face-to-face with the thing that's try-ing to kill me.

Even close-up, its camouflage is so effective that I'm having a hard time picking out the details of its body. Color ripples over its skin, shifting to blend in with the trees around us. It's almost as tall as I am, even crouched on its haunches. Its eyes are huge and violet-blue, like the Tau sunrise. The skin around the charred wound on its shoul-der is turning black, and the arm below it is hanging limp.

It pushes back up to standing, towering over me. I try to run. I end up falling instead. I crawl, dragging myself through the spinning, heaving trees.

The creature grabs my ankle, pulls up, and twists. I feel the bone snap. I roll and fire the laser welder again. I miss, but the burning white beam is close enough that the creature lets go of my ankle and stumbles backward a few steps. Its skin shifts constantly as it moves, from brown to green to gray and back again.

I re-aim the welder and fire another laser burst at my attacker, but my arm is shaking so hard that I don't even get close. The creature grins, revealing a mouthful of jagged teeth. It kicks me in the small of the back, and I go sprawling at the base of one of the wide tree trunks.

I try to roll back to my knees, but my body refuses to cooperate.

Something lunges out of a shadowy hollow at the base of the tree. It grabs my hand, yanks me forward and down into a hole that was invisible in the shadows. Pain screams through me as my broken ankle cracks against the tree's roots.

Then there's nothing but dark.

SIX

I'm so cold. Goose bumps run up my arms, rasping against the sleeves of my thermal. It's dark. I keep waiting for my eyes to adjust, but they don't. There's no light to adjust to.

Where am I? What happened? Where are my friends? The questions are heavy and slippery, sliding through my mind as I try to focus on them.

Something drips on my face and slides into my eyes. It stings. I shake my head to clear it away, and pain whips through the laser welder burn on my right shoulder and races down my body. Everything hurts except my left ankle, which is numb and tight. I can feel my blood pulsing through it, beating against my swollen skin like hands on a drum. I need to loosen the straps on my boot, so it doesn't cut off circulation.

As I struggle to sit up, a deep hum fills the air. It's weirdly tactile, like the sound is touching me. My heavy, aching mind soaks it up like a sponge until there's no more room for thought. I don't even notice when I lose consciousness.

"Joanna?"

I blink. Light stabs through my lashes like shards of glass. I squeeze my eyes shut again for a moment before trying again.

"Chris?" I croak as his red-rimmed eyes swim into focus. He's crouched next to me, close enough that I can see the flecks of gold around the irises of his black-brown eyes.

"Miguel says you shouldn't move too much until the pain patches kick in." His voice is wet and thick. He's been crying.

I can feel the tingle of a pain patch on the back of my neck. I cautiously roll my head from side to side. A headache thuds gently at the insides of my temples, but I can tell it would be worse without the painkillers flowing from the patch. The arm of my thermal has been sliced open, and most of my left shoulder is smeared with bright yellow dermaglue. The transparent wound sealant doesn't hide the angry blisters of the burn underneath.

I lift my head. The right leg of my jeans is rolled to my knee and a spray-on cast encases my ankle. Two more bright-green pain patches are lined up on my shin above the cast. They aren't enough to suppress the agony that roars through my leg when I shift my weight.

I flop back onto the cot and stare at the ceiling, fighting to catch my breath. The octagonal panels above me are impossibly familiar. We're in an ISA cabin. I'm lying on a cot just like the one I sleep on back at the Landing, except the sleeping bag spread under me is red instead of green.

Are we back home? No. We can't be. If we were at the Landing, we'd be in the medical center. Doc would be here. Mom would be here.

I wish Mom were here.

"Where . . ." My mouth is dry and sour. I lick my lips and swallow a few times. Then I try again. "Where are we?"

"I dunno," Chris shrugs, picking at the edge of the cot. "I don't remember much after Mom . . . Mom . . ." He presses his face into the pillow, like he's hiding from the memory.

"I'm so sorry, Chris," I whisper around the tears that clutch at my throat. I roll onto my side and rest my cheek against his hair. He smells like smoke and rocket fuel and grass, as though the horrors of that valley are clinging to his skin.

I push myself up on my elbow and look around. The cabin is sparsely furnished. There isn't even a chair—just the cot, a storage locker, and a portable combination recycler/3D printer. Beth is sitting cross-legged in front of the storage locker surrounded by neat piles of blankets and light sticks and protein packs. It looks like she's taking inventory. Leela is sitting on the floor with her back to me. Miguel is crouched beside her applying dermaglue to her arm.

"Hotshot?"

I look up to find Jay standing in the open cabin door with a light stick in his hand and a look on his face that's more intense than I can handle. I try to think of a joke or something to break the moment, but all I can come up with is "Hi."

He smiles. I smile back. I can't help it.

"You're awake," Beth says without bothering to look up from her inventory.

"'Bout time," Leela grumbles. "What the hell happened to you?"

"How did we get here?" I counter.

After that, the air fills with overlapping questions and answers as we all try to figure out what happened to us. Finally, a sharp whistle breaks through the jumble of interruptions.

Beth waits until she has everyone's attention before she announces, "This is unproductive and repetitive given that we discussed this ad nauseam while Joanna was unconscious. I'll summarize."

Beth lays out what I missed in her usual blunt style. The *Wagon* suffered an unexplained cascading systems failure and crashed. While preparing for an emergency landing, Leela figured out she couldn't eject the engines. She moved everyone on board into the cargo hold before emergency separation, because she knew the landing chute for the passenger pod was going to get screwed up by the fuselage.

"It was an innovative solution to an intractable problem," Beth says. Leela shrugs the praise away, staring at her boots.

Everyone on board survived the crash, thanks to Leela. But they had to scramble to deal with the engine fire before the fuel cells exploded. Chief Penny didn't even bother to find the *Wagon's* satellite phone and call in their location first.

Once they got the fire out, they thought they were safe. Miguel and Leela were in the cargo hold retrieving emergency supplies when the crash site was attacked. Leela wanted to go out and try to help the others, but then they saw Ensign Scott get ripped apart by two of the predators. After that, Miguel wouldn't let her leave.

I'm glad. As far as we know, all twelve of the other pioneers who were on the *Wagon* were killed. It's unclear whether Chief Penny managed to call the Landing for help before she was attacked.

Leela's face is carefully blank, and I can tell she's working hard to keep it that way. Reliving all of this is killing her. I'm not the only one who sees the pain bleeding through her neutral expression. Miguel puts a comforting hand on her back, but she waves him off.

"We arrived less than an hour after the initial attack," Beth says. "Your diversionary tactic was successful in leading most of the creatures away from us, Joanna, but we lost consciousness before we reached the cargo pod. When we awoke, we were here."

"What do you mean, you lost consciousness?" I say. "All of you passed out?"

"Yeah," Jay says. "It was even weirder than it sounds. One moment I was about to be gutted by this huge, green-skinned . . . thing, and the next there's a knife sticking out of its eye and it drops dead at my feet. I looked up and saw someone in a black robe with the hood pulled up over their face. Then I heard a really intense hum and passed out."

Uneasy recognition dances up my spine. "A hum?"

"I heard it too," Chris says. He sits up, scrubbing tears and snot from his face, then wipes his hands clean on his uniform pants. "It made me feel weird. Tingly, kinda."

I tell them about the strangely tactile hum I heard and felt after I got dragged into the cave. Then I have to go back and explain about my fight with the huge, chameleon-skinned creature. I'm not as organized as Beth, but the story gets told.

"Camouflage explains some stuff," Miguel says. "I swear, it felt like the grass had grown claws and was trying to eat me."

"Where are we?" I ask. "And how long have we been here?"

"Not long," Leela says. "We only woke up an hour before you."

"It has been ten hours and"—Beth checks the time on her flex—"thirty-six minutes since I logged our landing time at the crash site."

"As for where we are," Jay says, standing up, "it'll be easier if I show you." He points to the cast on my ankle. "Is Hotshot okay to walk on that thing, Miguel?"

Miguel shrugs. "Long as the happy patches have kicked in, she should be able to tough it."

Jay holds a hand out to me. "Come on."

I let him pull me to my feet. Curiosity does more to dull the hurt in my leg and shoulder than the pain patches.

"Beth, crack those light sticks you found and bring them," Jay says, wrapping an arm around my waist to support me as we hobble to the door. "And switch your flexes to flashlight, everybody." He swipes the lock and the door slides open.

There's nothing on the other side but dark.

"What the hell?" I breathe.

"It's a cave," Jay says, leading us out into the bubble of brightness cast by the cabin's exterior lights. "It's huge. I went as far as I dared, and I couldn't find the walls. But there's a second cabin about fifty meters thataway." He points into the darkness. "It's empty, but the components are all marked with *Vulcan* printing codes just like the ones in this cabin."

Beth passes each of us a light stick. The oasis of light around us grows, but that doesn't make me feel less like we're marooned in an endless void. It's dizzying. I look down at the solid ground under my feet, just to remind myself that it's there. Veins of crystal in the rock catch at the light from my flex and light stick.

"We're still in the Diamond Range," I say, pointing out the sparkle.

"Or under it, at least," Miguel agrees. "We might not even be that far from the crash site."

"Doesn't matter how far we are from the crash site if we can't find a way out," Leela says.

"Leela's right," Beth says. "There are only three pertinent questions right now: Where are we? Is it possible to get back to the flyer? And if it isn't, how are we going to reestablish communication with the Landing?"

"What about: How did we get here?" I say.

"The answer isn't relevant to our survival," she fires back. "Which makes it a waste of time."

"It's also obvious," Leela says. She points at the cabin behind us. "We know all this stuff was made on printers from the *Vulcan*. It's freaking weird that the Rangers are still on Tau and not in Wolf 1061, but they obviously are. They must have rescued us. No other explanation makes sense."

"The Rangers didn't save us," Chris says. "They're dead."

"How can you know that?" Leela demands.

Jay throws a raised eyebrow at me. I shrug. "There's no point in trying to keep it secret now."

"I agree," Beth says. She tells Leela and Miguel about finding the *Vulcan* and the abandoned settlement, and then the graveyard in Jannah.

"None of this makes sense." Leela shakes her head. "If something happened to the Rangers, why don't we know about it? Why would the ISA keep that a secret?"

"Speaking of things that don't make sense," Miguel says, "doesn't the Planetary Survey Report say that there aren't any large predators on this continent?"

"Correct," Beth says.

"Which means either the Rangers totally missed a species of massive chameleon beasts with claws and fangs, or . . ." Miguel trails off.

"I think Mom knew they were out here," I say, picking up the horrible thought. "That's why she made us hustle to get the shield up."

"Why wouldn't she just tell us?" Chris says.

"She didn't have a choice," I say. I tell them what Mom told me about the survey report being incomplete.

"Classified?" Leela says. "Why would the ISA classify parts of a Planetary Survey Report?"

Beth huffs an irritated sigh. "We're getting off topic. Again. We need to get back to Pioneer's Landing as quickly as possible. There is no scenario in which confronting the party that brought us here is a good idea."

"The party?" Miguel says, dubious. "I guess it is kind of hard to believe Dr. Brown rescued us alone."

"Impossible, in fact," Beth agrees.

It takes a second for that crazy hypothesis to sink in. There are no other humans on Tau. If the people who brought us here weren't Rangers or pioneers, that means they weren't human.

"You seriously think we were abducted by aliens?" I say, finally.

"No," Beth says. "If there is an intelligent life form on Tau, this is its home. We are the aliens here."

My heart sinks. If Beth's right, this could be the end of everything. The Galactic Frontier Project's mission statement is very specific—we will not settle on occupied worlds. No exceptions. Nobody wants to steal other people's homes the way our ancestors did when they built empires on Earth. If there's intelligent life on Tau, the mission is over. Everything we've been through, everyone we've lost, will have been for nothing.

"You should have gone back to the Landing for help," Leela says. She doesn't add, *Joanna*, but she's looking right at me.

"We were trying to save you!" I protest.

"Miguel and I were safe in the cargo pod," she fires back, "until we had to go out to save *you*."

"How could we possibly have known those things were out there?"

"You couldn't. Which is why you should have gone for help," she says, biting off each word. "But you had to be Joanna Watson, girl hero. And now we're stuck here."

"Take it easy, Divekar," Jay says. "This isn't on Jo. We made the call together."

"Uh-huh," she says. "You haven't been around the Watsons as long as the rest of us, Jay. They might act like they're listening to you, but they aren't. They decide, and you agree."

"Well," I say, "you don't have to worry about me deciding anything anymore, do you? You're cadet pilot. Whatever we do, it's going to be your call. Hopefully, you'll make better decisions than me."

"Be hard to do worse."

She's never stopped blaming me for Teddy. She won't forgive me for this, either.

Bitterness and grief tangle together inside my chest, turning each other toxic. I'm about to say something I know I'll regret when Chris blurts out, "It isn't Jo's fault! It's my fault! I wanted to come. I thought we could help Mom. Now we're stuck here because of me."

With that, he bolts into the dark.

"Chris! No!" Jay shouts.

"I got this," Miguel says, already moving after Chris. "Wait up, little dude!"

"God damn it," Leela mutters, swiping tears I didn't see before from her eyes and running after them.

I instinctively move to follow, but my bad leg folds under me. Jay catches me before I hit the ground. "Come with us, Beth," he says. "We shouldn't get separated." Then he sweeps me up into his arms and strides after the others.

"What are you doing?" I sputter.

"Would you rather stay behind in the cabin?" he counters.

"No."

"Then stop squirming."

The others are spread out ahead of us. The glows from their flexes look like beads of light rolling through the darkness. I can still see the cabin lights behind us, but what are we going to do if Chris goes too far and we lose sight of it?

Dampness rolls over my skin. It feels like a mist that's just becoming rain, which is weird, since we're in a cave.

I run a hand over my arm. It's not wet. But I can still feel droplets pattering over my skin.

"What the hell is that?" Jay says. "Is there water coming from somewhere?"

"Maybe we're getting close to an entrance," I say, relieved he feels it too.

The damp cold is abruptly replaced by a blast of tingling warmth, and then moist coldness seeps through the heat again. It feels like I've got a fever set in fast forward, chill and heat alternating at impossible speeds. Weird emotions are surging through me in response to the sensations. I don't know how to describe it, exactly. Anticipation, maybe? My stomach is tight and my muscles are tensed, but in a pleasant way. It's like I'm standing knee-deep in the ocean on a hot day, waiting for a cool wave to crash against my chest.

Ahead of us, Chris stops.

"Do you hear that?" he calls out, squinting to see past the glow of his flex. "Is something out there?"

I didn't hear it before, but now I do. Somewhere, voices are singing in a close minor harmony. The warmth and chill, the excited tingling, it's all part of the rise and fall of the song.

Chris screams and disappears into the dark.

"Chris!" I shout. There's no response. No sound of struggle. Nothing.

Jay puts me on my feet and tosses his light stick into the dark after Chris. It illuminates nothing but empty space. Chris is gone.

"The hell?" Miguel says.

Behind us, Beth gasps. I spin just in time to see her disappear, sucked into the darkness without so much as a scream.

I don't think, I just move, plunging after my sister. I can feel the pain in my ankle, but it doesn't matter.

"Beth," I shout. "Beth! Talk to me!"

There's a grunting shuffle ahead and to my right. I follow the sound, swinging my light stick like a weapon.

There's nothing there. She's gone.

"Beth!" I spin again, flailing out with my light. *"Beth!"*

My hand brushes something thick and scratchy—roughly woven fabric. Before I can react, a cold hand with fingers long enough to overlap around my arm yanks me against a hard, narrow body.

My attacker is unbelievably strong, and its arms feel like they bend in more places than they should. I buck and kick, ignoring the pain that ping-pongs through my limbs. I try to shout, but my captor squeezes harder, driving the air from my lungs. Sparks explode through my vision. I'm about to pass out. This is my last chance to fight.

I throw my head back as hard as I can. My skull cracks against a sharp, bony chin. My assailant lets out a buzzing growl and drops one of its arms. I grab the other and try to pry it away from my body, gasping and trying to scream. Just a little farther and . . .

A knife blade presses into my throat.

I freeze. My attacker growls into my ear once more, in a voice that's more like a choir. The harmonic sound feels like a thousand tiny slices all over my body. I don't need to understand the words to know the meaning. It's a threat.

Then light swells around us, temporarily blinding me.

"Pel, release her." The English words are spoken in another multitoned voice that cannot possibly be human. "Now."

The blade lingers, digging into my flesh. Then it falls away.

I collapse in a gasping heap.

After I catch my breath, I sit up, blinking furiously as my eyes adjust to the sudden light. A figure in a hooded black robe is kneeling in front of me. Beth is standing a few meters away, beside another kneeling being in an identical black robe. Yet another kneels beside Chris, who is still curled up in a terrified ball.

The light is coming from a being wearing a pale hooded robe that seems to glow in the dark. They're walking toward us, flanked by a dozen more beings in black who are almost invisible against the darkness.

The luminous being raises a hand. Their escort stops. They keep walking until they are standing right in front of me. Now I can see that their robes aren't actually glowing. The light comes from within, filling the cascading folds of fabric with layers of bright and shadow. The pistol holstered on their belt strikes a jarring contrast to their ethereal beauty.

The being pushes back their hood.

Huge, cupped ears flare over the being's skull in a crest of flesh and cartilage. Thin lines of blue-violet light trace branching fractal patterns over their cheeks and run down their neck to disappear below their translucent robes. The extraterrestrial is both fierce and beautiful. And they're wearing sunglasses.

"I believe some introductions are in order," the being says in their layered voice.

"As you wish, Ord."

One of Ord's entourage steps out of line and drops their hood to reveal a human face. It takes me a moment to recognize Dr. Lucille Brown. She's changed since the picture was taken with Dr. Pasha in the lake. She's thinner, and her skin is chalky white. It makes her look older than she is. So does her close-cropped hair, which has gone gray.

"Come forward, juveniles," she calls, looking past me to my friends. "You have nothing to fear."

I twist to see Jay approaching cautiously, his hand on his stun gun, keeping himself between Leela and Miguel and the robed beings. Beth cautiously edges past the being who still kneels beside her to join us, but Chris doesn't move. I want to go get him, but the glowing being is between him and us. I don't know how their guards will react if we get too close.

Dr. Brown turns her gaze to me. "You shouldn't be on your feet, Joanna. Your injuries are serious."

The way she says my name makes me think she recognizes me, but we've never met. I'd remember.

"You know me?"

"In a way," she says. A warm smile washes over her face. "The last time I saw you, I think you were about four. You were playing pioneers in the garden with your brother and sister. And your father and I were discussing a dream we called the Galactic Frontier Project." She turns her attention back to the bioluminescent being standing between us. "Ord, these juveniles are Joanna and Bethany Watson. They are daughters of the great leader I spoke of—Alice Watson."

"My name is . . ." The glowing being makes a series of gentle moans that brush across my skin like dappled sunlight. "But our language is too sophisticated for human voices, so you may call me Ord."

"Ord is Followed," Dr. Brown says. "He is the leader of the Sorrow."

"The Sorrow?" Leela says.

Dr. Brown nods. "It is a poor translation for this species' name, but human linguistic capabilities are quite limited. Thankfully, Ord was willing to learn English in order to communicate with me after he saved me when the same predators that attacked you killed my crew."

"It has been *our* honor to protect and nurture such a being." Ord's voice hums over my skin like a touch, even when he's speaking English. "As it is our honor to welcome you, Joanna Watson. You and your companions may consider yourselves guests of the Sorrow."

"No, please. My friends are over there," Chris's voice punches through the awe-inspiring moment. My head snaps around to see Chris on his feet, struggling against the restraining hands of the black-robed being beside him.

"Chris! Just wait for—" I call, but it's too late. Before I can get the words out, Chris throws himself back, harder than before. The being loses their grip. Abruptly freed, Chris stumbles a few steps, straight into Ord.

The being kneeling beside me lunges forward and snatches Chris off his feet. Their hood falls back as they press a long, slender knife against Chris's throat. The Sorrow warrior has a wide, gray strip of fabric wrapped over their eyes. The pale-green bioluminescent patterns on their skin flow out like organic lace around the blindfold-like cloth. Their delicacy is a striking contrast to the thick scar that slices down one side of the warrior's face.

Jay's hand darts back to his stun gun, but Dr. Brown holds a hand up to stop him. "That won't improve the situation," she says calmly. "Ord, this one is a child. He is overwhelmed by your presence and distressed. He meant no harm to you."

Ord hums something low and warm like a fire on a cold night. The scar-faced Sorrow replies with a shriek and a series of sharp sounds that feel like sparks popping against my skin. Ord opens his mouth in a wide oblong. Whatever he's saying must be out of the range of human hearing, but I can *feel* the sound. It's like a hard wind, the kind you think is going to knock you off your feet.

Nobody moves for a few painful breaths. Then the scarred Sorrow shoves Chris toward us, making their knife disappear into their robes in a single fluid movement. Miguel darts forward and grabs Chris around the waist and half carries him back to us.

Ord holds his hands out on either side of his body, palms forward. Bioluminescent light traces over his palms and down each long, triple-jointed finger.

"My apologies. Pel is one of my most devoted Takers. She is passionate about my safety."

"No kidding," Leela mutters.

"We're sorry she was alarmed," I say, trying not to sound terrified.

"Your apology is accepted, Joanna Watson," Ord says. "Do not be anxious. We have been waiting for your people. It pleases us that you are here."

They've been waiting for us? What does that mean? I badly want to exchange a *what the hell* look with Jay, but I manage to keep a straight face. "We're . . . um . . . thank you. But we have been in a, I mean, some of us have been in an accident. We need to return to our people and, ah, seek medical attention." It has the virtue of being true, and it can't possibly offend them.

"We will see to your well-being, juvenile," Ord says. "And return you to your people when the night has come and it is safer to move about on the surface. In the meanwhile, you will allow me to show you our city."

"No!" I twist to stare at Leela, who looks just as surprised as I am that she blurted that out.

"Leela," I start, but she cuts me off with an *I know* head shake.

She steps forward to address Ord. "I don't mean to offend, but we aren't trained for this, nor are we equipped to make sure that we won't inadvertently harm your people," she says. "It would be much better to wait for our leaders—"

Dr. Brown cuts her off. "Your thoughtfulness is admirable, but you take too much responsibility upon yourself, juvenile. I am an International Space Agency colonel. You are cadets. Children. For you, I am the Followed. Understood?"

Despite her strange choice of words, what she means is clear. She's giving us an order. But that doesn't mean we should follow it. Taking a bunch of, as she put it, cadets and children into an extraterrestrial city without even briefing us on the local culture is incredibly dangerous. Chris nearly got himself killed already. He's just a kid. What if he gets scared and does something like that again? What if I do? We know nothing about the Sorrow. Any of us could easily do or say the wrong thing and offend them, hurt them.

But to my surprise, Leela doesn't even argue. She says, "Understood, ma'am."

"Very good," Dr. Brown says. She smiles warmly at us. "Now, juveniles, please extinguish your light sticks and switch your flexes back to standby. The Sorrow tolerate artificial light sources here, but they are deeply offensive in the Solace."

"You want us to walk around in a cave with no light?" Chris asks, his voice shrinking from the idea.

Before Dr. Brown can answer, Ord slams his staff down on the cave floor. The resulting boom unfolds into a string of echoes as he strides up the row of black-robed beings. They turn to follow him in a single motion, stepping in time like dancers moving across a dark stage.

"Follow Ord," Dr. Brown says. "He provides as much light as you will ever need." With that, she flips up the hood of her cloak and disappears into the dark.

SEVEN

Thanks to his glow, Ord is easy to follow, but his light isn't bright enough for us to see anything or anyone but him. Especially not his guards, who are dressed to disappear. I can hear the whisper of their footsteps, I think, but that makes it worse. It feels like the darkness is alive and watching us.

"You cool, Jo-Jo?" Miguel calls out from somewhere ahead of me.

"I'm fine," I call back, even though I'm not. Pain sparks from my toes to my hip with every step, but Miguel doesn't have any medical supplies with him. There's nothing he can do, so there's no point in making the others worry.

Abruptly, a strong arm wraps around my waist. I recognize the shape of Leela's body as she levers her shoulder under mine. "I'm okay," I say. "I don't need—"

"You gasp every time you take a step," she mutters, hauling me forward. "Don't be an idiot."

"Fine," I say. "Whatever."

Walking is a lot less painful with Leela bearing some of my weight. I should thank her for the help, but I don't feel like giving her another opportunity to lecture me about my poor life choices.

"I didn't reboot the computer." Leela's voice is so quiet, I'm not sure I heard her right.

"Huh?"

"I had time," she says, ignoring my confusion. "The rear engines failed right after we crossed the stratosphere. I had twenty-four seconds before we were falling too fast to recover. I could have rebooted the computer and gotten the engines back online fast enough to do an emergency burn and land."

Oh. Now I understand. Leela has spent the walk dissecting the crash in her head and trying to figure out how she could have prevented it. I'd be doing the same thing if I were her. I've been doing it every day since Teddy died.

"You can't know whether a reboot would have brought the engine back online," I say. "And if it had failed, you wouldn't have had time to get everyone into cargo."

She grunts, neither accepting nor rejecting the reassurance.

"That was brilliant," I say. "I'd never have thought to use the cargo pod to get passengers down safely."

"No," she says, shifting her grip on my waist as we pick our way over a patch of uneven rock. "You'd have thought to reboot the computers."

"Maybe. Maybe not. And if it hadn't worked, we'd all be dead," I say. "Remember Mom's first rule—space is always trying to kill you. Some days it tries harder than others. That's all."

"But it didn't kill *me*," she says, choking on the words.

Sometimes, surviving sucks.

Leela's willingness to take orders from Dr. Brown makes more sense now. She's a cadet pilot. Chief Penny might have been the senior officer on board, but the *Wagon* and everyone on it were Leela's responsibility. Now the *Wagon* is wrecked and, except for Miguel, everyone who was on board is dead. With all of that weighing on her, it must be a huge relief to not feel like our lives are in her hands too.

"Thank you," she says abruptly.

"For what?"

"For not trying to make me feel better."

"Oh," I say. "You're welcome."

This is the longest conversation Leela and I have had since the accident. I don't know if it's the darkness, or the exhaustion, or the emotional chaos that's making it possible for us to talk to each other again. But I don't want it to end.

"Where do you think they're taking us?" I say, hoping curiosity is a neutral topic.

"Someplace with a little more light, preferably," Leela says. "Just when you think you're too old to be scared of the dark . . ."

"No kidding," I say.

"I am sorry the lack of illumination causes you discomfort," a harmonic voice says from somewhere to my right. A buttery yellow glow spills free as one of our Sorrow escorts pushes down their blackout hood. "May I share my light with you?"

Unlike the other Sorrow we've seen so far, this one's eyes are uncovered. They're round and liquid black. Up close, I can see that their skin is transparent. The shadowy outlines of their bones and muscles are visible underneath, highlighted by branching trails of pale-yellow light. I think Sorrow blood must be bioluminescent, and the glowing fractal patterns are actually veins and arteries shining through their skin.

"Oh, um, yes," I stutter. "That would be very nice. I apologize—we didn't mean to disrespect your home."

"It is I who must apologize for intruding on a private conversation," the Sorrow says, falling into step with us. "The Sorrow can hear many things humans cannot. Lucille says it is a matter of the process she calls evolution."

"Oh," I say cautiously. "That's . . . interesting." I'm not sure we should be engaging in casual conversation without Dr. Brown's guidance, but this Sorrow seems to be totally at ease with us. They must have spent a lot of time with Dr. Brown.

"We live in darkness, so we must see with our eyes *and*

our ears," the Sorrow continues. "Lucille calls this echo-location. She says that some of the lower beings on Earth have similar capabilities."

I wonder if that's what we've been feeling when the Sorrow speak and sing. If they can echolocate, then they must have natural sonar, like bats and dolphins. Maybe that's what gives their language its tactile qualities.

"Thank you for sharing your light," Leela says, before I can ask more about the Sorrow's sonar. "It makes us much more comfortable."

"It is my pleasure," the Sorrow says. "I find expressing myself in a language with only one dimension a pleasant challenge. My pouch mate and I have often commented that English is unexpectedly complex."

"Your pouch mate?" I say.

"My apologies," the Sorrow says. "I have not greeted you properly. Lucille calls me Tarn. I shared my father's pouch with the one she calls Ord, who is Followed. To use a human word, I am his brother."

I have so many questions, if I wasn't afraid of offending the Sorrow with the light from my flex, I'd start taking notes. If Sorrow carry babies in their exterior pouches like marsupials back on Earth, do they also give birth to them? Or do females do that? How many siblings share a pouch at once? Do they have lasting familial relationships, like humans do? They must, if Tarn is introducing himself as Ord's brother.

"When my pouch mate brought Lucille here to live

with us, he asked me to help him learn your language so that we could communicate with her," Tarn says. "I am glad he did. I find your people fascinating."

"So Dr. Brown has told you a lot about us, then?" I say.

"Yes." Tarn covers his face with his hands, palms out. It seems reflexive, like nodding or head shaking for us. "I have also learned much from the program Lucille used to teach us your language. Your educator is a wonderful tool."

"Dr. Brown used the educator to teach you English?" I clamp down on an inappropriate giggle at the thought of imperious Ord discussing verbs and nouns with that irritating panda avatar.

"Yes," Tarn says. "She used her three-dimensional printer to create several additional flex tablets for us."

"I guess she also used it to print your pouch mate's gun, right?" Leela says. I suck in a breath. I'd almost forgotten that Ord was carrying a human weapon.

"Yes," Tarn says, covering his face with his outturned hands again. "Ord is fascinated by human technology, and Dr. Brown often obliges his interest. Your printers are astounding."

So is the idea of Dr. Brown printing technology and weapons for the Sorrow. She's the one who created the ISA's First Contact Protocol. I can understand why she chose to violate it, when the other option was total isolation. But what consequences will that choice have for us? Or for the Sorrow?

"How long has Dr. Brown been with you?" I ask.

"The ways in which we measure the passage of time do not translate well into your language," Tarn says. "But Lucille has been with us since her crew was lost. I am glad you have arrived. I think she will be pleased to be among humans again, despite her expressions of desire that your people would never come."

"What?" Leela says. "Dr. Brown didn't want us to come here?"

Every new piece of information we get makes less sense than the last. The *Vulcan*'s satellites are still in orbit. If Dr. Brown didn't want the *Pioneer* to follow her here, all she had to do was inform the International Space Agency that Tau was already occupied. The ISA would have sent a rescue mission instead of an E&P ship. Wouldn't they?

The report is accurate. However, it is not complete.

Mom's words rebound through my brain. The ISA classified parts of Dr. Brown's survey report. Did they do that because she reported there was sentient life here and they decided to send us anyway? Even as the thought forms in my brain, I know I'm right. It's the only answer that makes sense. But I can't believe the ISA would do that. I can't believe my mother would go along with it. I must be missing something.

"Friend Lucille has expressed fear that your people and mine will not be able to cooperate adequately to share this world," Tarn says. "And she does not wish to endanger the Sorrow with your presence here."

"We had, um, similar concerns," Leela says. "We were

surprised that Dr. Brown wanted us to come with you."

"So I observed," Tarn says. "But Lucille follows Ord now, and he is confident that humans and the Sorrow can live together in harmony. She would never question his leadership. She trusts in Ord to show her the way."

Leela throws me a wide-eyed look. I'm as shocked as she is. Does that mean that Dr. Brown has sworn allegiance to Ord? Is that why she agreed to bring us here, even though it violates her own protocol? Acid twists through my stomach. We should never have followed her orders. We shouldn't be here. We probably shouldn't even be on this planet.

A percussive buzzing sound patters over my skin like a thousand tapping fingers. It makes me want to walk faster, despite the pain in my leg.

"If you will excuse me, juveniles. My pouch mate summons me," Tarn says. The Sorrow flips his hood up again, but this time the black cloak doesn't make him disappear. As Tarn walks ahead of us, I realize that the cave isn't as dark as it was a few minutes ago. In fact, it seems to be getting brighter with every step.

Smooth rock walls slip out of the fading darkness. We're in a tunnel. Actually, we're at the end of a tunnel. A few seconds later, we emerge into a sprawling underground city. It's still dark in here, but it's more like the two-moon darkness of a Tau night. There's enough light that I can see my friends' awestruck expressions.

This cave is enormous. You could fit the entire Landing

inside, and the *Pioneer*, and have room left over. Flecks of light sparkle in the soaring ceiling, getting brighter and denser as the cave narrows to its lowest point at the center of the city. The buildings are like honeycombs—towering scaffolding built in intricate geometric patterns and draped with some kind of fabric or paper. Some of it is see-through and some of it isn't. They're impressive, but strangely uneven. The shapes look like they should add up to something, but I can't figure out what.

Ord and his guards lead us up a wide avenue that wraps around the outer wall of the cave before spiraling into the city. As we walk, crowds of Sorrow emerge from buildings and fall in behind us. They wear the same long, hooded robes as Ord and his attendants, in a luminescent gray that mutes their natural light but does not hide it. No two are exactly the same color, so the crowd creates swirling rainbows as they move.

"Aliens on parade," Leela breathes, taking in the throngs. She's right. Ord is showing us off. I wonder if this is meant to be welcoming or intimidating. If it's the second one, it's working. Even if we could find a way out of here, we're totally hemmed in by Sorrow.

"Look!" Miguel says, pointing up at the cavern wall. At first I see nothing but the shadows cast by the city, shifting over the stone. Then the shades of gray organize themselves in my mind and I see it. The intricate honeycomb buildings are designed to cast images on the cave walls. Jagged shadow figures with multijointed limbs that are clearly Sorrow stretch the full height of the cavern, fighting against creatures with exaggerated claws and teeth.

"They paint in shadows," Jay says, staring up at the grayscale battle that rages as we walk and our perspective shifts. He has the same awestruck expression on his face as he did when we watched the sunset in Jannah. He sees as much beauty in the shadows as the light. I don't know why, but the look on Jay's face makes all of the nuances of darkness and light in the shadow mural come alive.

"Where's that light coming from?" Chris says, peering at the glowing heart of the city.

"That is our Solace," Ord says. His sunglasses are gone, and his round black eyes shine in the violet light of his bioluminescence. "The place where the Sorrow began." He holds out an imperious hand. "Come, walk beside me. Let me tell you our story."

Chris shoots us a wide-eyed look.

"It's okay, dude," Miguel says. "We're right behind you."

I don't think that makes Chris feel much better, but he lets Dr. Brown lead him to Ord's side.

"Once, the Sorrow lived in the light," Ord says. "A very long time ago." His attention is focused on Chris, but his voice is pitched so that we can all hear him. I think maybe the whole crowd gathered behind us can hear him too, thanks to the acoustics in here. I think they're meant to. This story isn't just for us.

"Our ancestors lived in the sun. They spent their days surrounded by the gracious beauty of these mountains," Ord continues, "but their lives were brutal and short because of the Beasts. The Beasts preyed on the ancient Sorrow, attacking the weak and feasting on the young. They crave light, so the Sorrow learned to live at night and hide themselves during the day. But there is no true darkness on the surface. The moons and the stars pollute almost every hour of the night. So our ancestors lived in fear. They had no direction, no purpose beyond survival.

"Everything changed when the First who was Followed discovered that the Beasts fear true darkness. They would not enter it for any reason. She explored these caves and she found this place, where there is enough light for the Sorrow but not enough for the Beasts to survive. She led our ancestors here, to the Solace. In the safety of this place, the Sorrow found possibility. Growth. Purpose."

"So those things, the Beasts, they don't come down here?" Chris says.

"No." Ord briefly raises his hands to cover his face, palms in. "Sorrow's Solace has protected us for many, many generations. But it also limits us. We do not leave this place, except to tend our gardens and gather food. And our Growers and Gatherers risk their lives every moment that they are on the surface. That means they can produce only the smallest amount necessary to feed our people."

"I find it unlikely that the Sorrow have no offensive

capabilities," Beth says quietly to Leela and me. "Given the weaponry and skill displayed in our interaction with their warrior class."

"You are correct, Bethany Watson," Ord calls, turning to us and throwing his arms wide to indicate his black-robed guards. "My Takers are brave and dedicated fighters. They can and do protect us from the Beasts, but not without the giving of many Sorrow lives. Those lives are given gladly, but not lightly. We stay where it is safe, unless absolutely necessary."

"I wish humans were smart enough to do that," Chris says. His voice is gruff and sticky, like he's trying not to cry.

Ord holds up an open palm, thumb to his cheekbone, fingers spread. Then he presses his hand forward to skim it across Chris's eyes.

"You have suffered a great loss, haven't you?"

Chris's voice creaks from the strain of not crying as he whispers, "Yes, I, my mother . . ." He trails off, choking on the words.

Beth finishes the sentence for him. "His mother was killed by the predators."

"I see," Ord says without looking away from Chris. "There is no shame in sadness. Or pain, or anger. Just as wind and water hone rock, these turbulent emotions help us find our proper shape, making us stronger and wiser. But fear also has the power to shape us. We cannot allow that."

Ord pulls a knife from under his robe. It has a black handle and a long, narrow, black blade that is only visible because its edges are so sharp they catch at his bio-light.

"This was my father's knife. He was a good father. He nurtured me and my pouch mate and we grew strong. But my father was a Grower. He left the safety of Sorrow's Solace each day to feed our people. On one of those days, the Beasts attacked and killed him."

Ord keens something in the Sorrow language that makes my stomach ache. The crowd responds in a soft hum that slides over my skin like freshly printed fleece. They're comforting him.

"My father died long before Tarn and I were ready to live beyond his pouch," Ord continues in English. "I was so afraid. I did not know if my pouch mate and I would survive without his care. Fear could have consumed me. Paralyzed me. But instead, it made me angry. I used that anger, and this knife, to carve the fear out of myself. Tarn and I didn't just survive. We thrived." Ord presses the knife into Chris's hands. "So can you."

Chris stares down at the blade. I can't see his expression in the shifting dimness.

"This is a gift beyond price," Dr. Brown says, putting a hand on Chris's shoulder. "Both the knife and the inspiration it will bring. Ord will help you find your way through this tragedy. As he helped me."

Ord holds a beckoning hand out to her. When she

comes to him, he cups her cheek. She leans into his long, many-jointed fingers. The delicate, blue-violet light from the veins in his palm leaches her eyes to black as he strokes her neck. Her eyes stay locked on his as she adds, "No one understands sacrifice better than the Sorrow."

The moment is so intimate that I look away. My eyes land on the scarred Sorrow guard, Pel. Her hood is down and her huge ears are spread out on either side of her head like cupped horns.

She's watching them too.

"Friends!" Ord calls, drawing my attention back to him. "Until now, the Sorrow have found only pain and fear in the light. But today it brings us something new. Humanity.

"The friendship between our species will help the Sorrow grow in ways that our fathers and their fathers never dreamed of as they carried us in their pouches. You have much to teach us, but we have much to teach you in return."

With that he spins, artfully twirling his glowing cloak around his body, and marches up the spiraling road toward the heart of the city.

The crowd surges forward to follow him as Dr. Brown leads Chris back to us, parting the flow of robed extraterrestrials like a stone in a river.

"What's going to happen now?" I ask her.

"Something sacred and extraordinary." She looks past my shoulder, and a radiant smile spreads over her face. "Don't struggle."

Don't struggle? What's that supposed to mean?

"Whoa," Miguel says, following Dr. Brown's look. "What the what?"

Before I can turn to see, my feet are off the ground and my body is being lifted into the air. Long, many-jointed fingers grip my head, shoulders, waist, and knees. I reflexively arch my back, trying to twist away from the grasping fingers. Pain ricochets from my wounds, exploding out of me in a scream.

"Leave her alone!" Leela shouts, lunging for my hand.

"I said don't struggle!" Dr. Brown snaps, holding Leela back. "Do not show the Givers disrespect. This great gift is given not just to you, but to humanity."

In other words, if I keep freaking out and offend these Sorrow, our whole species will be held accountable for it. But what exactly does *sacred* mean? Will it hurt? Will I survive it?

"Joanna!"

I twist to find Jay. He's holding his stun gun. He can't possibly win a fight in this situation, but he's willing to try. They all are. I can see it in their faces.

There's more at stake here than humanity's future on Tau. If I don't go along with this, my friends are going to get hurt trying to help me.

"I'm okay," I call back to them. "I'll be okay."

I'll be okay. I repeat the words to myself as the Givers carry me away.

EIGHT

I'll be okay.

The Givers glow almost as brightly as Ord. Their encir-
cling light is blinding. I can't see where we're going, or if my
friends are being allowed to follow. All I can do is stare up
at the cave ceiling and keep trying not to panic.

The cave is getting lower as we approach the center of
the city. The multicolored points of light that were just distant glimmers at the outer walls are closer together here,
and easier to see. They drip down from the ceiling like glowing stalactites, but they don't look like rock. What are they?

Boom! A sharp rumble rolls through the air.

Boom! Boom! Boom!

Just as the last echoes die away, the Givers carry me
between a pair of soaring white pillars carved to catch the
shadows and make them dance. The cave is only a couple of

stories high here, and the sprays of color and light that drip from the ceiling almost reach the floor.

They're roots, I realize, as the Givers carry me on through the clusters of light. These are *Chorulux neon* roots, like the ones we saw in Dr. Brown's abandoned cave campsite in Jannah, but much, much bigger. The trees growing over this spot must be ancient.

The enormous root clusters are trained into ornate designs. Narrow paths wander among the bioluminescent root sculptures, widening into little clearings near particularly striking displays.

Boom! Boom! Boom!

The hollow booming sound fills the cavern again as I'm carried between another set of carved pillars that support a soaring trellis. The root clusters at the center of the grove are woven through it, creating a luminescent dome.

The Givers carry me to the center of the living cathedral up what feels like a set of steps. They lay me down on a cold, hard surface and step back, forming a circle around me. They are absolutely still, like living statues.

My eyes are starting to adjust to the Givers' light. I can see past them now. What must be hundreds of Sorrow twinkle in the twilight dimness of the root garden. A silent cacophony of sonar spins over my skin, accompanying the melodic murmur of their voices. I can hear the sharper, thinner voices of my friends, too, poking through the thick hum. At least I'm not alone.

Without warning, the Givers pivot to their left.

The crowd goes quiet.

The abrupt silence is tight and tense, like the cavern itself is holding its breath.

Then the Givers start to move. They circle me. Each step is perfectly synchronized, as though they are a string of echoes stretching out behind a single figure.

After the third circuit, the Givers begin to sing. Their voices swell, filling the huge space with sound. Then the single tone shifts and multiplies, weaving together into . . . I don't know exactly what to call it. The word *melody* feels like an understatement. The Sorrow's multifaceted voices form harmonies that are beautiful but sound, I don't know, incomplete. I wonder if there are more layers of sound there, notes that go beyond the range of human hearing.

The sonar under the sound buzzes against my skin like an electric shock, except it doesn't hurt. It doesn't feel good, either. It just is.

The Givers stop walking. Still singing, they turn back to face me. The buzzing sensation of their voices gets stronger, flowing over, around, and through me.

I float in the sound.

Empty.

Full.

Here.

Gone.

I don't know how much time passes.

My brain snaps back into focus as something cold and

wet winds around my left ankle. I try to lift my head to see what's happening, but fingertips press on my temples, holding me down. Seconds later, another Giver whips a thin, wet cloth over my face and shoulders.

I reflexively suck in a breath, and the moist wrappings suction into my mouth. I gasp for air, but that just makes it worse. My body gets tighter and tighter, like my skin is shrinking. I think I might implode.

There's a sound like bubble gum popping inside my brain, and pain crashes through me. It's loud, like every cell in my body is screaming.

And then everything goes quiet.

The Givers silently remove the wet cloths from my leg, face, and shoulders. Then they turn their backs on me and walk straight out, into the crowd.

I lie there for what feels like a long time, waiting to see what happens next. But the Givers don't come back. Finally, I move my head just enough to look around. I'm lying on a long white slab at the center of a raised platform. My friends are standing at the foot of the stairs with Dr. Brown. Miguel has an arm around Chris's shoulders. Jay's hands are clenched at his sides, like he's braced for a fight. His eyes find mine. I nod, trying to reassure him. I'm okay. I think. I still have no idea what they did to me, but nothing hurts.

Wait. Nothing hurts.

Whoa.

The pain from my injuries is gone.

I wiggle my toes. There's no stiffness. No pain. I cautiously rotate my ankle as far as I can in the cast. It doesn't hurt. It doesn't even feel like it's broken anymore.

"Rise, Joanna Watson!" Ord's harmonic voice sings through the unnatural silence. I twist to watch as his glowing figure sweeps through the crowd. "You have fought bravely. And now, thanks to the generosity of our Givers, you have strength to face the light once more."

He jogs up the steps to the platform and grabs my left hand to pull me to my feet. I brace myself, but the pain I expect in my burned shoulder never comes. My eyes dart to the wound, but it's gone. I can see unbroken skin under the layer of dermaglue.

"What . . . how . . ." I'm so stunned I can hardly put the words together. "How is this possible?"

A pulse of white light burns through Ord's glowing veins. I think he's enjoying my reaction.

"Your people have built powerful machines to do your bidding," he says. "But the Sorrow find our power within. Givers spend their lives learning to shape sound and mend flesh with their voices. In times of need, they can be called upon to heal the brave and the deserving."

Shape sound. I'd never have thought of it, but that's exactly what it felt like—the Givers kneading and molding their voices around me like clay. Given their bio-echolocation, it makes sense that they have more control over sound than humans do. But it's still astounding to think that they can heal broken bones and third-degree burns just by manipulating sound waves. Even with nano-surgical bots and bone-growth stimulation, it would have taken Doc weeks to get me back on my feet. They did it in minutes.

Ord takes my hand and walks me down the steps.

"You have been given a great honor, juvenile," he tells me as he escorts me to Dr. Brown. "It is usually reserved for our greatest Takers. But today, we are happy to share it with our new friends."

"I, ah, thank you," I stammer. "I'm very grateful."

Ord bounds up the steps again. When he reaches the center of the dais, he hoots a bright, coppery sound, raising his hands as though to embrace the crowd. The Sorrow return the greeting in perfect harmony, their choral voices raised as one.

Ord begins to speak in the layered tones and harmonies of Sorrow language. He's giving a rousing speech to the assembled crowd. I can't understand it but I can feel it. The sound feels like jumping on a huge trampoline—tingly and exciting and just a little terrifying. I wish I could understand the words.

That's when I see Ord's brother, Tarn, slipping through the crowd. He stops at my side. "Allow me to translate."

He continues in English, speaking a few seconds after his brother. "Our friends from the stars have come to us needing haven and help. And we, the Sorrow, have demonstrated our graciousness by welcoming them in their hour of need. Our new friends have suffered . . ."

Dr. Brown throws a *be quiet* look at Tarn. He meets her eyes in acknowledgment and raises his hands to cover his face, palms out. But he doesn't stop.

"Now that our pain allows us to understand each other," he translates, picking up Ord's speech again, "and the Givers have healed the physical wounds of Joanna Watson, daughter of the human leader, they will offer a Mourning, that our new friends' emotional suffering may be healed as well."

There's a rumbling sound. It's faint, like thunder that's really far away. But it's getting louder. For a moment, I think the cave is collapsing. Then I see the lantern robes of at least a dozen Givers cutting through the crowd. They're walking toward the dais, moving so slowly it looks like they're out of sync with the rest of the world.

Pressure builds in my chest as their woven voices crescendo. My body throbs, every muscle shuddering. Clenching. Then the tension explodes into a cascade of emotions I can't begin to name. The outpouring feels like water running over my skin inside and out. It's exhilarating and peaceful at the same time. I feel like I could run for kilometers or lie down to sleep and never even think about bad dreams.

The Givers fall silent as they reach the steps of the raised platform where Ord stands. They turn to face the crowd, creating a rainbow of light around his brighter form.

It's so quiet that I can hear myself trying to catch my breath.

Ord's voice booms into the reverent silence. Tarn's quiet translation follows: "People of the Sorrow, sacrifice is never without purpose. This is not just a day to grieve with our new friends. This is a day of destiny. Today, we begin again. We step forward into a new world. A safer, stronger world. A world we now share. Every single loss we have suffered has led us to this day. And the brave dead have made every step possible."

The brave dead.

Teddy's last, bittersweet smile floats to the surface of my memory. I can still see every detail—from the soot in his hair to the constellation of tiny burns across his face to the fear and determination in his eyes. But for the first time, the memory isn't painful.

"The brave dead have given of themselves so that we can build a new future," Tarn translates. "So that we can reclaim this world, above and below, once and for all."

With that, Ord raises his staff in the air, triumphant. The Sorrow around us cry out in response. The explosion of sound ricochets off the cave walls, building into a pulsing roar that sweeps me up in a tumbling current of loss and joy and sorrow and triumph.

Beth stands up and walks away.

The sudden movement jars me out of my reverie. I'm not the only one. I can see little clusters of nearby Sorrow peering after her as she shoulders her way out of the crowd.

I bolt to my feet and hurry after her, into the glowing garden. The root sculptures flex and spin around me as I hurry past them. I catch up with Beth beside a root topiary waterfall that glows a pale green-blue. It undulates gently, reaching out to us as I grab Beth's arm and pull her around to face me.

"What the hell is wrong with you?" I snap. "We're representing the whole human race right now, and storming out in the middle of a religious ceremony is just . . . just . . . rude!"

Beth blows out a frustrated sigh. "I know."

"If you know, then why—"

"I found Ord's hyperbolic rhetoric about sacrifice offensive and manipulative," she says without looking back at me. "The Givers' ritualistic stimulation of our emotions was bad enough. But that speech . . ." She shakes her head. "I just . . . couldn't."

"What's wrong with honoring the people who died to get us here?"

Beth spins to glower at me. "People *lived* to get us here," she snaps. "Our family has lived and breathed for the Galactic Frontier Project every single day for as long as I can remember. So have hundreds of other scientists and engineers and ship designers. They've spent their lives making this happen. People don't die for a reason or some greater purpose. They just die."

"You are unbelievable!" I hiss the words through clenched teeth. Then I walk away before I say something I really regret.

"I sat in your hospital room watching your skin grow back for twelve days," Beth calls after me. "Did you know that?"

I stop. I don't turn around.

"No," I say. "I didn't." But I can picture it. The image makes the tiny hairs on the back of my neck stand on end.

"I could have saved you from that," she continues. "I could have convinced Teddy to make you get back on the *Wagon* with us and fly away. But I didn't, because you were both correct. It was worth risking your lives to save the *Pioneer* and her crew. But that didn't make it easier. It still doesn't. And I dislike being told that it ought to."

I turn around.

We stare at each other.

"I didn't . . ." The words catch, tangling around themselves before I can get them out. I try again. "I didn't mean . . ."

"I know," she says.

How is it that in all this time I've never stopped to think about what it was like for Beth after the accident? She didn't talk about it, and I didn't ask. I should have asked. I should have said . . . something.

I should say something now.

Instead, I say, "Let's go back. We don't want to get separated from the others."

"Agreed." Beth turns and walks toward the root cathedral without a backward glance.

I follow her slowly, allowing the winding paths of the root garden to take me where they will. I'm feeling so many different things that I'm not sure I can pick out the separate thoughts and emotions. Why is it that nothing about life ever seems to get *less* confusing?

As I walk past a series of pure-white root sculptures, I hear a human voice murmuring nearby. I follow the sound to a cluster of roots that have been woven into a hollow rainbow of light. There's a small gap in the weaving, just big enough to step through. Inside, I find Dr. Brown sitting cross-legged, holding a flex up to record herself as she talks.

"You know, as I do, that this will have consequences," she says. "Let us just hope the price is worth paying." With that, she calmly ends the recording and wraps the flex around her wrist.

"Solace tree groves like this one are the Sorrow's primal habitat," she says pleasantly, ignoring what I just overheard. "These structures weren't always decorative. They were nests. The early Sorrow lived in these roots. They only went to the surface to hunt for food. Now the nests are sacred places. Cherished and preserved. Imagine if humanity had such restraint."

"There are a lot of sacred places on Earth," I say.

"And many more that have been destroyed," she says. "Many times over."

"But we always build new ones." I pull out the charred flex I took from her campsite in Jannah and offer it to her. "You built one here. At Jannah."

"Pasha named that valley," she says, taking the flex from me and turning it over in her hands. "He was quite devout. I always found that an odd trait for a scientist, but I think I understand him better now. The Sorrow have taught me a great deal about faith."

She runs her fingers over the flex, and the picture of her with Dr. Pasha crackles over the charred screen. She drinks it in.

"Dr. Brown?" I wait for her to look up at me, then ask, "Do you think humanity is going to hurt the Sorrow?"

She lifts a single eyebrow. "Who suggested that remarkable idea?"

I don't answer. I don't have to.

"Tarn." She shakes her head. "Of course. He has always struggled to follow."

"Tarn wasn't disagreeing with Ord or anything," I say hurriedly. I don't want to get him in trouble. "He was just telling us how he was glad we'd come, for your sake, and it just slipped out. That's all."

Dr. Brown smiles. "You are so young. Consider the intention as well as the words, Joanna. Why raise the subject at all, if he didn't want you to question my choices, and thus Ord's wisdom?"

I hadn't thought of it that way, but she's right. Tarn guided that conversation to exactly where he wanted it to go. And Dr. Brown is doing the same thing right now.

"So Tarn was right?" I say, sidestepping her attempt to change the subject. "You don't think humans should be on Tau?"

"What I think does not matter," she says, her eyes drifting back to the image of Dr. Pasha on her charred flex. "You're here. My fears are meaningless."

Dr. Brown tucks the flex into her robes and unfolds herself from her seated position, groaning softly as she straightens. She's leaving. Who knows when I'll get her alone again? This might be my last chance.

"Did you approve Tau for E&P?"

Dr. Brown turns to stare at me with an expression somewhere between shock, anger, and a weird sort of satisfaction. Then she bursts out laughing. "My god, the ISA is even more foolish than I imagined."

She reaches into her robe and pulls out the charred flex that I just gave back to her. She presses it into my hand. "I suspect you'll wish I'd never returned this to you. Understanding is a double-edged blade, and you cannot sheath it once it's been drawn."

She pulls her hood up. "Come, Joanna. We will rest until nightfall. Then I'll take you home."

NINE

The walk back feels a lot shorter without a broken ankle.

Pel wanted to escort us, but Dr. Brown told her it was unnecessary. I'm glad. Pel makes me nervous, and not just because she nearly killed Chris for crashing into Ord. She always seems to be watching us. And I might be imagining it, but she seems brighter than the others. If the Sorrow's internal glow comes from the blood pumping under their transparent skin, does brighter mean her heart is beating faster? Is she afraid? Or angry? Neither would surprise me. Actually, I'm shocked the Sorrow have been so calm about this. I can only imagine the chaos if Mom took Tarn and Ord for a stroll in a major metro back home.

The others seem happy to take Ord at his word that we're welcome. They're whispering together in quiet amazement as we walk back to the cabin. All except for

Chris, who is lagging behind us.

I drop back to walk with him. He doesn't acknowledge me. I don't say anything either. There's a lot I want to say, but when I think about Chief Penny being dead, all the words get wrung out of me like water from a cloth.

A speck of light flares up ahead. It swells as we approach, until I can pick out the details of the cabin. The door is still standing open. It's hard to believe it's only been a couple of hours since we met the Sorrow.

"Stay here until I return," Dr. Brown says. Then she flips her blackout hood up and disappears back into the dark expanse of the cave.

"Harsh," Miguel says as we go inside. "I thought for sure she'd drop the mysterious thing once we were alone."

"I don't think she wants us to know more about the Sorrow," Leela says. "Jo and I had a little chat with Ord's brother, Tarn. He said that Dr. Brown has sworn loyalty to Ord. She doesn't actually want us down here at all, but Ord does, so she's going along with it."

"That's disturbing on several levels," Beth says.

"Why?" Chris asks. "Ord wants to share his world with us. What's so terrible about that?"

"That depends on why he wants us here," Leela says.

"Better question," Jay says. "Why does the ISA want us here?"

"We're an Exploration and Pioneering Team," Miguel says. "Title kinda speaks for itself."

Jay shakes his head. "That's not what I meant. The commander told Jo that the Planetary Survey Report we have isn't complete because parts of it are classified, remember? She has to have been talking about the Sorrow."

"You think the ISA intentionally violated its own rules?" Leela says.

"It would explain why they decided to keep parts of the report secret," Jay points out. "If they hadn't, who knows how many countries and corporate sponsors might have pulled out?"

"Not to mention the E&P team," Miguel says. "My mothers would have peaced if they'd known."

"But why would the ISA bother?" Leela says. "It's not like it was going to stay secret once we got here. Why not keep looking for an unoccupied world?"

"I think Dr. Brown knows," I say, pulling her old flex from my pocket. "When I asked her, she gave this back to me and said all the answers were here."

Miguel makes a face. "Cryptic much?"

"The Sorrow appear to be an authoritarian society," Beth says. "If Dr. Brown has sworn fealty to Ord, contradicting him might be seen as a violation of that oath."

"The ISA would feel the same way about sharing classified information," I say. "But that doesn't stop her from letting us figure it out on our own."

I press the flex against the wall screen to sync it with the cabin, and then tap on the file icon labeled Backup. It pops open, revealing hundreds of subfolders. One of them is labeled Planetary Survey Report: Tau Ceti e.

Wow. I didn't think it would be that easy.

It isn't.

There's only one file in the folder: Appendix G, a detailed taxonomy of all the plants and animals the Rangers surveyed on Tau. I pull it up on the cabin wall screen so the others can see and skim through the web of Latin.

"Looks just like the taxonomy in our version," Leela says.

"No," Beth says. "It doesn't." She taps a name to enlarge it.

Lucifossor sapiens.

"The *Luci* prefix obviously refers to *lucifer* which means 'light bearing,'" Beth says. "The root *fossor* means 'underground digger.'"

"And *sapiens* means wise," Jay says.

Beth nods. "It is only used once in Earth's taxonomy. For Homo sapiens. 'Wise man.'"

Human.

"Sentient Underground Light Bearer," Chris says. "That has to be the Sorrow."

"Dudes," Miguel says, "if this is part of the original report, that means Jay's right."

"They knew," Leela breathes, staring up at the web of words. "The Rangers knew about the Sorrow, and they told the ISA, and the ISA sent us here anyway."

I feel stupid for being so shocked. It's not like we hadn't

already put most of the pieces together. I guess I was still hoping we were wrong.

"Interesting," Beth says.

While the rest of us have been staring at each other like the whole universe just grew a second head, Beth has been studying the Tau taxonomy. She double-taps another species on the chart, and the wall screens zoom in on the words:

Chorulux phytoraptor.

"This species has also been redacted from our version of the report," she says.

"You sure?" Jay says.

Beth nods. "I paid special attention to the Tau hybrids. I'd planned to write a paper once the terraforming program is up and running."

"So *Chorulux* is what?" Miguel says, talking it through. "*Chorus* for 'dancer' or 'singer,' and *lux* is 'light,' obvi."

"Light Dancer," Beth says. "It's the classification for a genus of Tau plants that are unusually active. It includes *Chorulux fidus* and *Chorulux neon*, the roots of which the Sorrow have cultivated at the center of their city."

"Dr. Brown called them solace trees," I say. "She said those woven roots were originally nests for the Sorrow's ancestors."

"That fits with the origin mythology Ord shared with us," Beth says.

"So is *Chorulux phytoraptor* another kind of tree?" Chris asks.

"Maybe," I say, my pulse skittering as I close the file and skim through the other folders in Backup. "But *phyto* means 'plant,' and *raptor* means . . ."

"Badass predator," Miguel says, just as my fingers come to a stop on a subfolder labeled *Chorulux phytoraptor*. I open it. There are a dozen folders, plus hundreds of photographs and vids. The first few that I try are corrupted. Finally, I find one that will open.

A picture of the predators that attacked the crash site expands across the wall screen.

Chris sucks a hiss through clenched teeth.

"Seriously," Miguel says, bobbing his head in agreement with Chris's involuntary reaction.

"Fascinating," Beth mutters. She yanks off her flex and presses it over Dr. Brown's to copy the files. "Absolutely fascinating."

"This has to be a mistake," Leela says. "How could a species of pack-hunting predators be plants?"

"According to their placement in this taxonomy, phytoraptors are related to plants in the same way that we are related to monkeys," Beth says, pulling her flex free and swiping open the newly copied files. "They evolved in the same genus as the hybrid trees, but that doesn't make them plants, per se."

"Still," Leela shakes her head in disbelief. "How is that even possible?"

"Different planet," Miguel says. "Different evolutionary pressures."

Leela rolls her eyes. "It was a rhetorical question, Captain Obvious."

Miguel grins, "Doctor Obvious. Technically speaking."

"But why would the phytoraptors have been left out of the survey report?" I say. "The fact that Tau has dangerous predators wouldn't have ruled it out for E&P."

"Unless they're sentient too," Jay says.

"You think the plant monsters are intelligent?" Leela asks, skeptical.

Jay shrugs. "The only other species that got redacted was the Sorrow, so . . ."

"Those things aren't people! They're monsters!" Chris shouts, abruptly. "How can you even think . . . They *ate* Mom."

The pain that grates through his voice is almost more than I can bear. I don't know how to comfort him. I guess nobody does, because it gets really quiet after that.

Finally, Miguel says, "Okay, people, we're all crazy exhausted right now. We've got a couple of hours, so we should grab some shut-eye while we can."

"A prudent suggestion," Beth says. "However, I need to continue and learn what I can about *Chorulux phytoraptor* from Dr. Pasha's notes. Given the threat they pose, we can't afford to be unprepared."

"Good call," Leela says.

"Better you than me, B," Miguel says. "I'm beat." He grabs the pillow from the cot and tosses it to Leela. "Let's share the cozy, shall we?" He takes the blanket and turns to Chris. "You want the cot, bro?"

"I'm not tired," Chris says, so quietly I can hardly hear him. He stalks across the cabin and collapses cross-legged on the other side of the 3D/recycler combo, pointedly putting it between us and him.

"Suit yourself," Miguel says, flopping down on the cot.

Leela and Miguel both fall asleep quickly, despite Beth muttering to herself as she skims through the phytoraptor files on her flex. I spread the blanket out on the floor and lie down, but I'm not even slightly tired. I'm probably imagining it, but I feel like my skin is still buzzing from the sonic energy the Sorrow used to heal me.

Jay sits down next to me with his back against the wall. As usual, he doesn't make a big deal about it. He's just there.

I consider telling him about the crazy reactions I've been having when I hear the Sorrow's language, but I don't. Trying to put the tactile and emotional sensations into words makes me wonder what it would be like to touch his skin. Or have him touch mine.

The thought makes me feel warm all over. I'm pretty sure I'm blushing. I need to change the subject, even if I'm only having this conversation with myself.

"Not reading tonight?" I say, hoping he can't hear the residual embarrassment left by my internal monologue.

"No flex," he says, showing me his bare wrists. "I took it off while we were trying to help the chief. Got left behind in the commotion."

"Oh. Right." Jay's flex was monitoring the chief's pulse when we abandoned her body to the phytoraptors. My brain keeps trying to forget.

"I can't believe she's gone. And Chris . . ."

I look across the cabin to where Chris is studying the knife Ord gave him.

"I almost took it away from him on the walk back," Jay says, following my gaze. "But I figure he doesn't need us treating him like a little kid right now."

"Still . . . ," I say.

Jay nods. "Makes me jittery too."

I give up on sleep and sit, propping my back against the wall beside Jay. "We shouldn't have gone into the city," I say. "We should have waited and let Mom deal with Ord."

"Dr. Brown gave us an order," Jay says. "We didn't have a good reason to refuse it. Sucks, but it is what it is. My mom always told me taking orders was the hardest part of military life. Don't think I really understood what she meant until today."

"Is your mom a marine, too?" It's a relief to talk about something that isn't a mind-blowing revelation or an emotional quagmire.

"Nah," he says. "She was North American Army Nursing Corps when she was young. She only did it to pay for school. She was so mad when I told her I wanted to enlist, but my grandfathers had my back. They're both Marine Corps. They met doing peacekeeping work in the Pacific after the 2040 typhoons. One of their buddies from back then helped me apply for Space Operations School."

"So you always wanted to leave Earth?"

"Nope." He chuckles softly, like he's amused with his past self. "I wanted to come to Tau. When the GFP announced that they'd found a viable world, I watched the survey report vids they put on the public channels. The second I saw this place, I knew I had to be a part of it. Busting my ass in basic training to land a spot in the *Pioneer*'s marine squadron was a hell of a lot more feasible than coming up with a PhD in eighteen months."

I've always known I wanted to explore other planets, but I never questioned whether I'd get the chance to do it. I never had to. What would I have done to get here if I hadn't grown up a Watson?

"What?" Jay says, and I realize I've been staring at him. "You thought I was in it for the sexy uniform?"

"You say that like I think your uniform is sexy," I counter, hoping that I'm not blushing. Again.

He grins. "You say that like you don't."

Damn it. I'm definitely blushing. This is why I can't talk to him. Ever.

Before I can think of a comeback that might salvage my dignity, Beth huffs a theatrically irritated sigh. "I'm trying to educate myself on a grave threat to humanity's future on this planet, and I find your flirtatious banter highly distracting. So, if you don't mind—"

"Beth!"

Jay bursts out laughing. "Sorry, B." He shoots me a grin. "Sometimes I can't help myself."

With that, he leans back against the wall and closes his eyes. Like he can just go to sleep now and not be at all preoccupied by either the flirting or the public acknowledgment of the flirting or the fact that we're stuck in a massive underground cave system and completely dependent on the hospitality of extraterrestrials whose world we've accidentally invaded.

I hear the soft whisper of a snore. He's asleep.

Unbelievable.

I'm positive I'm never going to sleep again, so I pull Dr. Brown's flex off the wall and open the *Chorulux phytoraptor* file again. I swipe through the pictures and the anatomical drawings. They're kind of beautiful, in a terrifying way. No two look alike, but that's true of most species. I tap open a subfolder called Encounters. It contains four video files: Bob. Blue. Spike. Sunflower. I open the first one, and Dr. Pasha's face fills the screen.

"This is interaction six with subject *Chorulux phytoraptor* 345, affectionately known as Bob."

"Pretty sure you shouldn't be getting affectionate with a superevolved carnivorous plant," an amused voice calls from behind the camera. I recognize the rich alto. Dr. Brown.

"Jealous?" Pasha smirks.

"You know me," her disembodied voice replies. "Always have been territorial."

"Anyway," Pasha says, smothering a chuckle, "CP345, otherwise known as Bob, has been visiting us on a daily basis for the last three weeks. Though phytoraptors are predators, Bob has never displayed any overtly aggressive behavior toward us. In fact, I believe he is attempting to communicate."

"Uh-huh." I hear Dr. Brown's disbelieving snort behind the camera. So does Pasha. He makes a face at her through the lens as he continues.

"Some of us find it improbable that an intelligent life form might have evolved from carnivorous flora. But there are stranger things in heaven and Earth, and on Tau Ceti e; and as scientists, we have an obligation to explore even the improbable. To that end, I have been trying to teach this subject, and several others, American Sign Language. The other subjects in Bob's . . . oops, we need a group noun."

"Bouquet?" Dr. Brown suggests from behind the camera, chuckling.

"Cute," Pasha says, mock glowering. "You get to edit this, you know." He squares his shoulders and starts over. "The other subjects that Bob travels with are not interested. But Bob has engaged. He has two dozen signs so far. Today, I'm going to attempt a simple conversation."

The camera swings to reveal a trio of phytoraptors on the other side of a particle shield. They're not bothering to camouflage themselves, so I can see them clearly, despite the shimmering warp of the force field. Instead of blending in, their skin is rippling through shades of green and brown and the turquoise of Tau's sky. They're sitting back on their haunches, watching Pasha. They're bipedal, like the Sorrow, but I wouldn't call them humanoid. Their arms are nearly as long as their legs, and each has different . . . what's the right word? . . . foliage, I guess, since they're plants. One of them has long black spines all over its head and running down its back. Another has whorls of electric-blue petals clustered on its shoulders that seem to bend and flex with every move of its head. The third is plain in comparison. It's shorter and broader than its fellows, with a smooth, round head that makes its wide eyes look even bigger.

Pasha disengages the shield.

"Do you have to do that?" Dr. Brown says from behind the camera.

"You're armed," Pasha says. "So is Amahle." He points off camera to his left. "We're fine."

He cautiously approaches the three phytoraptors.

"I'm going to start simple," he says, narrating for the camera. He brings his hand to his forehead and then brings it out at an upward angle.

"Hello," he says out loud as he signs. "Nice to see you." He points to himself, then taps the extended index and middle fingers of both hands together. "My name is . . ." He makes the sign for *p* and shakes it. "Pasha."

The plain, burly phytoraptor shuffles forward on his feet and knuckles. Pasha takes a tiny, inadvertent step back. The camera jitters—Dr. Brown pulling her stunner, probably. But the phytoraptor doesn't attack Pasha. He just studies him.

Pasha repeats the sequence of signs two more times.

"I think you owe me twenty bucks, Pash," a female voice with a delicate Nigerian accent calls. That must be Amahle.

"Damn," Pasha says.

Then Bob raises one hand to his forehead and draws it out and up at an angle.

Hello.

All three human voices on the recording speak at once: "Yes!"

"Did that just happen?"

"I knew it."

I find myself leaning forward in anticipation.

Pasha repeats the full greeting again in sign and English: "Hello, Bob. My name is Pasha."

Bob raises his hand to his forehead once more. *Hello.* Then he shifts his weight back to his haunches and taps two straight fingers on both hands together. *My name is . . .* He makes the sign for *p* and shakes it. *Pasha.*

Pasha wilts. "It's not responding. It's imitating."

"Hey," Dr. Brown calls from beyond the camera. "There's no pouting in science."

"Who says?" Pasha grumbles.

The recording ends.

I drop the flex in my lap, relieved. If Pasha had actually managed to teach the phytoraptors sign language, it would seriously complicate our relationship with the Sorrow.

I watch the next video—Blue. It's a lot less interesting.

I have no idea that I'm asleep until Beth shakes Jay awake, which wakes me up too, since my head seems to have fallen on his shoulder.

"What's wrong, Beth?" Jay says, quiet but instantly alert.

"Is Dr. Brown here?" I mutter, scrubbing grit from my eyes.

"No," Beth whispers. "And I need to find her."

"Beth," I groan, checking my flex for the time. "It'll be night soon, and then Dr. Brown will find us."

"This can't wait," she insists. "I need to speak to Dr. Brown now. Jay, can you take me to the second cabin? That seems like her most likely location." Jay nods, already climbing to his feet. As she follows him to the door, she whispers, "Go back to sleep, Joanna."

Jay chuckles softly as I scramble after them, "Not Hotshot's style, B. You know that."

My sister shoots me a quick look. "Indeed. In fact, I count on it."

What's that supposed to mean?

We slip out of the cabin quietly, so that we don't wake the others.

"Left, four o'clock," Jay says, taking the lead as we strike out into the dark expanse.

"Beth, what's going on?" I ask. "Why are you so freaked?"

My sister almost growls in frustration. "The redactions in the Planetary Survey Report have resulted in an error in our terraforming strategy. It may lead to ecological collapse if we don't prevent it."

"Ecological collapse?" Jay says. "As in . . ."

"As in we destroy our new planet before the first town is even built." Beth cuts him off, hurling out the words. "How far away is this cabin?"

Before Jay can answer, our lights haul a gray geodesic dome out of the darkness a few dozen meters ahead of us.

Beth bolts to the door. She knocks once, then shoves it open without bothering to wait for a response.

Jay and I follow her in.

Dr. Brown isn't there.

"Damn it," Beth snaps, glaring around the cabin as though she can make the Ranger materialize through sheer force of will. But the cabin's single room is completely empty. There's no furniture, just a flat cushion at the center of the floor.

A three-sixty video is paused on the wall screens. It's frozen on a shot of Tau's turquoise sky crisscrossed by solace tree branches. The angle is strange. Unintentional. Something about it makes me nervous. Like someone I can't see is standing right behind me.

"Maybe we should just sit tight," Jay says. "Dr. Brown said she'd come back for us."

Beth shakes her head. "This can't wait. We'll have to go back to the Sorrow city. Ord or one of his people will know how to find Dr. Brown."

I'm only half listening to their conversation. I can't stop thinking about the paused three-sixty on the wall screens.

"You really think going in there on our own is a good idea?" Jay says, dubious.

"No," Beth says, heading for the door. "It's a terrible idea. But we don't have a choice."

I give in to my instincts and call out, "Computer, can you play this three-sixty from the beginning, please?"

"Joanna!" Beth almost sobs my name. "We don't have time for this!"

"I know," I say. But I don't move.

The cabin comes alive. With no furniture to interrupt the three-sixty, it feels like we've been transported into a sunny day up in the Diamond Range. I think this is the same valley from the video of Dr. Pasha's attempt to communicate with the phytoraptor he called Bob. It looks kind of like Jannah, but bigger and with fewer parrot palms.

Dr. Pasha steps into the shot.

"We've got a new visitor today," he says. "I'm designating it *Chorulux phytoraptor 352*. But I think we'll call it Sunflower."

I can hear Dr. Brown's amused snort as she pans to

a huge phytoraptor with a ruff of what looks like yellow wildflowers running down its spine.

"Subject is larger than the others who have approached us," Pasha continues. "I can only speculate as to whether this is a gender-based anatomical difference. Phytoraptors don't display exterior genitalia, so for the moment, it is impossible to classify them."

A low hum swells from the wall screen. Static, I think, until Pasha says, "Do you hear that? Is someone humming?"

That sound isn't static. It's part of the recording.

"I don't know, babe," Dr. Brown says from behind the flex. "Wind in the trees, maybe?"

"That's not what I'm talking about," Pasha says. "I swear, there's something . . ." The hum snaps to silence. Like someone flicked a switch. Pasha grimaces, looking around him like he's confused. "It's gone."

"'Cause it was a figment of your imagination?" a voice I recognize as Amahle's calls from the somewhere left of camera.

That's when Sunflower jumps on Pasha's back and rips out most of his throat with its teeth.

The image tumbles as Dr. Brown drops the flex. The three-sixty panorama is mostly sky now. Someone in the background screams. Dr. Brown runs into the frame, stun gun out and firing. Sunflower casually reaches out, snags her around the waist with a claw, and flings her out of the frame again.

Sunflower goes back to eating Dr. Pasha. He's still alive.

There's more screaming. Another Ranger runs past. There's a roar and crunch, and then he gets dragged back through the off-kilter frame. His intestines are bubbling out of a gash in his stomach and stretching out behind him in the dirt. He isn't screaming anymore.

The vid cuts out. The wall screens return to flat gray.

"Worse than I imagined it would be," Jay says quietly.

The squishy warmth of Chief Penny's insides sliding through my fingers oozes up from my memory. I clench my hands into fists, trying to drive it out of my brain. "I guess we shouldn't be surprised," I say. "We knew they were killed by phytoraptors."

"Human arrogance killed my crew," Dr. Brown says from the cabin doorway. Her black robe is hanging open, and the black tank top underneath does nothing to hide the trails of scar tissue that run up her chest and over her left shoulder. Claw marks. "As a species, we have a bad tendency to assume we can go anywhere we please without consequences."

She isn't talking about her crew. She's talking about us.

"We didn't mean to intrude on your . . ." What is this? It isn't a living space. It's clearly designed for watching three-sixties. For watching that three-sixty, I'm guessing. This is a shrine to her guilt.

"We don't have time for social niceties," Beth says, jumping in. "Tau Ceti e is facing a possible extinction-level

181

event. If we want to prevent it, we must communicate with Pioneer's Landing in the next thirteen hours and"—she checks the time on her flex—"twenty minutes."

Dr. Brown's face shifts from surprise to skepticism.

"You must learn to follow, juvenile," Dr. Brown says. "If you have detected this threat, surely your mother has as well."

"My mother doesn't have the information stored in your backup files," Beth fires back.

The disapproving look on Dr. Brown's face dissolves into horrified recognition as Beth continues, "I ran a comprehensive analysis of *Chorulux phytoraptor*, based on Dr. Pasha's records. That analysis included a genetic interaction projection with our Stage Three terraforming bacteria, which I designed to alter Tau soil for Earth crops. The phytoraptors have a unique genetic structure that makes them vulnerable to the bacteria. Once cross-infection occurs, it is impossible to predict how the Stage Three bacteria will mutate, but they *will* mutate. Those mutated strains *will* infect and destroy other Tau species. It's just a question of how many."

"I thought you genetically engineered Stage Three not to interact with the indigenous ecosystem," I say.

"Correct," Beth says. "But I didn't factor the phytoraptors in, because they weren't included in the data set I was given. I had no way to predict this."

"You accidentally created a pathogen that will wipe out

the Beasts?" Dr. Brown says. The look on her face is not exactly excited. It's something darker than that.

"Yes." Beth grinds the word out between her teeth. "And many other species. Our hosts could be among them. Stage Three could easily wipe out the whole *Chorulux* genus, including the so-called 'solace trees,' which would effectively destroy the Sorrow's primary habitat."

In my mind's eye, I can see the glowing root garden at the heart of Sorrow's Solace withering and rotting. The cathedral dome collapsing. The great city disappearing into darkness. The mental image makes my skin crawl. But it doesn't change the look of bleak calculation in Dr. Brown's eyes.

"You're speculating," she says thoughtfully. "The bacteria could just as easily die out with the Beasts."

"Or they could turn this whole continent into a rotting wasteland," Beth snaps. "This is not something we can control, Dr. Brown. If Stage Three is released, Tau's ecosystem will never recover. We need to return to the Landing now and stop the deployment."

Dr. Brown turns and stares up at the blank gray wall screens. I can almost see the gory three-sixty playing out behind her eyes. Remembered pain and fear warring with logic and science. Then she flips her hood back over her head and says, "Come with me."

She turns and strides out into the dark without another word.

"Can't we just go back to the crash site, Dr. Brown?" I ask as we scramble after her. "Our flyer is still there—we can use it to get to the Landing. Ord would understand—"

"No," she says. "He would not."

"Do you really think he'd be angry that you did something to protect Tau from destruction without asking him for permission first?" I ask, stunned.

"Ord is Followed," she snarls. "We move as one, and he chooses the way."

"We? We don't follow Ord," I blurt out. "*We* are human."

"And if humanity had just stayed where it belongs, we wouldn't be in this situation," Dr. Brown fires back.

"Let it go, Joanna," Jay says. "Dr. Brown is an expert in Sorrow culture. We have to trust that she knows what she is doing."

He's probably right. But I can't shake the feeling that Dr. Brown's respect for the Sorrow is about to doom their planet.

"Do you really think the botany team will initiate Stage Three without you?" I ask my sister.

"If they don't, the bacteria will run out of nutrient and die," Beth says. "It's possible that the loss of the *Wagon* and our disappearance will disrupt the process, but I doubt it."

"So our team is going to poison this world and there's nothing we can do to stop them," I say, tasting sour bile at the back of my throat.

"Humans will not harm our home," a harmonic voice hisses. "Because I will not let you."

Pel's scarred face slides out of the darkness as she pushes back the hood of her blackout robe. She's holding a long-handled hammer made of a solid crystal shard that's bigger than my head.

She's been there, this whole time. Following us. Listening.

"I see you've learned English, Pel," Dr. Brown says calmly. How can she be calm? I'm shaking like my whole body is going to come apart.

"Ord's inability to prevent your poisonous influence from spreading through our city is just one of his failures in leadership," Pel replies. "I knew following Ord was the path to destruction. Now I can prove it."

"Nothing will be destroyed," Beth says. "We can prevent this, if you'll allow—"

"I will allow you nothing, juvenile," Pel snarls. "You are blinded by foolish human ambition, just as you are blinded by your foul, false light. You will not blind me as you've blinded Ord." She moan-hisses, and three more heavily armed Sorrow reveal themselves around us. "Come with us, human poison. You follow me now."

TEN

Pel doesn't bother with the spiral road to Sorrow's Solace. She cuts through the city and leads us straight into the root cathedral.

Chris, Leela, and Miguel are already there, guarded by a pair of heavily armed Takers. As we approach, Leela takes off her flex and hands it to a Taker holding a long staff studded with the razor-sharp crystal. The Taker drops her flex on the ground and smashes it with the barbed end of their staff. The shards spark and flare in the Taker's acid-green bioluminescence.

My anxiety congeals into dread. Where is Ord? Why is he allowing his Takers to do this to us? We need to get out of here. With every passing second, our chances of getting to the Landing in time to save Tau are getting smaller.

Dr. Brown must realize that too, but she has an expression of calm disinterest on her face. She could be waiting in line for chow, for all she seems to care what's happening here.

Pel growl-moans something loud and hot. Another pair of Takers hurries to her side. One glows bloodred and the other an icy blue.

"Give them your flexes," Pel hums to us, in English.

She strides back into the root garden without waiting to see whether we comply.

My hands are shaking so hard that it takes a couple of tries to get my flex off my wrist. I hand it to the blue Taker. Dr. Brown's old flex is in my pocket. I leave it there. It's a risk, but Blue doesn't bother to search me. They just destroy my flex and move on to Jay.

He holds out his bare wrists. "I don't have a flex."

The green Taker stalks over to us, brandishing their barbed staff. They snarl at Jay. The Sorrow word feels like a slap.

"I don't have a flex," Jay repeats, slower this time. "I lost it during our fight with the phytoraptors."

I bite back a scream as the green Taker swings their staff in a whistling arc that stops abruptly, centimeters from Jay's head. They snarl the harsh Sorrow word again. The verbal impact makes my ears ring this time. They aren't taking no for an answer.

My hand closes around Dr. Brown's flex, still hidden in

my pocket. Would it satisfy the Taker's demands if I handed it over? If I do, we'll lose a lot of priceless information about Tau. And I'm not even sure it would work. But if I don't do something, they might kill Jay. I can't just stand here and let that happen.

Just as I start to pull it out, a knife blade presses into my throat, and a many-jointed hand traced with blue light grips my waist.

Oh.

They aren't going to kill Jay for his flex. They're going to kill me.

Jay holds up his hands. "Steady. There's no need for that."

The blue Taker presses their blade harder against my jugular and hums something at Jay that feels like bleeding.

These Takers clearly don't speak English. Jay can't talk them out of this. I'm going to have to give them Dr. Brown's flex. I don't have a choice.

"Steady," Jay says again, his eyes still locked with mine. He's talking to me, I realize, not to the Taker holding me hostage. He keeps his left hand out to the side and slowly reaches for his stun gun, which is still holstered on his utility harness.

My heart skitters, tripping over itself in terror. Does he really think he can draw fast enough to stun this Taker before they cut my throat?

Instead of drawing his weapon, Jay unsnaps the holster from his belt and tosses the stun gun to the ground.

"There," he says. "It's a weapon, not a tablet, but it's all I have."

The blue Taker keeps their knife planted against my skin as Green scoops up the stun gun and studies it. Then Green leans in and shrills something in Jay's face that makes him flinch.

They aren't going for it.

Out of the corner of my eye, I see my captor's biolight flare. I stiffen, bracing myself for the bite of the knife.

Then the green Taker drops the stun gun and smashes it repeatedly with the barbed end of their staff.

The knife at my throat drops and the blue Taker shoves me, hard.

Jay catches me before I go sprawling to the rock floor of the cave, steadying me against him. We cling to each other.

"Is it too much to hope you've got a brilliant idea?" he murmurs into my hair.

"Definitely," I breathe, pressing my face into his shoulder, trying to stop shaking.

Now that they have our flexes, the Takers herd us all into one corner of the root cathedral. "What the hell is going on?" Leela whispers.

Beth quickly explains what she discovered about Stage Three and how Pel and her Takers were following us and overheard it all.

"Question is," Jay says, "what is Pel planning to do about it?"

Boom! Boom! Boom!

Pel strides back into the courtyard, her crystal hammer in one hand and a slender black knife in the other. Her robe is gone. She's wearing a tight garment that looks like the body stockings we wear under our spacesuits, but thicker and segmented like armor.

She slams her hammer against the cave floor.

Boom! Boom! Boom!

The other Takers herd us back toward Dr. Brown. She's standing where they left her, hands tucked into her robe. Her eyes are closed, like she's meditating.

Boom! Pel slams her hammer into the cave floor again. *Boom! Boom!*

The noise reverberates into echoes that consume all other sound.

Boom! Boom! Boom!

"I accept your challenge," Ord calls out in English as he strides into the courtyard.

Ord is clad in the same sort of molded body armor that Pel is wearing, and he's carrying a crystal-spiked staff in one hand and a knife with a nasty-looking pronged tip in the other. Hot white light is pulsing rapidly through his blue-violet bioluminescence. That's his heart beating, I realize. Pounding.

Ord shouts something in Sorrow that blasts over my skin like a hurricane wind. Pel responds in a lower tone that smacks into me with just as much velocity. Her voice is hotter than his and sharper edged, but just as resonant.

Pel swings her hammer at Ord's head. He blocks it with his staff and lunges at her, pronged knife flashing. She drops her hammer and dives under Ord's knife arm just in time to catch it as she rolls out of his reach.

Ord and Pel circle each other in poisonous silence. It's like you can see the anger flowing through their bodies as their bioluminescent blood flares and sparks under their transparent skin.

Pel darts in again. She and Ord exchange a lightning-fast series of blows before falling back once more. They're evenly matched. Quick, ruthless, and brutally strong.

My brain is racing. Ord called this a challenge. I think it's a coup. What happens if Ord loses? Pel obviously isn't a fan of humanity. What if she decides to just kill us all? Then the team will initiate Stage Three, and Tau will be ripped apart.

I swing on Dr. Brown. "We need to get out of here while there's still time."

"Ord has been challenged before," she says without taking her eyes off the fight. "And he knew it might happen again if he brought you here. He chose to fight for us. I won't abandon him now."

"What if he loses? What happens to us? What happens to Tau, if we don't get back to the Landing and stop Stage Three?"

"Ord won't lose."

A trio of Takers emerges from the root garden behind us, dragging Tarn between them. As they march him under the dome of roots, he trips one of his captors, tackling them into a roll. They grapple. For a moment, I think Tarn's winning. But then the Taker flips their positions, grabs him by the back of the head, and smacks him face-first into the rocky cave floor.

Tarn collapses.

Ord sees it happen.

He shouts something so hot it feels like the sound is burning my skin. Pel takes advantage of his distraction, swinging her hammer like she's hitting a home run with Ord's skull.

Ord flies into one of the carved white pillars and slides to the floor in a heap.

Is he dead?

No. I can see his chest heaving. He's alive, but not for long. Pel is stalking toward him, ready to deliver a killing blow.

A bright, tangy sound blasts past me. I twist to see Tarn pushing himself up to hands and knees.

He shouts the battle cry again. It's still reverberating as Ord rolls to his feet, knife low, already charging. Pel throws herself backward, but Ord's knife catches her hip, tearing through armor and flesh. She screams, stumbling as Ord hurls himself into an airborne roll that drops him behind her. Before Pel can turn to meet him, Ord drives his knife into her shoulder.

Pel reaches back and grabs Ord's wrist. She spins, sending

him sliding across the courtyard. This time, Ord rolls back to his feet and charges Pel again without hesitation.

As the fight surges on, Tarn's captors drag him to his feet and march him to the corner where the other Takers have us contained.

"Tarn!" I whisper. "Are you all right?"

"I will heal," he says. "If my brother wins this challenge."

"What if he doesn't?" Jay says.

"Then Pel will be leader of our people," Tarn says. "It is then likely that she will kill me before I have the chance to recover."

Crap. I was right.

"So this is a mutiny?" Chris says.

"This is a rightful challenge," Tarn says. "Any one of the Sorrow may challenge our leader, if they believe he or she is taking us in the wrong direction. The one who survives the challenge is Followed thereafter."

"We have to get out of here," Leela says.

"And go where?" Jay says. "This cave system must go on for kilometers. We'll never find our way out alone."

"Dr. Brown knows the way," I say.

"That'd be super useful, if she was still here," Miguel points out.

"What?" My head snaps back to where I left the Ranger, but she's nowhere. I can hardly believe the words, even as they slip out of my mouth. "She left us."

Ord roars, pulling our attention back to the fight. He's got Pel pinned against the dais at the center of the dome. She's lost her knife and hammer. He looms over her, spiked staff high. But before he can strike, Pel swings her legs in a roundhouse kick, knocking the knife from Ord's hands and locking her thighs around his throat. With a piercing scream she flips herself up and over his head, using her momentum to slam him backward into the stone steps.

Pel scrambles to her feet again and dives for her hammer.

Ord doesn't move.

"We have to get out of here," Jay says.

"They aren't just going to let us leave," Chris says.

Jay nods in grim agreement. "I'm not planning to ask for permission."

Ord finally staggers to his feet, but he's leaning hard on his staff. He's hurt. Badly. Pel circles him, tossing her hammer from hand to hand. Taking her time, like a cat entertaining itself with a mouse. Ord stumbles again, collapsing to his knees before painfully pulling himself back up.

He isn't going to last much longer.

I'm not the only one who thinks this is almost over. The Sorrow around us are breathless with anticipation, our guards included. If we're going to go, now is the time.

Jay points to Leela, then to the blue Taker. Leela nods.

He looks at me. I read the silent question in his face: *Ready?*

I nod.

"Okay then." Jay throws a hard elbow into Green's torso, then grabs their staff and slams it into the blue Taker's chest, sending them flying. Before the acid-green Taker can react, Leela drives her fist into their face. Green reels backward. Leela grabs their knife hand and twists, snapping their wrist. The green Taker roars in pain as she flips their knife away into the root garden.

Green staggers back, clutching their arm and moaning. The sound boils over my skin. The red Sorrow rushes Leela, but Jay swings his stolen staff again, knocking Red's feet out from under them. Red's head slams against the stone, and they slump back, motionless.

"Move!" Jay shouts. "Go, go!"

The others follow him as he plunges into the garden. I twist, searching the crowd for Dr. Brown one more time. We need her if we're going to have any hope of finding our way out of the caves.

"Come on!" Leela shouts, grabbing my hand and pulling me after Jay. I yank her backward as a black-robed body stumbles across our path.

It's one of Tarn's guards. Tarn is locked in combat with the other two. And he's losing.

I have an idea.

I shake Leela off and hurl myself back through the roots.

"Jo! What the hell?" Leela shouts, but there's no time to explain.

She darts after me anyway as I race back to the red Sorrow, who is curled in a ball on the cavern floor, moaning. I search the root clusters behind it, but I don't see what I'm looking for. Come on! Where is it?

There!

I snatch the Taker's staff and charge back toward Tarn. The staff is even heavier than it looked, but I ignore my screaming muscles and pull it up over my shoulder.

"Tarn! Duck!"

Tarn hits the floor as I swing the staff, the same way I saw Pel attack Ord minutes ago. The barbed end cracks into the skull of one of Tarn's attackers. Tarn rolls with the other, flipping them over his head into a cluster of roots that close around them like a net.

"Come with us, Tarn!" I shout. "Please!"

He's about to answer when Pel bellows. We both look up just in time to see Pel swing her hammer into the small of Ord's back. It connects with a wet thud. He falls. He doesn't get up.

Tarn keens a hum that makes me want to weep.

"Please, Tarn," I say. "You can't help Ord now!" I ache for him. I know the weight of abandoning a brother to die. "You can't help him, but you can help us. And we can help you," I say. "Ord wouldn't want you to die here too."

A Sorrow shrieks behind me. I spin just in time to see the Taker I hit staggering toward us, knife flashing. I freeze just a fraction of a second too long. Leela steps between us and grabs their swinging knife with her bare left hand.

"Leela!" I scream.

Leela doesn't flinch as her blood wells over the blade. She also doesn't let go. She shoves the knife back into the startled warrior's face and throws a punch with her other hand, sending the Taker stumbling.

I swing the staff again. It slams into the Sorrow's back with a crackling thud I can feel all the way up my arms. The Taker collapses.

"Can we go now?" Leela groans, clutching her wounded hand to her chest.

I stop waiting for Tarn to decide. I grab his arm and drag him along as we plunge into the writhing glow of the root garden, leaving the fight, the Sorrow, and Dr. Brown behind.

ELEVEN

Tarn leads us through the back streets of the cavern city. Sorrow peer at us from the skeletal buildings, but nobody gets in our way or tries to help. I'm guessing they'll stay neutral until word spreads that Pel won the fight. We need to be gone before that happens.

Leela is keeping up, but she's pale and sweaty. I'm pretty sure she's going into shock. We bandaged her hand in some strips I tore from the hem of my T-shirt, but she refuses to let Miguel do anything else until we're safe.

Tarn takes us to a crevasse in the cavern wall that leads into a low, narrow tunnel. It's another of the massive geode formations. It's less than half a klick long, but by the time we reach the end, my whole body aches from walking in a tense crouch, and my arms and scalp are bleeding from brushes with the clusters of crystal that jag out of the walls and ceiling.

The tunnel ends in expansive blackness.

"Even the smallest light will give us away now," Tarn whispers, taking my hand. "Do not let go."

Then he pulls up his blackout hood and disappears.

"Hold on to each other," I whisper to the others, grabbing Chris's hand as Tarn tugs me forward.

We follow Tarn through the dark, holding hands like little kids on a school field trip. There's no way to judge the passage of time, but my aching feet tell me that we've been walking for at least an hour when I finally see light up ahead. It's faint and far away. I probably wouldn't even be able to see the whispers of green and blue and white if I had my flex on flashlight mode.

I want to ask Tarn what it is, but I have to stay quiet. Light isn't the only thing that could give us away if Pel's Takers are out there looking for us.

After a few more agonizing minutes, the pale, distant lights come into focus. It's another grove of solace tree roots. The glowing clusters aren't artistically shaped like they are in the root garden. They drip down from the cave ceiling in wild, ropy tangles of all different lengths. Only a few of them make it all the way to the floor.

Tarn walks a little faster now, leading us through the forest of roots to a lime-green cluster that's at least three times wider than I am. Its outer branches have been braided into loops that run up the length of the thick taproot at its center.

It's a ladder.

Tarn drops my hand and momentarily disappears; then the light of the root ladder picks his silhouette out of the dark. He starts to climb. Clearly, we're meant to follow. I tug experimentally on a loop of root. It seems sturdy enough, so I swing myself up after him. Suddenly, I want to be in the open air so badly, I can hardly stand it.

The starlight is coming from a triangular hole in the cave ceiling. Tough, woody surface roots frame its edges. I hook my hands over the nearest one and pull myself through.

Tarn is waiting to help me up. He's got a strip of gray cloth tied over his eyes, like the Takers did when we first encountered Ord in the caves. It's thin—I can see his round black eyes through the cloth. This must be how the Sorrow protect their eyes from excessive light. It's the middle of the night, but with my eyes still adjusted to the caves, the light of the twin moons seems bright. I can only imagine how glaring it looks to Tarn.

Chris is right behind me, but Beth is taking her time coming up the root ladder.

I look around while we wait for her to reach the surface. We're back in the woods near the crash site. The fan-shaped leaves of the solace trees are stiff and still in the night shadows. They smell sweet and sharp, like the blue Jell-O they always served with dinner in the rehab center.

I half expect to see work lights dancing through the trees. Actually, *expect* is the wrong word. It's more like I was hoping that Chief Penny managed to call in their location to Mom before she was attacked. But it's been almost 27 hours since the *Wagon* fell out of the sky. The valley is dark. If Mom and the others knew where the crash site was, they'd be here. That means we're on our own.

Beth reaches the top of the root ladder, and Chris and I help her up. Then I climb halfway back down to help Miguel and Jay get Leela to the surface without using her wounded hand, which is swollen and black with bruises. She's breathing hard, and her bangs are matted with sweat by the time we get her out.

"You're a little green around the gills there, boo," Miguel says as he rewraps her makeshift bandage. The torn strips are crusted with blood.

"I'm fine," she insists. "Let's just get to the flyer and get out of here."

With that, she starts toward the crash site. She makes it only a few steps before her legs buckle. She grabs a low branch to steady herself. Miguel wraps an arm around her waist to support her. She doesn't argue with him.

We follow them through the trees.

"I should return to Sorrow's Solace," Tarn says quietly, so that only I can hear him.

"But you said Pel would kill you," I say.

"She may," he says, covering his face with his hands, palms out, for a few seconds. The yellow glow of the bio-luminescent blood pumping under his skin is faint in the moonlight. "But now that Pel is Followed, she chooses the way for all Sorrow. Including me."

"Even if it leads to your death?" I say.

Tarn walks in silence for a while. Thinking. Then he says, "This is why the Sorrow follow. It helps us to make the right choices, despite personal consequences."

"Dr. Brown said you struggled with following Ord," I say.

"Lucille knows us well," Tarn says. "But she is still human. She will never truly understand us. I followed Ord long before our people did. He kept me alive after our father was taken by the Beasts. I trusted him completely. If I questioned his choices, it was only in the service of clari-fying his vision. Pel will look to others for such clarity. Perhaps that is why I am reluctant to return now. Perhaps my selfish desire to have influence over our direction is misleading me."

"How can wanting to stay alive be selfish?" I say.

"Very easily," he says. "Our Growers and Gatherers risk their lives every day when they go to the surface to retrieve food for our people. If they all chose to preserve their lives rather than following, would that not be selfish?"

"I guess so," I say. "But this is different. Nobody's going to starve if you stay with us."

"That may be so," he says. "But if one Sorrow chooses not to follow, then another may do so, and another. Then all will be lost."

I understand what he's saying. The Sorrow follow for the same reasons that ISA officers obey orders. Nothing would get done if everyone argued with Mom every time she made a decision. But Mom always taught us that we shouldn't follow an order if we know it's wrong.

That makes me wonder all over again what we're doing on this planet. Mom has access to the classified parts of the survey report. She knew about the Sorrow. There's no way she thought that coming here was the right thing to do. So why did she go along with it? And why did she keep the classified sections of the report secret? She might not have anticipated the problems with Stage Three, but she had to have known that keeping the Sorrow and the phytoraptors secret would put us all in danger. And she did it anyway.

"What if Pel is leading the Sorrow in the wrong direction?" I say. "Following someone just because you're supposed to doesn't help anyone."

"Perhaps," Tarn says. "But is it my place to say whether she is right or wrong?" Tarn raises his hands in clenched fists in front of his face, then drops them. "I should return. I have no reason to stay here. You are safe, and your vehicle is ahead. You do not need me."

"Maybe we don't need you," I say. "But you didn't need Dr. Brown, either. You and Ord protected her because she needed you. It's our turn now. Come back to Pioneer's Landing with us. Let us protect you from Pel."

Tarn doesn't respond, but he stays with me as we cross out of the trees into the high grass. From here I can see the silhouette of the flyer against the starry sky. For some reason, Jay and Chris are walking on the wings. What are they doing up there? Why isn't Jay inside doing the preflight sequence?

It takes me another few steps to realize that the flyer's skinny wings now end in bare stumps. The rotors are gone. Without rotors the flyer can't take off.

We're stuck here.

"What happened?" I shout, running the last few meters through the waist-high grass.

"Someone cut off the rotors," Chris calls back. "They cut a lot of the solar paneling off the wings too."

"Cut?" I say, confused.

"Yeah," Jay says, swinging himself down to hang from the wing by his hands and then dropping to the ground. "Real carefully. If I didn't know better, I'd think it was a pro-salvage job."

For an irrational half second, I wonder if Mom and the others already found the crash site, salvaged the wreckage, and left us for dead. But I dismiss that paranoid fantasy immediately. I can see the burned-out hulk of the *Wagon*'s engine fuselage from here. There's no way they'd leave that much recyclable material behind. Not to mention the fact that this was a perfectly good flyer. They would have taken it, not salvaged it for parts.

"Tarn," I say, "would Pel know our flyers can't take off without their rotors?"

"I doubt she would bother with sabotage," Tarn says. "If the Followed wished to stop you from leaving, she would be here waiting for us with Takers."

"It doesn't matter what happened to the flyer," Beth says. "We need to retrieve the *Wagon*'s satellite phone and use it to call for help."

"The chief had it," Leela says. "She pulled it from the emergency kit and stowed it in her harness first thing. She didn't want to risk losing it if we couldn't get the engine fire out and something happened to the cargo pod."

"Are you sure?" I say.

"Of course I'm sure," Leela snaps. "I watched her do it."

My heart sinks.

"She didn't have it when we found her," I say. "Her harness was shredded. It must have fallen out during the attack."

"Then it's over," Beth says, grim. "Unless the Landing happens to find us in the next seven hours, this whole ecosystem will collapse, and it will be my fault."

"Yeah," Leela says. "It will."

"Excuse me?" I say, turning on her. "This is not Beth's fault. She didn't know about—"

"If she's just giving up now, it's totally her fault. Yours

too," Leela says, cradling her swollen hand. "And mine. All of ours. We're pioneers. We don't give up. Especially you two. You're Watsons. You're not allowed to have doubts. It's in the Project bylaws, remember?"

I swallow hard to stop myself from bursting into tears at the stupid old joke. I remember what it felt like, to be so sure of everything. It's such a long way from how I feel right now.

"I'm not giving up," Beth says. "I'm facing reality. Our flyer has been destroyed, and we have no way to communicate with the Landing. We're stranded."

"What about the Rangers' hot spots?" Chris says.

The words are like a light switching on in my brain.

"What hot spots?" Leela says as I pull Dr. Brown's flex out of my pocket and shake it out.

"There's a map of these mountains saved on this thing that's way more detailed than the one in the survey report," I say, opening the file as I speak. "Her team set up a ton of hot spots out here. We may be close enough to get to one of them." I pull our coordinates from the flyer's autopilot history and enter them into the map.

An orange dot marks our location as in a broad puddle of green that's closer to the ocean on the western side of the mountain range than it is the prairie and the Landing. I can see the distinctive waterfall with its shining cliff wings. That's our valley.

And there's a green plus sign a little less than a centimeter away.

"Is that close enough?" Jay asks.

I double tap the waterfall, then the plus sign. A jagged yellow line pops up as the map suggests the quickest route between the two.

A tiny, relieved sigh darts through my lips.

"That's less than an hour hike," I say, amazed by our luck. "We can definitely make it there before the Landing initiates Stage Three."

"Are you sure we can network that thing?" Leela says. "It's ancient, and it looks like Dr. Brown tried to set it on fire."

"All its other systems work," I say, but I pull up system preferences and open the wireless settings anyway. "I'll run a diagnostic, but . . ." I trail off, staring at the flex in disbelief. "It doesn't have comms."

"What?" Chris says, grabbing the flex from me and swiping through the wireless settings menu. "All flexes have comms."

"Nope," Miguel says. "Fun fact: They made a couple of models with no wireless connectivity, back in the day. Mama Alejandra still has a bunch. She uses them for movies and games and stuff 'cause they have sweet battery life."

"And that's exactly what Dr. Brown has saved on this one," I say, trying to keep my panic to a dull roar. "It's useless."

"Isn't there a spare flex in the medical kit?" Leela says.

"There's no medical kit," Beth says. "Mom prioritized

arming the marine squadron over properly kitting out the flyers."

"We'll search the wreckage then," Jay says. "There has to be a flex somewhere in this valley."

Beth throws her arms wide to encompass the sea of night-black grass that stretches between the high cliffs behind us. *"Somewhere in this valley* isn't exactly helpful, Jay."

She's right. It was dumb luck that we found the chief, and that was in daylight. Finding the rest of the bodies in that grass could take all night. And who knows if their flexes even survived the attack. I can't remember if I saw Chief Penny's flex on her wrist or not. When I try to think back, all I see is the look on her face as she watched Chris cry for her, knowing she was dying with every red pulse of the flex draped over her neck.

Jay's flex. He left it behind when he went to get Beth's first aid kit. Then we abandoned the chief's body. Which means . . .

"I know where we can get a flex with comms," I say. "Jay, come help me. Miguel, see what you can do to keep Leela from keeling over before we get back."

"Copy that," Miguel says.

"I'm coming with you, too," Chris says.

"No!" The word pops out of my mouth like a burst bubble.

"Why not?" Chris says.

I really don't want to tell him that Jay and I are about to go scavenge his mother's corpse. I don't have to. I can see the realization pour over his face, transforming his indignation into horror.

"Oh," he says, choked. Fighting tears.

"Come on, bro," Miguel says. "I need you and Beth both to help me scrounge for medical gear."

"Just find me a couple of dozen pain patches," Leela says. "I'll stay in the flyer and sleep it off until you guys come back with reinforcements."

"We aren't leaving you behind," I say.

"I'm not walking two klicks," she says. "Not like this." She's leaning against the side of the ramp, sweating and shivering at the same time. She looks gray under the flyer lights.

"You've got an infection," I say, panic jabbing at me. Whatever Tau bacteria got into her wound, it's moving fast. And her immune system has no antibodies to fight it.

"Duh," she snaps. "Stop worrying about me. That's Miguel's job. You need to go find the stupid flex and save the world."

She's right, but I don't care. If Leela already looks this bad, we can't risk waiting to deal with this infection. Who knows what it might do to her? Even if we get in touch with the Landing and get her back to medical before morning, it might not be fast enough.

I turn to Tarn. "Could you heal her?"

"I am no Giver," he says. "And my understanding of the process is theoretical at best."

"Try anyway," I say. "Please. I know you're meant to go back and follow Pel. But saving a life can't be wrong."

Tarn's shielded gaze meets mine, and he rumbles a moan that makes my muscles clench like a sob. Then he says, "I will try."

"Excellent," Miguel says. He turns to Leela. "May I?" She waves her good hand weakly in a *whatever* gesture, and he scoops her into his arms. "C'mon, Chris. I need your help clearing a place for Tarn to work in the flyer."

"I'll plan our route to the hot spot," Beth says, following them up the ramp.

I turn to Jay. "Let's get this over with."

It's easy to retrace our steps. There are swaths of thinned and broken grass left behind where we walked and ran. Was that really just yesterday? I feel like a different person. Again. How many different people is it possible to be in seventeen years of life?

"Tau to Joanna," Jay says.

"Sorry," I say, dragging my brain back into the moment. "Did you say something?"

"Nah," he says. "But I could tell you were wandering."

"I was just thinking about . . . I don't know," I say. "The attack. The Sorrow. Ord . . ."

"You think we'll stay?" he says. "When everything's said and done?"

I shrug. "I don't know what's going to happen. Respect for indigenous species was built into the GFP's charter from the beginning. No one wants to repeat Earth's history of colonial atrocities out here. That's why the Rangers weren't supposed to approve occupied worlds for E&P teams. But we're already here, so . . ."

"Do you want to go home?"

Wow. Talk about questions I don't know how to answer. Tau Ceti e is so much more than I ever imagined. More beautiful. More dangerous. Harsher and sweeter at the same time. But so many people have died because we're here. Not just humans—Ord is probably dead, and who knows what will happen to Tarn?

But does that mean I want to go home?

"No," I say. "I don't want to go. But I don't think Pel's going to agree to share Tau with us, and we should respect that."

"Yeah," Jay says. "It's a bummer, but—" He cuts himself off, his voice abruptly sharp. "Is the grass getting thicker?"

"Huh?"

I look down. He's right. We're surrounded by pristine, waist-high grass.

"I think we're past the point where we found the chief," Jay says, turning to look behind us. "The grass should all be beaten down between the flyer and her body. We walked back and forth on that route a couple of times."

"And we've never walked through here," I say, dread closing around me like a fist.

"Did we miss her?" Jay asks.

"Maybe." I circle back toward the beaten-down grass behind us. "But I'm pretty sure we . . ."

My boots slip-slide on something. I stumble back a few steps to find my balance. Then I look down.

Sour bile rises in the back of my throat. I have to swallow it back to get the words out. "She was right here."

Jay follows my gaze to the blood-smeared hollow I nearly fell into. This is where we left the chief's body. It's gone. And so is Jay's flex.

"You'd think there'd be more left," Jay says in a choked voice. "If they ate her."

I've seen big predator kills in the extinction-reversal preserves back home. They don't look like this.

"There would be," I say. "Just like the flyer would have been ripped to shreds if the phytoraptors were the ones who destroyed it."

"You think the Sorrow took her body?" Jay says, catching up with my train of thought.

"No . . . yes . . . I don't know. Maybe," I say. "But if Tarn is right, and Pel wouldn't care about stealing our technology, then why would she steal our bodies?"

"We aren't going to figure it out now," Jay says. "We need to start looking for another flex."

"It'll be faster if we split up."

Jay shakes his head. "Not fast enough. Remember, Ord

said even the darkest hours aren't safe up here."

"If there are phytoraptors out there, we aren't any safer together than we are apart."

"Yeah, maybe," he says. "But it makes me feel better to pretend that's not true."

"Jay—"

"You know what's not going to find us a flex?" he says, cutting me off. "Arguing about this. Come on."

I give in.

Most of the bodies should be near the *Wagon's* fuselage, given what Leela and Miguel told us about the phytoraptor attack. But we don't find anyone, just a lot of blood in the grass. We look in the wreckage of the passenger cabin next, but it's empty, so we move on to the cargo pod.

Jay leaves me to stand watch as he climbs the side of the pod and crawls through the emergency hatch on top. I bounce a little to keep warm and distract myself from the despair that's winding up my insides. It's still dark and getting darker as the moons set, but it won't be for long. Morning is coming. And Stage Three is going to be initiated in four hours and fourteen minutes.

There's a small thud as Jay shoves the cargo pod hatch open and pulls himself up and out.

"Did you find a flex?" I call up to him as he walks to the edge of the pod and jumps down.

He shakes his head. "There's nothing in there. Someone took the cargo, the float carts, the manifests. Everything."

"It has to have been the Sorrow," I say. "But when did

Pel and her Takers find time to come out here and steal it all?"

"I don't think Pel did this," Jay says.

"You think Ord had his people salvage the crash site?" I say. It hadn't occurred to me before, but it makes sense. Ord carries a gun, and Tarn said that Dr. Brown had printed other technology for them. "You think he was planning to recycle this stuff with Dr. Brown's equipment?"

"Something along those lines," Jay says. "With the added bonus of being sure we needed him to save us." He looks around and sighs. "It's going to be light soon. We should get back to the flyer. If we seal it up, we can keep the phytoraptors out until it's dark again."

"By then, it's going to be too late to stop Stage Three," I say.

"Maybe not," Jay says. "We made it this far. Maybe we can figure out another way to get in touch with the Landing in time. Or maybe Dr. Howard will put it off. After all, with Chris and the chief both MIA, he must be pretty distracted. He might just hit the pause button. Wait to find Beth."

"Beth doesn't think so," I say. "Beth thinks Stage Three is going to destroy everything."

Jay takes my shoulders and turns me around so I have to meet his eyes. "Beth is brilliant, but she only sees what's true. You see what's possible. So don't stop looking now."

A tear slips down my cheek. He wipes it away with his thumb. I move closer and wrap my arms around his waist, burying my face in his shoulder.

He sighs like he just walked into a warm house on a cold day. His arms settle around me, pulling me closer. It feels weird and good and kind of embarrassing. This is so not the time to be getting all gushy, but I can't seem to give this moment up.

Something catches at the corner of my eye. I pull back. There's a bright-orange light in the grass maybe a dozen meters away. It fades and then swells again, but this time it's purple. Then blue and then green.

"What is that?" I say, pointing.

Jay turns to look. Then he swears and starts running.

"What?" I demand, racing to keep up. "What is it?"

"My flex!" he shouts back. "I set the flashlight to celebration mode the night before we left. The squad was out partying—last night on Earth and whatnot. I haven't used the flashlight since, so I never changed it back."

I can't believe we actually found it. And we've still got more than three hours to get to the hot spot and call the Landing. We're going to stop Stage Three. We're going to save Tau.

Jay slams to a stop so fast that I run right into him.

"What are you . . . ?" The question dies as I look over his shoulder and realize we're less than a meter from a phytoraptor. It's sitting on its haunches, watching us. Its chameleon skin has gone blue-gray, blurring its body into the night sky at its back. I'm not sure we'd be able to see it at all if not for the strobing light from Jay's flex, which is wrapped around one of its powerful forearms.

"Turn around and walk back to the flyer," Jay whispers without looking away from the phytoraptor. "Don't run. Predators chase things that run."

"On Earth," I whisper back. "We don't know how a phytoraptor is going to react to anything."

"Joanna—"

"I'm not leaving you."

Abruptly, the phytoraptor rears up on its hind legs, throwing its powerful arms wide. The strobing light of Jay's flex catches on its huge claws as they unsheathe from its thick fingers.

Jay spins, wrapping himself around me and burying his face in my hair. Braced for attack.

I can't look away from the towering form outlined in the pulsing rainbow light. My heart thuds against my rib cage, once, twice, three times as the beast looms over us. Then it sinks down again into the deep grass and ambles away, the flashing light of the flex on its arm dwindling and disappearing into the night.

TWELVE

A Sorrow song scratches over my skin as Jay opens the rear doors of the flyer. The sonar that flows under the sound feels hot and ragged. What is Tarn doing to Leela?

I vault onto the ramp before it hits the ground and hurry inside.

Leela is sitting in one of the passenger chairs. Miguel is checking her vitals. I can't see her hand, but the gray tinge is gone from her skin. Beth and Tarn and Chris are gathered around Dr. Brown's charred flex, watching something. The terrible sound is coming from the flex.

"Amazing," Tarn says, taking it from Beth and turning it over in his hands. "The recording is imperfect, but the shape of the sound is there. Even that which your people cannot perceive."

"If Pel's Takers had not destroyed my flex, I could have captured the higher frequencies more completely," Beth says. "But this is an old model, and in disrepair."

"You recorded Tarn healing Leela?" I ask.

"With his permission," Beth says. "It was an excellent opportunity to expand our understanding of his people."

"It was not a true healing," Tarn says. "When a Giver heals, the body is restored to its true state. My attempt was a poor substitute."

"Don't sell yourself short, Tarn," Leela says, holding up her hand. It's still bruised and purple, but the wound has closed and the swelling is gone. "Our doctors couldn't have done what you did, even with a full medical suite."

"You were gone for a long time," Chris says. "Did you find a working flex?"

"Sort of," Jay says.

"Woot!" Miguel crows.

"Don't get too excited," I say. "This is going to suck."

While Jay explains that his flex is currently on the arm of a phytoraptor, I switch the wall screens to three-sixty mode. The moonless predawn darkness outside snaps into place around us.

I pivot, searching the grass until I find what I'm looking for.

"There!" I say, pointing to a flare of hot-pink light. "That's Jay's flex. It's less than a dozen meters away. All we have to do is get it back from that phytoraptor."

"That's an ambitious use of the word *all*," Miguel says.

Beth turns to Jay. "Would your stun gun knock it out long enough to grab the flex?"

"Not an option," he says. "Pel's Takers destroyed it."

"I lost my laser welder during the phytoraptor attack," I say. "But it was pretty effective. Is there anything else in here we could use as a weapon?"

"It would have to be formidable," Tarn says. "The Beasts are very hard to kill." He pulls his robe back to reveal a molded body suit like the ones Ord and Pel wore to fight. It's made of layers of something smooth that shifts from blue to green to a charcoal gray that almost matches his black robe as the light hits it. "Their skin is nearly impenetrable. We use it as armor."

"What about this?" Chris says, holding out the knife that Ord gave him.

Tarn keens softly. The sound feels like repressed tears, pricking at the corners of my eyes.

"A fine weapon," Tarn says, "capable of cutting through Beast hide. Unfortunately, we'd never get close enough to use it."

"But your people do know how to kill them," Leela says.

"Yes," Tarn says. "We hunt and kill the Beasts. But as my pouch mate told you, this requires great sacrifice. We cannot take their lives without giving our own. I do not recommend approaching a Beast."

"I don't think we have a choice," I say. "We need that flex if we're going to stop the Landing from initiating Stage Three."

"What is Stage Three?" Tarn asks.

I watch his face as Beth explains. His expression doesn't change. Not that I would know what it meant if it did. My stomach is flip-flopping like a hooked fish. I know it isn't our fault that Stage Three might cause a catastrophic environmental collapse, but our species is endangering his world. It would be hard not to see that as a betrayal. I like Tarn. I don't want him to feel that way about us.

"So this Stage Three will kill the Beasts?" Tarn says.

"Yes," Beth says. "But it would do a lot more than that. My preliminary simulations indicate a near certainty that the Stage Three bacteria will jump to other species. One of the most vulnerable are the solace trees that light your city."

"And if we can't kill that thing, we'll never get Jay's flex back," Chris says. "Then we won't be able to stop it."

Tarn looks up at the wall screen, where the pulsing light of Jay's flex reveals the phytoraptor's presence in the grass. "There might be a way, if we can find its nest."

"Nest?" I say.

"They return to their nests at dawn and dusk to rest," Tarn says. "That is the only time they are vulnerable."

"You want to take a single knife into a whole nest of those things and try to kill one of them?" Jay says.

"I don't think we'd need to kill it," Beth says. "I read most of Dr. Brown's file on the phytoraptors last night. According to Dr. Pasha's notes, the whole nest enters a catatonic state for short periods at dawn and dusk. Pasha frequently used that time to run tests and take blood and tissue samples. There's no reason we can't use it to steal back Jay's flex."

"If we find the nest," Tarn says. "Which is uncertain. The Beasts build their nests in hidden places. We can attempt to follow this one back to its home, but it will be a challenge."

Beth pulls Dr. Brown's flex from her utility harness and unfolds it. She swipes up the map of the Diamond Range. "Computer, please overlay phytoraptor nesting and hunting data."

Half a dozen red dots appear on the map. Each has a shaded area around it.

"The Rangers found and recorded six different phytoraptor nests and accompanying hunting grounds," Beth says.

"I wonder why Lucille never spoke of this to my pouch mate," Tarn says, studying the glowing dots.

So do I.

Beth puts her fingers on one of the red dots and pushes outward, zooming the map in to show the shaded area around it. This valley and its winged waterfall are right in the middle. "If Dr. Pasha's data is correct, I suspect that any predator we encounter in this valley belongs to this nest."

"Weird," Chris says. "It's right next to the Ranger hot spot." He's right. There's a green plus sign on the map right next to the red dot that marks the nest.

"Not weird," Beth says. "Expected, given the likelihood that these hot spots were built to facilitate Dr. Pasha's study of the phytoraptors."

"We can make this work," I say. I'm actually starting to believe it. "If we steal Jay's flex back while the phytoraptors are sleeping at dawn, that gives us two hours to get in touch with the Landing and stop Stage Three."

"You're crazy," Chris says, pointing at the wall screens, where the strobing light from Jay's flex has settled in the branches of a solace tree on the edge of the woods. "It's right there. Alone. If we go to its nest, we'll be outnumbered. And if those things wake up . . ." He shakes his head. "We should figure out how to kill it now. There has to be a way. I'm not scared."

But he is. I can feel the fear vibrating through his words. Maybe I'm imagining it. Or maybe being around the Sorrow is making me listen to human voices differently.

"I'm scared," I say. "All of our options right now are terrifying. It seems like every choice we make is scarier than the last one. But maybe, I don't know . . . Maybe it's good to be afraid." I shake my head. This isn't coming out right. But I keep going anyway, as much for myself as for the others.

"A lot of people made choices that brought us here. To this. Choices that we didn't have any say in. Choices we didn't even know about. The ISA, Mom, Dr. Brown . . ." My eyes find Tarn's blindfolded ones on the other side of the flyer. "Ord. We followed their orders because we respect them and because that's the way it's supposed to work. We were supposed to be able to trust them. But their choices put us in danger. They got people we loved killed. And they might end up wrecking the whole planet, if we can't get home in time to stop them. So maybe . . . I don't know, I think I'd rather make my own choices and live with the fear."

The others are staring at me. I must sound like a sanctimonious idiot. They're never going to let me live this down.

"Well said," Beth says quietly.

Miguel bobs his head. "Agree. Two thumbs up."

"Sure," Leela says. "It was a great speech, but that doesn't make this a good plan. If we hike to that nest, we'll be out in the open for at least an hour. Do we really think we can get all the way there without running into a phytoraptor and getting ourselves eaten?"

"Our Growers and Gatherers come to the surface to tend our gardens and gather food during the night hours," Tarn says. "They often survive."

"Often?" Leela says dubiously.

"Hey, that's better than rarely," Jay says, "but this doesn't have to be an all-or-nothing thing. Jo and I can go alone. You guys can stay here."

"Don't be dumb," Leela says.

"I think it's a very reasonable offer," Miguel says. "But I'm gonna pass anyway. This little field trip is exactly the kind of deal where you need a doctor along for the ride."

"Sorrow's Solace is in danger. I must help you," Tarn says.

"We have less than an hour to sunrise," Beth says, pointing to the east, where the stars are starting to fade. "And less than three before Stage Three will be deployed."

"No time like the present, then," Jay says.

"But procrastinating is so much fun," Miguel quips as he swipes up the lock pad and opens the rear doors.

The others troop down the ramp, Chris and I bring up the rear. He stops halfway down, looking out over the valley.

"You can stay here," I say. "We'll come back for you when it's over."

"What if you all die?" he says.

I open my mouth to tell him that won't happen, but then I close it again. We might. There's no use pretending otherwise. "That would be pretty bad."

"Yeah," he says. Then he walks down the ramp after the others. Watching his narrow form wade into the grass, I feel all those fears I was talking about congeal in my chest. They weigh so much that I can hardly put one foot in front of the other. But my friends believed me when I said we could do this. I guess that means I have to believe me too.

"Joey?" Miguel calls back. "You okay?"

"Yeah," I say, walking to the bottom of the ramp and tapping the lock screen to close it behind me. "I'm coming."

The stars continue to disappear as we slog through the grass. When we reach the cliffs at the southern end of the valley, Jay and Chris free climb to the top. They're going to plant anchor spikes up there so the rest of us can tether in and rappel up the cliff. They're almost to the top when I see a flicker of colored light out of the corner of my eye. Before I can react, the phytoraptor wearing Jay's flex barrels right past me and leaps up the cliff. It's so close I can hear the twang of its claws scraping over the crystal.

Leela swears. "Did you see that?"

I dart back from the cliff face and look up, holding my breath. I let it out again in a rush when I see Jay and Chris crawling over the top. They don't seem to have even noticed the passing raptor.

"Why didn't it attack?" Miguel asks, craning to look up. "Not that I'm complaining."

My hands are still shaking. "Maybe it didn't see us," I say. "It is pretty dark."

"No," Tarn says. "If the Beast was hungry, it would have taken us."

"*If* the Beast was hungry?" I say. "So they aren't always dangerous?"

Tarn raises his hands to cover his face, palms out. "They are not always hungry. This doesn't make them less dangerous."

"They're ready," Beth says, pointing up to where Jay is waving at the top of the cliffs.

"Yay," Leela says dryly. She presses the autoconnect button on her harness. Her tether line shoots out, snaking up the cliff face to connect with one of the anchors. She plants her boots on the cliff and starts climbing, favoring her still-bruised hand. Miguel tandem-tethers with Tarn and I tandem with Beth, just in case my pacers freak out about the exertion and the altitude change. But I make it up just fine. We even beat Miguel and Tarn to the top.

I walk a few meters into the woods at the top of the cliffs while we wait for them. Blue parrot palms arch over burly solace trees here, just like they did in Jannah.

There's a ripple of movement to my left. My head snaps around to scan the forest, but there's nothing there. Am I imagining things? No. There it is again. And again. Now that I'm focusing on them, I can see flickers of motion whisper through the trees all around me. It looks kind of like a faulty wall screen warping a three-sixty. Except we aren't in an entertainment center. We're in the forest on Tau. And those flashes of movement are phytoraptors.

It takes precious seconds to persuade my feet to move. Now that I'm looking for the creatures, I can see them all around us. I don't know if I'll even make it back to the others. With every step, I expect to feel claws sinking into my back or meaty fingers ripping me off my feet. But the attack never comes. The phytoraptors don't even acknowledge my presence.

When I get back to my friends, Jay and Leela are helping Tarn over the cliff's edge while Chris and Beth dig our anchor points out of the rocks.

"Stop," I say. "We have to go back. Now."

"Joanna," Beth says, "if we're to have any hope of—"

"The woods are full of phytoraptors," I say. "They're camouflaged. You can't see them unless you're looking. But if you're looking—"

"They're everywhere," Jay says, alarm sparking in his voice as his hand reflexively goes to his utility harness, where his stun gun used to be. He swears. "God damn it."

A thick, pulsing hum floods through the trees. The sound races over my body like the surge of adrenaline I used to feel when I put Grandpa's Cessna into a controlled dive.

What is that? And where is it coming from?

Tarn whistles a minor chord in the Sorrow language. I can't feel the sonar as clearly as I could in the caves, but the sound is still tangible. Like nausea, prickling over my skin.

"What's wrong, Tarn?" I ask.

"I fear we have chosen poorly," he says.

Before I can ask what he means, a huge phytoraptor hurtles over the cliff and barrels straight between us, knocking Chris and Beth aside like bowling pins. Chris fumbles for Ord's knife, but the Beast doesn't attack—it just keeps running.

"What the hell is going on?" Leela shouts.

"I don't know," I say, as more phytoraptors charge past, headed in the same direction.

"They are being called," Tarn says. He hoots again in that melancholy tone that makes me feel like I'm going to vomit. Real anxiety layers over the sonar-induced emotional reaction as I see the rainbow-colored strobe of Jay's flex racing through the trees. Our phytoraptor has reversed course, just like the others.

"Did you see that?" I call.

"Yeah." Jay swears. "Come on! We're going to lose it!"

We follow the phytoraptors. There's no point in trying to stay out of sight. They're totally focused on that sticky, surging hum. It has to be a Sorrow song. No regular sound could make me feel so . . . itchy. But why would the Sorrow want to call phytoraptors to them?

Whatever their reasons, it's working. Phytoraptors are all around us, running past us and climbing through the branches overhead. They're heading for an open space in the trees up ahead.

Now that I can see where we're going, I try to pick up the pace, but Tarn grabs my arm, holding me back.

"No! Please!" he says. "We must not interrupt the hunt!"

"Why not?" I ask, hushed.

He whistle-moans something in Sorrow that makes me feel like my clothes are too tight. "Please, Joanna. Just do as I say."

"Sorry, Tarn," Jay says. "But we need that flex." He looks to the rest of us. "Stay back here, okay?"

With that he slips ahead, cautiously weaving through

the trees. I follow him. So does Tarn. He whistles in distress as we creep closer. He desperately doesn't want us to go into that clearing. I understand why Jay is insisting, but ignoring Tarn this way feels wrong, and not just because it's disrespectful. Tarn has always been so open—if he doesn't want us here, there must be a good reason.

Jay finds a dense cluster of parrot palms at the far side of the clearing. The narrow, flexible trunks are so close together we can barely squeeze between them, but they're good cover. Tarn and I slide in behind him.

This isn't a natural clearing. It looks more like a huge arena cut out of the forest. A pair of Givers are standing back to back at its center, singing. Their layered voices make them sound like a whole host of beings, but they seem to be alone. Their translucent robes glow in the navy-blue predawn.

Phytoraptors are oozing out of the trees from all directions, circling the Givers. They don't seem to care. They don't even react to the seething mass of muscles and teeth and hunger that's swirling around them.

The Givers' song takes on a percussive quality—a tactile drumbeat so undeniable, my heart feels like it's pounding in time. Pulsating. Throbbing. Growing louder and faster with every passing moment. The circling phytoraptors are moving faster too, closing in on the Givers. This is going to get ugly fast.

Moving in unison, each of the Sorrow pulls a knife

from under their robes. Wide, heavy blades with wicked pronged points like the one Ord used in his fight with Pel.

The Givers' voices grow even louder as they raise their knives to eye level, blade out. The sonar under the song thuds under my skin, churning through my stomach like ravenous hunger. Charging up my spine like uncontrollable fury. I want to run, as far and as fast as it takes to chase that noise out from under my skin. I also want to kill something. To rip flesh with my bare hands.

What the hell is happening to me?

As one, the two Givers swing their knives down and drive the blades into their own abdomens.

Air punches out of my chest, as though the pronged blades just slammed into my intestines instead of theirs. I can hardly breathe, but the Givers continue to sing as they drag their knives across their bellies. Silver-gray viscera and luminescent blood spill out of their bodies onto the grass. They sway on their feet, but they don't stop singing. There's no pain in the deep, tactile thrum of their sonar. It's victory. Lust. Hunger.

The Givers collapse.

For a breathless moment, the silence is deafening.

Then the phytoraptors attack.

They swarm over the robed bodies, their shrieks and groans cracking through the clearing as silver blood and lumps of flesh fly. They aren't just feeding. There's a manic ferocity to it that feels unnatural.

"What just happened?" I whisper to Tarn. "Why did those Givers do that?"

"This is why they are called Givers," he says, his eyes still locked on the gory display at the center of the clearing. "They give their lives so that Beasts may be taken."

"Taken?" I say. "Like killed? By who?"

As if in answer to my question, a projectile whistles through the trees and thuds into one of the swarming phytoraptors. Then another, and another. Phytoraptors are collapsing all over the clearing, bleeding viscous white where the spinning missiles strike home. But the predators are so swept up in their bloodlust, they don't seem to notice. I look up, searching the trees. In their blackout robes, the Takers look like dense shadows crouched in the branches. I count seven of them up there, raining death down on the phytoraptors.

Suddenly, it all makes a sick sort of sense. This was a trap, and the Givers were the bait. The Sorrow lured the phytoraptors here and then sacrificed themselves to keep the predators in a feeding frenzy so that the warriors could kill them.

"I told you, we give lives in order to take the Beasts. It is the only way," Tarn whispers. "This hunt is a celebration of the new Followed, I am sure of it." He whistle-moans again. I can't describe the physical sensation of the sound. It's too complicated. But it makes me want to cover my ears and run screaming.

"We have to stop this," I whisper.

"I doubt we can," Jay says. "Besides, it'll be a lot easier to just grab my flex off that thing's dead body after the Sorrow leave."

"The Takers will not leave the bodies," Tarn says. "No part of a hunt is wasted. They will bring everything they find back to Sorrow's Solace. They will either collect the flex or destroy it."

"Okay," Jay says. "Guess we're going with Hotshot's plan then."

If only I had one.

The Givers have been consumed, but the frenzied phytoraptors don't stop. They turn on their own dead, ripping into the fallen raptor bodies with as much enthusiasm as they did with the Sorrow.

"If the Givers lured them here with that song, could another one snap them out of it?" I whisper.

"I do not know. No one would ever do such a thing," Tarn says, humming urgently in Sorrow. "To disrupt a hunt . . . it would be wrong in ways I cannot express in your language."

"Even knowing what's at stake?" Jay asks quietly.

Tarn brings both hands in front of his face in clenched fists and keeps them there, groaning something that makes my heart pound and my head swim like my blood sugar is crashing. *Desperation.* We can't ask him to do this.

"There has to be another way," I say. "We just have to distract them."

Tarn moans again in Sorrow. "Please," he says, switching to English. "If the hunt is disturbed—"

"They're going to kill it!" Chris exclaims, behind me. I didn't even realize he'd snuck up to join us until he spoke.

I spin to see one of the Takers slam a massive crystal-shard hammer into our phytoraptor's shoulder. The phytoraptor hardly seems to notice the impact. It's busily tearing long strips of flesh from the body of another raptor and draping itself in the gore.

The Taker draws their hammer back for another strike. A death blow.

We're out of time. Unless . . .

I yank out Dr. Brown's flex, crank the volume, and smack the audio file Beth recorded of Tarn healing Leela.

Tarn hisses as the harsh, warped recording of his own voice blasts through the clearing.

Our phytoraptor snaps upright as though noticing its surroundings for the first time. The Taker who was about to kill it freezes in midstroke. In that split second of shock, the beast bellows and throws itself at the Taker, sending their hammer flying. The Taker uses the raptor's momentum to toss themselves free. Then the Taker spins, drawing their knife and charging the phytoraptor again before the creature can react.

The knife connects, driving into the predator's torso.

The phytoraptor screams and backhands the Taker, its massive claws catching them across the throat. The Taker's head lolls back, nearly severed from their shoulders. The body stays upright for a heartbeat, as though they're as shocked as I am by their sudden, brutal death. Then they collapse.

Sorrow shouts careen around us. Sonar bursts of panic, fear, anger, and pain splash over me from all directions. The hunt has suddenly become a battle. Some of the surviving phytoraptors leap into the trees, chasing Takers into the forest. Others simply disappear, camouflaging themselves into the trees around us as they flee. I search the quickly emptying clearing. I don't see the flashing lights from Jay's flex. Our phytoraptor is gone. I hope it's heading for its nest.

In seconds, everyone and everything left in the clearing is dead.

Without a word, Tarn steps through the trees and crosses to the dead Taker, staring down at the body.

"We need to keep moving," Jay says to me quietly.

"I know," I say. "Just . . . give him a minute."

I try to figure out what I'm going to say as I pick my way through the carnage of phytoraptor corpses. "Tarn, I know you didn't—"

"I made my choice," Tarn says, cutting me off before I can get my lame apology out. "And so did you." He looks up at the pale tendrils of turquoise on the horizon. "Time is short. We need to run."

THIRTEEN

The sky fades slowly as we hike through the mountains. Tarn can take the steep, uneven terrain a lot faster than we can with his long, trijointed limbs, so he ranges ahead of us, scouting the best path forward. My muscles ache and my lungs are burning, but I hardly notice the pain. I can't stop thinking about that Taker. We got them killed. No, *I* got them killed. Was it worth it, to save the flex? To save Tau? I thought so at the time. But after I saw what happened, the way they died . . . I don't know.

"Chill, Joey," Miguel says, falling back to walk beside me. We're almost to the nest, so Tarn made us slow down so we don't miss it. "Stress is bad for your blood pressure."

"This is not exactly a relaxing moment."

"This is not exactly a relaxing place," he cracks. "But

so far, we've been takin' care of business, saving the world, etc., just fine. Why start worrying now?"

"You didn't see what this phytoraptor did to that Taker," I say. "And we're walking into its nest to try to steal a flex off its wrist."

"You got a better idea, you should definitely speak up," Miguel says.

"I wish," I say. I shake my head. "If we had just gone back to camp after we saw the *Wagon* crash, like Leela said—"

"Then maybe you'd have come back with a rescue team, and they'd have all gotten eaten by phytoraptors too," Miguel says. "Walk in the present, Joey. That's the only way we get to see the future."

He's right. He usually is. Miguel doesn't make a big thing of it, but he's pretty wise.

Wait.

"Are you quoting Doc's coffee mug?"

"Sure." Miguel flashes an unrepentant grin. "But I figure the trite oversimplification of Zen Buddhism applies. Am I right?"

"Holy crap," Jay says. Ahead of us, he stops so abruptly that he has to grab the nearest tree to check his forward motion.

Miguel and I scramble up the last few meters of the slope.

"Careful," Jay says, holding up a hand to slow us down.

A few seconds later, I see why. He's standing on the edge of a cliff. It's a sheer drop into a narrow box canyon that hugs the curves of a tumbling river. The canyon must be three stories deep, but it's only five or six meters across, and the forest continues on the other side.

"You weren't kidding about these nests being hard to find, Tarn," Leela says, looking a few meters upstream, where the rocky cliff walls bend away from the water, unfolding into a deep, wooded ravine. "You'd never know this was here until you were falling into it."

"If my people knew of this place, it would no longer exist," Tarn says, staring down at the phytoraptors that are wading up the river toward the ravine in groups of three and four.

Electric-blue parrot palms cluster across the ravine floor, digging their roots into its steep walls. Fleshy, brownish-green vines cover the riverbanks and wind up the narrow trunks of the trees. Their muted leaves fold around bloodred flowers that stretch open like screaming mouths, thrusting their bright orange stamens up to the sun.

Phytoraptors are now pouring into the ravine from all directions, throwing themselves down the cliffs like gravity is a minor annoyance. The shifting color palettes of their skin make it hard to see where one member of the crowd ends and another begins.

"How many of them are down there?" Leela whispers.

"Too many," I say. "And they don't look sleepy."

"They don't sleep," Beth says. "Dr. Pasha described it as a trancelike state. He recorded several videos of phytoraptor hibernation, but the files were corrupted. I can only assume we'll know it when we see it."

I turn to see that my sister is crouched next to a jagged spire of crystal that juts out of the cliff. She's about two centimeters from the edge, leaning out over open space.

"Beth!" I hiss, racing to grab the back of her utility harness. "What the hell?"

"Thank you," she says, leaning out farther now that I'm bracing her. "I just need—got it."

She straightens, holding a scrap of solar paneling.

"Where did that come from?" I say.

"Our flyer, presumably." She points to flecks of *Pioneer*-green tint along the panel's sharply cut edge.

"Seriously?"

"Look," Jay says, pointing across the ravine to another spire that bristles with wide, metallic spikes.

"No way," I say. A chill prickles up the back of my neck at the realization. "Is that . . ."

"Yeah," Jay says. "It's one of the missing rotors from the flyer."

"I thought the components were removed," I say. "Not ripped out."

"They were," he says. He looks as mind-blown as I am.

"There's another one," Leela says, pointing across the canyon. "These little towers are all over the place."

Now that I'm looking for them, I can see at least a

dozen pillars built of carefully balanced crystal and metal positioned at odd intervals along the clifftops.

"They're down there, too," Chris says, pointing down to where the odd little structures scatter through the river and across the ravine floor. "What are those things?"

"Dr. Pasha mentioned that the nests were engineered," Beth says, carefully fitting the scrap of solar panel back into the crystal spire. "I assume that he was referring to these structures. But he didn't elaborate on their purpose."

"If the phytoraptors can build something like this, does that mean Pasha was right?" Jay says. "Are they intelligent?"

"These structures are surprisingly sophisticated," Beth says.

"Crows and beavers use human trash to build dams and nests," Chris says. "That doesn't mean they're sentient."

"We don't have enough data to know one way or the other," Beth agrees. "But it is very possible that these pillars are what made Dr. Pasha attempt to communicate with this species. Of course, that attempt failed."

Failed seems like a pale word for being eaten alive.

A web of light explodes through the ravine, and the fear clenched around my rib cage shatters in a single moment of awe. The crystal spires snatch the blue morning light and splinter it into fractal patterns that dance through the ravine. It's breathtakingly strange, like nothing I've ever seen, or even imagined. And it's definitely not an accident. This is what the spires are designed to do.

"Whoa," Miguel says, finally.

"Yeah," Jay says. "I think that about sums it up."

"They make their nests out of light," Leela breathes.

This isn't a nest. It's a work of art.

"Have your people observed this phenomenon before?" Beth asks Tarn.

"The Takers have," he says. The intense light must hurt his eyes, but he doesn't look away. "But it has always been assumed that this was a naturally occurring phenomenon. The Takers don't examine the nests. If they are lucky enough to find one, they take the Beasts inside and then burn the nest itself to ash."

"The Takers slaughter them in their nests?" I say. "While they're sleeping?"

"Yes," Tarn says. He turns to look at me, impassive. "You have seen the consequences of confronting the Beasts while they are alert."

My stomach clenches, twisting at the memory of the Taker's head lolling back, its throat gaping. I guess the Sorrow have to take any advantage they can get. They don't stand a chance in a fair fight. Neither will we.

"Guys," Leela says, "something's happening down there."

The phytoraptors have spread out across the ravine floor. They are planting themselves, hands and feet digging into the silver-gray soil. Thick, leafy tendrils sprout from their arched backs, reaching up to the web of light. Flowers unfurl along the tendrils, blooming into a riot of color—blue, white, and deep purple. Even a few striking pinks. In less than a minute, the crowd of dangerous predators has been transformed into a field of otherworldly wildflowers.

"I think they're feeding," Beth whispers. "The focusing effect of these structures must amplify and condense the light for their consumption."

"Like ants under a magnifying glass," Miguel says. "Except they don't mind getting fried."

"Let's move," Jay says. "We don't know how long they stay down, once they're out."

He and Leela pick their way along the cliff to a steep wash littered with chunks of crystal. As they pick their way down, Miguel says, "I'm gonna stay here. Keep a lookout so I can warn you if they start waking up. Chris, you should—"

"No," Chris says. "I'm not scared. I'm going."

He starts down the wash before I can argue with him.

"I will stay as well," Tarn says. "I do not believe I can help you now."

"Of course," I say. "You should stay where it's safe."

"I do not fear for *my* safety," Tarn says, turning to look down at the blooming raptors. "Sorrow have already died because I chose not to follow. And if you succeed, you will prevent the destruction of the Beasts." The pain and confusion in his voice are palpable. "That will lead to more Sorrow deaths. Deaths that might have been prevented if not for me."

"It isn't that simple," I say. "The solace trees—"

"I understand the threat Stage Three poses," Tarn says. "That does not make protecting the Beasts any less treacherous to the Sorrow who will die at their hands."

"Joanna! You coming?" Leela whispers back to me.

Conflicting anxieties grind through me. I don't want to make Tarn feel like he's betraying his people. But we can't let Stage Three happen. Even if Beth could somehow stop it from spreading, we can't wipe out the phytoraptors just because they're dangerous.

"Go," Tarn says. "As you have said, we must make our own choices."

As I scramble after the others, I throw a look back to where Tarn stands silhouetted against the dawn sky. I wish I could see his face, but he's retreated under his deep hood. Not that the look on his face would tell me much, I remind myself. Tarn isn't human. It's surprisingly easy to forget that, considering that's he's transparent and his blood glows in the dark. But I can't help but think of Tarn as a friend. I feel like I understand him, even though I'm sure I don't. Not really. Tarn is just as alone with us as Dr. Brown was with the Sorrow.

By the time I reach the ravine floor, the others are already picking their way among the phytoraptors. At first we try to stay hidden in the trees, but the predators are oblivious to our presence. Finally, we give up on being sneaky and cut straight through the sleeping crowd.

The blossoming phytoraptors aren't as still as they looked from the cliff tops. Subtle undulations roll through their bodies, making their flowering tendrils flex and sway. I can see the huge muscles rippling under their skin as we pass. A few of them have chunks of crystal and flecks of metal and plastic knotted in their tendrils or driven through their flesh like piercings. They've been using bits and pieces of human technology to decorate themselves as well as their nest.

The strobe of Jay's flex is hard to see in the brilliant light that fills the ravine. It takes an unbearably long time to find our phytoraptor, which has planted itself in the shallows of the river. It's in bad shape. Most of its tendrils aren't flowering and some of them are hanging limply into the water. But when we get close enough, I can see that the flesh around the jagged slice on its chest is knitting itself back together. It's healing so fast, half of the wound has already been transformed into a scar.

Our phytoraptor shifts its weight, rolling its head back to let the light run over its face. The top of its head is smooth and round, almost like a human skull.

Recognition snatches at my breath.

"That's Bob!" I breathe. "The phytoraptor the Rangers were trying to teach sign language."

"Guess that explains why he knew how to wear a flex," Jay whispers.

"That's good, right?" Chris whispers. "Maybe he likes humans."

"Maybe," Leela whispers. "But his buddies still ate the Rangers."

"Right," Jay mutters. "On that note . . ."

He eases one foot into the river. When Bob doesn't react, he takes a step closer, then another, working his way toward the phytoraptor. He's moving painfully slow, but I don't want him to go any faster.

Finally, Jay is in arm's reach. He settles onto his haunches and extends one hand, very, very slowly toward Bob's forearm.

Jay's fingers slip under the flex.

It sags into his open palm.

Jay starts to pull his hand back.

Bob wakes up.

Huge blue eyes lock with Jay's.

Nobody moves.

After a while, Jay starts pulling his hand back farther, a centimeter at a time. Never taking his eyes off Bob. I expect him to tuck the flex into his harness. Instead, he reaches back and presses it into my hand.

"Get out of here," Jay breathes without moving his lips. "I'll keep him busy."

"We've already had this conversation," I hiss. "I'm not leaving you."

"This time you have to," Jay says. "Tau's future depends on it."

He's right, of course. But I'm not ready to admit that yet. There has to be another way.

I look past Jay to Bob. To my surprise, he locks eyes with me immediately.

Bob's eyes aren't just blue. I can see all the shades of the Tau sunrise in their depths, radiating from navy-blue pupils. The phytoraptor looks me up and down, studying me. Is he looking for weaknesses? Waiting for us to run?

My brain unfreezes abruptly. The last time Bob interacted with humans, Pasha was teaching the raptor sign language. Bob is waiting, but not for us to run.

He's waiting for me to talk.

Basic sign language was part of my extravehicular training at the academy. It comes in handy on space walks. But that was a long time ago. Do I remember enough to do this?

I jam Jay's flex into my harness and zip the pocket closed. Then I bring my hand to my forehead and make the tilted salute that means hello in American Sign Language. Next, I try to sign friend and human, but my hands are shaking so hard I can hardly form the signs.

Bob tilts his head, like he's confused. I shake my hands out and try again, making the motions clearer this time.

The phytoraptor's broad forehead flexes, widening his eyes in a way that makes him look almost comically startled. Is that recognition?

I try again.

Something lights up in his eyes this time. He raises a broad, double-opposable-fingered hand and touches it to his head, just above his eyes. Then he draws it out, and up.

Hello.

"No way," Jay says quietly. "Did he just . . . ?"

I nod. I raise my hand and echo the gesture. Then I add *Nice to meet you* in slow, careful motions.

I expect Bob to mirror me. Instead, the raptor points to himself, then taps two fingers on each hand together. He stops for a moment, like he's confused. Then he puts his thumb together with his gnarled forefinger in a circle, the other fingers straight. That's a B. Then he closes them, so his hand forms a round O, and then he raises them again. Another B.

Hello. My name is Bob.

FOURTEEN

The signed words set my brain on fire, rewriting the scene even as I'm living it. Bob spoke to me. He isn't mimicking. He's talking. I am officially making First Contact.

Bob smacks an open hand to his chest. It isn't sign language, but I get the gist: *Pay attention!*

When he's sure I'm watching, Bob points at me. *You.* Then he hooks a finger and swipes it downward. *Must.* Next, he raises his hand to eye level and makes a pinching gesture with his fingers as he draws the hand away from his face.

Crap. I don't remember that one.

Bob repeats the sequence even more emphatically.

"You must . . . ," I say, hoping that speaking the words out loud will help my brain translate. It doesn't. "Damn. What is that sign?"

A sharp whistle punches through the air.

I look up to where Miguel is standing on the top of the cliffs, waving his arms to get our attention. The web of light above us is starting to fade. The phytoraptors around us are stirring. Shifting and kneading the soil.

They're waking up.

Bob slaps the surface of the river, pulling my attention back to him. He points at me, then plunges one hand behind the other and pulls it out again.

That one I know.

You. Out.

"It wants us to leave."

"Yeah," Jay says, scanning the stirring around the canyon. "I second that motion."

"Move slowly," Beth says, already starting upstream, slipping between the restless phytoraptors.

"Or we could run really fast," Chris says, looking around nervously as we follow Beth. "Just a thought."

"Stay frosty," Leela says. "Let's keep the 'Do Not Disturb' on as long as we can."

That's easier said than done. The phytoraptors are still asleep, but they are no longer quiet. Their blooming tendrils writhe and snap as they retract. I have to turn sideways to slide between a small phytoraptor that bristles with thorns the size of my hand and a huge one covered with tiny, close-packed pink flowers that run up their back in neat rows like stripes. They look like a linebacker dressed up for a sorority party.

I clamp down on the inappropriate giggle that bubbles in my chest, carbonating my adrenaline into something close to hysteria. I just have to hold it together a little longer. Then we'll call Mom, she'll bring us back to the Landing, and I can have a meltdown in peace.

A cloying smell like burning maple sugar billows around me. It's coming from a phytoraptor covered in wide, meaty leaves. They drip with some kind of viscous liquid that splatters as each one folds back into their body.

We give that raptor a wide berth, which leads us straight into a cluster of phytoraptors covered in hair-thin vines. They're tangled together like a blackberry patch, pulsing in the shifting morning light. There's no way through, so we have to go around. By the time we reach the ravine wall, a few of the phytoraptors are already sitting back on their haunches and stretching thickly muscled limbs.

I think this might be more fear than I can live with.

"Just keep moving," Jay mutters, urging me on with a hand on my back.

We creep forward, low and slow. It's the slow part that's killing me. We're so close. Leela and Beth are already scrambling up the cascade of boulders that leads out of the ravine. Every muscle in my body wants to charge up the rocks and hit the top running. But this is no time to panic. We're almost out of here.

Chris is about to start climbing when a phytoraptor covered in dense, curling tendrils that sparkle with bits of metal and crystal throws their head back, smacking into Chris as they stretch.

Chris shrieks in terror.

Behind me, Jay whisper shouts, "It's okay, Chris! They're still asleep!"

But before Jay can get the words all the way out, Chris yanks Ord's black knife from his belt and drives it upward into the phytoraptor's eyes. The raptor explodes from half-sleep into a scream of agony and collapses forward on top of him. The sound snaps through the valley, whipping through the phytoraptors as though an invisible hand has jerked them awake.

"Run!" Jay shouts, shoving me forward. It takes both of us to drag the phytoraptor corpse off Chris. He almost stabs me as he flails with his knife, shrieking blindly in terror. Jay heaves the corpse into the path of the vine-covered phytoraptors who are still detangling themselves even as they seethe toward us.

I grab Chris and half throw him up the trail ahead of me. I don't look back at Jay. It would slow me down and put us all in more danger. I know he's right behind me. I can hear his boots scrambling up the rocks.

Then he isn't.

Jay screams.

"Keep going, Chris!" I shout. Then I twist my body, leaning into my uphill leg and letting my momentum skate me down the wash to Jay. I reach him as he punches the phytoraptor who just clawed his leg. I plant my downhill foot and let gravity spin my slide into a kick. My boot thuds into the phytoraptor's head, and they tumble backward off the narrow path. I lose my balance too, but I manage to fall back against the cliffs instead of over the edge.

Jay swears continuously as he tries to push himself upright. I find my feet again and duck under his shoulder, supporting his injured leg.

"Are you okay?" I pant, ignoring the shrieking apocalypse of my muscles as I pull both of us up the rocks again.

"I'm great," Jay says. "Except for the about-to-get-eaten part."

"We're not going to get eaten."

"Oh yeah?"

As if to prove me wrong, heavy footsteps churn up the wash behind us. The phytoraptors are swarming straight up the cliffs ahead of us too, blocking our way out. Any second now, we're going to be surrounded. Shortly after that, we're going to be dead.

A spark of light zips past my head.

There's a fleshy thud and a shriek behind me.

Another sparkling object arcs just in front of us. It's a chunk of crystal! It smacks into a phytoraptor clinging to the cliffs ahead of us. The raptor shrieks as they lose their grip and fall.

"Take that, swamp thing!" Miguel shouts from the top of the cliff. Then he hurls another chunk of rock straight down onto another phytoraptor climbing below him. They fall with a howl.

Miguel keeps pelting the phytoraptors as we scramble up the last few meters. It's working. Even when Miguel misses, the light catching on his glittering missiles seems to distract and disorient the raptors.

I pull Jay up the last meter. Leela and Chris are waiting at the top to help him over the edge of the cliff.

"You're a genius, Miguel!" I shout, scrambling out of the wash.

"I know, right?" He turns to throw me one of his classic, face-splitting grins. Enjoying the moment.

A huge phytoraptor with a lion's mane of blue-purple tendrils sprouting all over their head springs over the edge of the cliff behind him.

"Miguel!" I shout as the raptor charges, but it's already too late. The lion-maned phytoraptor tackles Miguel off the cliff.

The phytoraptor leaps free, hitting the ground in a rolling bounce. Miguel doesn't bounce. He smashes, his body shattering against the rocks.

My stomach clenches and flips, vomiting up a sob that is also a scream.

A thick, muscular hand closes around my ankle.

I look down. A huge phytoraptor with a crest of bold yellow petals running down their spine grins up at me. It's Sunflower.

The raptor yanks down hard, pulling me backward off the cliff.

I fall.

I throw myself forward, reaching for the jagged face of the cliff. The rocks cut into my palms but I hang on, scrambling my feet against the cliff face until my boots snag on a narrow foothold.

I cling, gasping for air.

I can hear Sunflower hooting and growling below me. They must have dropped to the canyon floor when they pulled me down, expecting me to fall. Now they're coming back up the cliff after me. I can hear them grunt with each leap upward.

I try to climb, but the razor-sharp crystal digs deep into my hands, making my fingers go numb when I try to pull myself up.

Leela calls over the cliff above me, "Jo! Hold on! I'm coming!"

"No!" I shout. The word is out before I know why I'm saying it. Then I realize, "I need an anchor!"

Leela catches on immediately. She's already ripping an anchor stake from her harness as she shouts, "Tarn! Help me!"

Sunflower reaches for my ankle again. I kick down hard. My foot connects with their head. The impact radiates up my leg and nearly jars my numb hands free of the rocks, but it works.

Sunflower screams in outrage as they slide down the cliff face below me. The tearing shriek almost drowns out Leela as she shouts, "Do it, Jo!"

I slap the control panel on my harness. The tether

shoots out, winding around me like a living thing. Searching. But not finding. It can't sense the tether point on Leela's anchor.

The cliffs are blocking its sensors. I need a clear line of sight.

I'm going to have to jump.

The image of Miguel's shattered body slams through my brain, followed by an even more terrifying thought. Jay's flex is zipped up in a pocket on my harness. If I fall and die, the others won't be able to get back to the Landing in time to stop Stage Three.

The future of this whole planet is riding on me. On a single leap.

Fear wraps itself around me, paralyzing me for precious seconds. Then another memory runs over my panic, dissolving the stiff helplessness. Miguel's beautiful smile fills my mind.

Walk in the present, Jo.

He's right. He was right. He still is.

I plant my boots against the cliff and shove myself upward with all my strength.

Everything gets really slow as my body arcs up and away from the cliff face. The pale sky above me is flecked with the last hint of stars. I feel light, as though I could simply evaporate into the morning.

Then my tether line snaps taut, slamming me back against the cliff face.

Crystal cuts into my face and bare left arm.

I scream.

The tether holds.

Claws slice through my jeans as I smack the control panel on my harness again. The tether retracts, dragging me free of Sunflower's grip, over the top of the cliff, and straight into Leela's arms.

A dozen meters ahead, Beth and Chris are helping Jay jog-limp down the mountain after Tarn.

"Miguel—" I start to say, but Leela cuts me off.

"He's gone, right?"

I nod.

"Then we gotta keep moving," she says. She shifts her grip on my waist and propels me forward without asking any more questions.

We're moving downhill now, running in long, leaping strides as gravity shoves us forward. The sun is rising over my left shoulder. We're going south, toward the hot spot. I feel light and strange. Like my brain is still falling off that cliff. The image of Miguel grinning at me as the huge phytoraptor charged at him from behind burns through my brain on loop. The memory feels fake. Like a dream that doesn't make any sense. We were out. We should have been okay. But we aren't. We never were. Nothing about this place has been right, from the very start.

The ground is suddenly crumbling under my feet. The vegetation is thinner here, and the hard mountain soil is getting softer, fading into blinding-white dunes up ahead.

As we cross onto the powder-fine sand, it billows up in clouds around us, sticking to my lips and crusting around my eyes, clinging to tears I didn't know I was crying. My feet sink up to my shins with every step. It's impossible to run, but that doesn't matter. The phytoraptors don't seem to be willing to go into the sand. They stop at the last of the scraggly trees and prowl there, watching us from their branches.

I crest the dune, and an outrageously bright turquoise ocean crashes below me. Perfect waves curl up onto the sand, shining like blown glass in the morning light. I stop and stare, snatched out of my pain by the glory of the water and the sunlight and the sand.

Miguel will never see this. He'll never sink his toes into this sand. He'll never surf those waves.

Walk in the present, Joey.

I hate the present. The present sucks.

But I'm in it now. The empty lightness is gone, and with it the paralyzing sense of unreality. Miguel died. We're alive. We have the flex. And we still have time to use it.

"Where's the hot spot?" I call to Leela. She's a few paces ahead of me now.

She points to a big rock jutting out of the water just offshore. I don't see it at first, but then the artificial gleam of solar panels catches my eye. Once I know where to look, I can see the bristle of antenna poking out of the rocks above the panels.

As I watch, Chris lunges out of the water and grabs the rock, hauling himself up to the hot spot.

"Chris swam out there?" I say. "By himself?"

"He's the engineer," Leela says. "Let's just hope he can get it running."

I fish Jay's flex out of my pocket. It comes to life under my fingers.

"Computer, call Jo's Mom."

"Searching for wireless network," the flex replies. "Searching for wireless network. Searching for wireless network."

Leela and I exchange a look.

"Searching for wireless network," the flex says again.

"What are we going to do if Chris can't get the hot spot back online?" I say.

"He's going to get the hot spot online," Leela says firmly. But I can hear the doubt under her confident tone.

"Searching for wireless network."

My heart feels like it's crumbling. This isn't working. Miguel died for nothing.

"Searching for—" the computer cuts itself off. "Connected."

"He did it," Leela breathes.

"Computer, call Commander Watson," I say.

"Connecting," the computer says promptly. "Please wait."

My mother's face appears on the flex. Time and space blur around me as the familiar sound of her voice fills my ears. I'm not sure what she's saying. Or what I say to her. All I know is she's going to stop Stage Three, and then she's going to come for us.

I close the call and walk down to the water. I pull off my boots and sit down on the wet sand where the waves can lick at my toes. No one follows me. I expect to be glad, but I'm not. I don't want to be alone.

That's new.

Actually, it's old. I never liked being alone before Teddy died. I'm not sure I liked it after, either. I just felt like I deserved it. I think I've been growing a hard shell since the accident. An invisible carapace, holding the sharp edges of the world away from my aching skin. I didn't realize it was there until now. I don't know where it went. But it's gone.

"Don't get melodramatic about this," Leela's voice says behind me.

I turn to see her walking down the beach toward me. She drops to the wet sand at my side.

"I'm doing my best," I say.

"Good," she says. She swipes tears from her eyes. "'Cause Miguel would be pissed if you used him as an excuse to get all withdrawn and edgy again."

We stare at the water. There are so many things to say, but the words have knotted around each other in my head. I can't find a loose thread to pick and let them out.

Miguel would know. Miguel could always find the simplest way to look at a problem.

So what's the very simplest thing I could say right now?

"I'm sorry," I say.

Leela rolls her eyes. "You are such a drama queen. I know you love to take credit for things, but you can't blame yourself for the GFP playing E.T. surprise party with us, neglecting to give Beth pertinent information, and nearly causing us to terraform Tau to death. It's their fault Miguel died. Not yours."

"No," I say. "I meant . . . I'm sorry I was a jerk about you being cadet pilot. And everything else. Basically."

"Oh," Leela says. She takes a deep breath and looks back out at the waves. "Well, I was a pretty big jerk, too. About a lot of stuff. So . . ." She trails off, but it doesn't feel like she's done talking, so I don't say anything.

She just sits there for a while, digging out a hole in the sand with the toe of her boot. Finally, she says, "It's not like I wanted to be cadet pilot, you know. I like protecting people. That's why I was going into the marines. Being a pilot feels like I'm risking other people's lives all the time."

"I never thought of flying that way," I say.

"That's why you're good at it," Leela says.

"That's why I *was* good at it," I say.

We get quiet again, but that feels okay. Something has changed between us. I don't know if I can really describe it. I feel like Leela's been far away for the last two years, and suddenly we're sitting next to each other again.

The tide is coming in. The waves aren't just licking at my toes anymore, they're splashing over my jeans and spattering what's left of my shirt and hair with water so salty it stings. I get up and hold a hand out to Leela. She takes it and lets me pull her to her feet. I try to let go, but she hangs on.

"I was so mad at Teddy after he died," she says.

"What?"

"You heard me," she says quietly. "I know you thought I was mad at you, and I guess I let you think that, but I wasn't. Not really. I was mad at him."

"Why?"

"Because he left me behind." Her voice is so quiet that I can hardly hear her over the waves that are sucking greedily at our legs. "Stupid, stubborn Watsons. Always thinking you can do everything alone. If I'd been with you guys, if there'd been three of us instead of two, maybe . . . He didn't have to die."

I can almost see the *what if* unspooling like a movie in my head. The three of us working together in the engine room. Getting the clamps released thirty seconds earlier. The airlock doors slamming, with all three of us safely back in the corridor.

Teddy standing next to me on this beach.

But that's not the only *what if* I see.

"What if you came with us and something else went wrong?" I say. "What if one of the clamps was stuck or the engine blew up a few seconds earlier or the hull breach was a meter to the left and we couldn't get through the access hatch? If we'd failed, and you had been with us, then Beth and Chris and Miguel and all those people in their insulated-sleep crates on the *Wagon* would have died too."

Leela nods in a *whatever* sort of way that both accepts and dismisses my point.

"I didn't say it was reasonable. I said I was angry. There's a difference." She gets a complicated look on her face then, somewhere between respect, pity, and irritation. "I'd never have thought to use explosive decompression to blow the engine module clear of the ship. Or to steal a flex from a phytoraptor nest. My brain doesn't work that way. I'm glad. It seems . . . stressful."

It isn't an apology. Not really. It's an acknowledgment. Understanding.

The *whomp whomp whomp* of a flyer's rotors overcomes the roar of the ocean.

"Mom's coming," I say. I thought I'd feel more relieved than this. I mean, I'm glad we're going back to the Landing, where it's safe. But our settlement was built on lies and ethical choices that I've been taught my whole life are wrong. Choices made by people I love and respect. Choices made by my mother.

And now I have to ask her why.

FIFTEEN

Dr. Howard is waiting for us when we touch down on the airfield. Chris runs down the ramp and hurls himself into his father's arms. They stand there, clinging to each other for a long time. Then Dr. Howard leads Chris away.

Once they're gone, Doc takes Jay and Leela to medical, and Beth has to explain the dangers of Stage Three to the rest of the botany team. That leaves me to introduce Tarn to Mom and Dad. After they welcome him to the Landing, Mom asks him to wait in an empty office in Ground Control while they debrief me. I have to repeat myself a lot, because my parents are constantly being interrupted by calls and texts from Sarge. He's scrambling a salvage crew to the crash site.

Sending people back to the phytoraptor-infested valley

is a risk, but we can't start work on a new shuttle until we recycle the wreckage. Building the new shuttle can't wait. According to Chief Penny's logs, she repaired the superluminal transponder on her last, ill-fated trip to the *Pioneer*, but apparently we still can't connect with Earth. Mom urgently needs to report our contact with the Sorrow and the phytoraptors to Central Command, so we need to get back up to the ship and fix whatever is wrong with the transponder.

After they're finished with me, Mom suggests that I go to medical so Doc can check me out while she and Dad talk to Tarn. I'm covered in cuts and bruises, but I decide to take a shower first. I tell myself it's because I smell, but tears start running down my face the moment I step into the cubical and turn on the water. My knees fold under me and I slide down the wall, weeping.

I cry for a long time. For Miguel. For Chief Penny. For all the people we've lost in the last three days. I cry until my head feels thick and my throat feels raw, and it hardly makes a dent in the grief. Still, I feel lighter now. Empty. I'm not sure if that's good or bad.

I wash my hair and scrub days of dirt and sweat from my skin. Then I switch the water to cold and turn my face into the spray for a full minute, cooling my tear-swollen eyes.

Once I'm dressed, I realize that I'm starving. I decide to grab some food before I go to medical. Doc is busy with Jay and Leela anyway, and physically I feel fine despite my various abrasions. Actually, I feel better than fine. It's like someone turned up the O_2 mix on the whole planet. Maybe I'm still coasting on the leftover adrenaline from averting the apocalypse while almost getting eaten alive.

Town square is mostly empty except for Mrs. Divekar and the little kids, who are helping to transplant a pair of the fido trees from the river to the garden plots in front of Ground Control.

Their giggles catch at my memory, pulling up a half-forgotten rainy afternoon when I was ten, Chris was six, and Teddy and Miguel were twelve. They took turns putting Chris on their shoulders and stomping around with his oversized rain poncho covering their heads, pretending he was a giant. We thought it was hilarious. My face hurt from laughing so hard.

At one point Chris and Miguel fell into the lake and got completely drenched. Chris started crying, but Miguel had him laughing again in no time. Miguel never let anyone feel bad for too long if he could help it. That's what made him a good doctor. Now he's gone. Evaporated into memory and smashed bones and broken skin.

I don't want to start crying again, so I stop thinking and go into the mess hall.

Tarn is standing by the window, watching the children in the square through the blindfold that shields his eyes from the daylight. I expected him to insist on returning to the Solace once we were safe, but to my surprise, he accepted

Mom's invitation to come to the Landing. I didn't expect to find him here. Mom had several hours' worth of questions for me, and she must have had at least as many for Tarn.

"Hello, Joanna," he says as I join him at the window.

"I thought you were with my parents," I say.

"Sadly, I could not answer most of your mother's questions," Tarn says. "The decision to share that information belongs to the Followed. Not to me."

"I'm sure Mom understood," I say.

"She was disappointed," Tarn says. "But she accepted my reservations." He gestures to Dr. Kao. "And Mohan Kao has been very kind. They have both attempted to make me comfortable."

"But you aren't?" I ask, hearing what he isn't saying.

Tarn covers his face with his palms in. "I am unsettled," he says. "I feel as though your world has already wrapped itself around mine, and I can no longer see the world as it was."

I look out the window to where the trees are being planted in the garden. The scene is totally different when I imagine what it looks like through his eyes. A gaggle of alien children, uprooting the wildlife.

"They didn't mean any harm, moving the trees. I can tell them to—"

"No," Tarn says. "It is lovely. It reminds me of the gardens where my father labored when I was still pouchborne."

"Oh," I say. "Okay."

"It is not this place that disturbs me; it is the things I have learned on the journey that led me here. The things your people know. The ideas you have. . . . You spoke to the Beast with your hands, and it spoke back to you."

"Is that a bad thing?" I say.

Tarn covers his face with his hands again, this time with his palms out so I can see the delicate veins of light that run up his fingers. "You cannot understand, Joanna. These creatures are like the cold and the rot and the sun. A force of nature that cannot be reasoned with or controlled. But you *spoke* to one of them. It spoke to you. That means that the Beasts cannot be what I *know* them to be. And it makes me feel as though I am not what I know myself to be either."

"Isn't it better that they aren't an unstoppable force?" I say. "If we can talk to them, maybe we can help you make peace."

"Can there be peace between the hunter and the hunted?"

"Tarn, you're wearing armor made of phytoraptor skin," I say. "You hunt each other."

He turns to stare at me. We're close enough that I can see his round, black eyes through the thin blindfold. "Humans make the truth feel like water slipping through my fingers. I don't like it."

"I'm sorry to interrupt," Dr. Kao interjects. We both look up to see him at the door with Doc. "Dr. Divekar is here to see you, Tarn. He's thrilled that you're willing to discuss Sorrow healing techniques with him."

"Of course," Tarn says. "If you will excuse me, Joanna."

Doc and Tarn leave.

Dr. Kao makes me a bowl of beans and rice and then grabs a rag and starts wiping down tables. He doesn't ask if I want to talk, but the invitation to spill my guts is clear. I sort of want to, but most of what I'm worried about is stuff I'm not supposed to know, and Dr. Kao isn't supposed to know either. The only person I could talk to about it is Mom. And I don't want to talk to Mom. Not yet.

I take my food outside and sit by the cold fire pits so I can watch the kids play while I eat. Tarn said this looked like a Sorrow garden. I wonder if some of the grasses and ferns that Mrs. Divekar and the kids planted around the fido trees are food crops for the Sorrow. I hope Tarn will stay here long enough to teach us about them.

"Joey?"

I turn to see Chris standing behind me. He's wearing a clean thermal and cargo pants with a new utility harness. The shoulders of his shirt are damp, and I can see water still dripping down the back of his neck from his wet curls. It drives the chief nuts when he doesn't bother to dry his hair after a shower. *Drove*. It *drove* the chief nuts. The past tense makes the back of my throat ache with a sudden surge of grief. She'll never remind Chris to dry his hair again. It's a stupid, tiny thing. It makes me want to weep.

"Hey," I say, squeezing the words past my looming tears. "Where'd you get to?"

"Shower," he says, in an *obviously* tone of voice. Then he adds quietly, "Dad and I were talking to Dr. Kao before that."

I nod, cautious. I feel like Chris is hollow glass vibrating at a frequency that's going to make him shatter if he doesn't relax.

"Dr. Kao isn't nearly as annoying as you'd think," I say, carefully keeping my voice light. "Not like the ISA HQ wonks they made me see back on Earth."

"I guess," Chris says, rocking from toe to heel like he's having trouble standing still.

"You hungry?" I say.

"No," he says. "I don't . . . Sarge went back to the nest to get Miguel. And they're coming . . . the flyer is coming back, and I thought . . ."

"Let me recycle this," I say, gesturing to my bowl and spoon as I stand up. "Then we'll go wait for them."

We walk to the airfield in silence. Night is starting to fall. The sun has almost disappeared behind the Diamond Range, and the mountains' dusk light show is fading. I can just pick out the flashing red and white beacon lights on the flyer's wings in the distance.

The airfield still isn't paved, but the stiff Tau grasses have been mowed short and marked off with a crosshatched square to make a landing pad for the flyers.

Chris says, "It's my fault. What happened to Miguel is my fault."

"No, it isn't," I say. "None of this is your fault. I know it can feel—"

"This isn't like the way you feel guilty about Teddy," Chris says. "I'm not just saying it's my fault because I feel guilty that Miguel died and I didn't. It's my fault that he's dead." Before I can contradict him again, Chris pulls something shiny from his pocket and thrusts it into my hand. It's a metallic starburst with stringy brown stuff clinging to its points.

"Is this one of your mom's Scout badges?" I say.

He nods. "I saw . . ." He trails off on a gasp, like the words are too heavy. Then he tries again. "That phyto-raptor. The one I killed? Remember how they had a bunch of shiny crap wound into their tendrils?"

Abruptly, I know what he's trying to tell me. I don't want to, but I do.

"Oh, Chris."

He sucks in a dry sob. "I saw Mom's EVA badge in their tendrils and I knew, I knew, I knew they must have killed her. They killed her and took her badge, and there they were, just waking up, and I had Ord's knife and . . . It just happened." He stares down at his hands like they belong to someone else. "I didn't . . . I don't feel like I decided to do it. I know that's wrong. I am responsible for my own actions. I know that. But it didn't feel that way. It just happened. And

269

then the raptor screamed and they all woke up and Jay got hurt and . . . Miguel. And it's my fault."

I try to snatch the horrified expression back before Chris sees it, but I'm not fast enough.

The pain in his face twists into a sharp, bitter point. "See?" he says. "Dr. Kao can't help me. Nobody can. Nobody will want to."

"That's not true," I start to say, but a voice interrupts me.

"Hello, my dears." I turn to find Miguel's moms walking toward us. Dr. Vega is part of the botany team. She has a protective arm around her wife, Alejandra, who is one of our architectural designers. Alejandra tries to smile at us, but the half-formed expression melts into tears instead.

Chris bolts.

I look after him, then back at Dr. Vega's and Alejandra's sad, concerned faces.

"Oh my," Dr. Vega says. "Poor little thing. And after losing the chief."

I nod. I don't trust my voice yet. I feel like I should go after Chris, but I can't. I'm too angry. I don't know if I've ever been this angry. I'm not angry at him. I'm angry at all of us. At this place. At the ISA. At all of the lies and assumptions and mistakes that led to Chris pulling out that knife. My mistakes. He's just a kid. I should have insisted that he stay on the cliffs with Miguel. And Jay and I definitely should have taken that knife from him. Of course, Ord shouldn't have given it to him in the first place. And our parents shouldn't have brought us to Tau. So many wrongs. I wish I didn't know about any of them. But I do.

So what am I going to do about it?

The roar of the flyer's rotors crescendos as it settles on the airfield grass. Miguel's mothers walk toward it as the ramp unfolds. I don't. My body feels like poured concrete.

Sarge guides a float cart bearing a black body bag down the ramp.

It looks so small.

My stomach heaves as I try not to imagine how little is left of Miguel.

Miguel's moms help Sarge guide the float cart across the airfield and into the Landing. I could help. I should.

I can't.

Instead, I watch the lights of the Landing come up and the rainbow sparkle of the Diamond Range die as the night gets thicker and darker. I don't realize how cold I am until Mom slips her hand into mine. The warmth of her skin makes me break out in gooseflesh all over.

"Come on," she says, tugging me back toward the Landing.

I hang on to her hand as we walk across the airfield. The floodlights throw shadows down her face, highlighting creases that weren't there two days ago. She looks like she's aged years.

"I'm sorry, Mom," I say.

"For what?" she says.

"Sneaking out?" I say. "Accidentally making First Contact with extraterrestrials? I can keep going . . ."

She huffs a little laugh. "I'm not sorry. It was the longest thirty-four hours of my life, not knowing where you and Beth were or what was happening to you. But if you hadn't gone, we would have initiated Stage Three this morning. We wouldn't have known it was a problem until it was far, far too late. You and your sister stopped us from causing an ecological disaster." She squeezes my hand. "Besides, we raised you this way. We have no one to blame but ourselves."

She's right. Mom and Dad raised us to ask questions and challenge authority. Dad used to joke that Mom was promoted to commander because her superiors got tired of arguing with her. She would never have just accepted an order she didn't believe in.

I stop walking. "Why didn't you resign?"

"I need more context to answer that question," Mom says, but she doesn't sound surprised that I'm asking it.

"I know the ISA edited the Sorrow and the phytoraptors out of the survey report, but you had access to the original. You knew they were here."

"Yes, I did," Mom says.

"Then why did we come?" The words explode out of me. "You helped write the charter. You and Dad fought to include the rules against settling occupied planets. So when the ISA decided to violate those rules, why didn't you resign?"

Mom sucks in a long breath and lets it out slowly, watching it mist in the chilly air between us. Then she nods, like she's just finished a debate inside her head.

She looks me in the eye. "Earth's ecosystem is on the brink of total collapse."

"I know," I say. "But the Earth Restoration Project is repairing that. Isn't it?"

She nods. "It is, to a point. But it doesn't matter how well the ERP's nanoscrubbers and ocean filtration systems work. Even if we completely restore the climate and the oceans, the current human population is unsustainable. We need to reduce it by thirty percent before 2165, or the ecosystem will collapse despite all of our efforts. That means we have roughly fifty years to move three billion people."

"That's impossible," I say. "We can't even build enough ships to do that in fifty years."

"I know," Mom says, grim. "But we're going to move as many people as we can. We have to try. That's why teams were sent to Tau and to Proxima Centauri b, despite the fact that neither world is . . . ideal."

Abruptly, I understand what Tarn meant about humans making the truth feel like water running through his fingers.

"Pel is right," I say. "We're here to steal their planet."

"*Share,*" Mom says. "When we came here, we planned to make peaceful First Contact with the Sorrow and negotiate a treaty that would allow us to share Tau with them. Obviously, that's going to be a little more complicated than we hoped, but it's the best chance for the human race."

"Does that make it right?" I say.

Mom thinks about the question for what feels like a long time. Finally she says, "I'm not sure *right* matters. Not when we're talking about the potential extinction of our species."

That gives me a horrible thought.

"What happens if Pel won't negotiate with us?" I ask. "What will we do if the Sorrow tell us to go?"

Mom doesn't answer right away. She doesn't have to. I can guess.

I think I might be sick.

"I hope that doesn't happen," Mom says, finally. "But no matter what, nothing that comes next is going to be easy." She scrubs a hand over her face and through her hair. "God, Jo, I'm so sorry. I wish you were still a little girl I could protect. But I'm glad you aren't. I'm going to need your help to get us through this."

And by *get us through this* she means "save the entire freaking human race." But no pressure or anything.

I'm furious. I'm terrified. I'm confused. I'm so incredibly sad. Big complicated emotions feel like they're slam-dancing under my skin, tearing me apart.

Then it's all gone.

Suddenly I feel good. Wonderful, actually. And warm, too. Like I'm standing in the sun. But none of that is true. It's still dark. It's still cold. And the hurricane of emotion is still there, screaming silently under a smothering, artificial coating of happiness.

Mom feels it too. "What is that?" she says, putting her hands against her cheeks.

"It's Sorrow sonar," I say. "I don't hear anything, but . . . wait. There it is. Can you hear them?"

Mom nods. The song is getting louder now. More intense. It sounds like a whole choir of Sorrow are out there, weaving their tactile voices together to create the warm and sunny sensations we're feeling.

"But that's impossible," Mom says, tapping into her flex. "They couldn't have gotten past . . ." She swears. "The particle shield is down."

"How . . . ?" I answer my own question. "They have Dr. Brown's command codes, don't they?"

Mom nods, texting furiously. "We kept her log-in active, so no one would question the official story that the *Vulcan* was in the Wolf 1061 system. Damn it. I should have thought to lock her out."

The exhilarated sonar is getting closer and stronger. It's making me feel like I'm bouncing on a giant trampoline. It's getting hard to focus on the real world and my real feelings.

Pounding footsteps cut through my sonically induced giddiness. Dad is racing down the street toward us with Sarge and four other marines on his heels. Jay and Tarn are only steps behind them, though Jay is still limping on his injured leg.

The marines are all carrying rifles.

"Guns? No!" I say. "Can't you feel it? That chant isn't a threat. It's . . . I don't know what it is, but it isn't hostile."

"Hacking our shield and coming into the Landing uninvited is hostile enough for me," Mom snaps, but then she turns to Sarge and says, "If we can avoid a confrontation, we should. Stay back where you won't be seen unless things start going south."

"Do not hide your weapons," Tarn says as he and Jay reach the group. "Whatever her intentions, Pel will appreciate an honest show of strength."

"That song isn't a threat, is it?" I say.

He holds his hands in front of his face, palms out. "It is a welcoming song," he says, dropping his hands again. "I am most surprised to hear it. The new Followed has always expressed great fear and anger toward your people."

"Would Pel use a welcoming song as a trap?" Jay asks. "To make us think she's friendly, so she can attack while our guard is down?"

"My pouch mate would not have done so," Tarn says. "But I cannot say what Pel might do. I'm sorry I cannot be more illuminating."

The air is so thick with Sorrow sonar that I feel dizzy with it. Happy tears prick my eyelids. My body can't tell the difference between real emotions and the manipulation of the song.

A line of black-robed Takers emerges from the darkness beyond the airfield's floodlights. Then another. There must be at least thirty of them. Maybe more. They're marching in a tight square formation around another, smaller square of Givers in glowing lantern cloaks.

"Fall in, marines," Sarge says. Jay's eyes find mine as he joins his squad mates behind Sarge. It feels so strange to not be standing shoulder to shoulder with him, facing this together.

"Tarn, Jo, stay close to us," Mom says, beckoning us to stand behind them as my parents turn to face the Sorrow.

The Takers are bristling with weapons. I see crystal-spiked staffs, massive war hammers, and lots of black-bladed knives. I hope Tarn is right, and Pel is just putting on a show of strength. Even with our guns, I don't think we'll win if this comes to a fight.

The Sorrow formation stops as they hit their final note. They hold it, letting the tactile sound flow over us and fade into the night. My ears ring in the silence, and suddenly I'm so cold that I'm shaking. I probably was freezing the whole time—I just didn't notice because of the effects of the Sorrow song.

The Takers expand their square by a single step, moving in absolute unison.

Mom is standing close enough to me that I can feel her body go tense at the eerily synchronized movement. The Sorrow formation opens like the covers of a book and the Takers fall back into two straight lines. The Givers melt back as well, their movements as fluid as the Takers' are sharp and precise.

Dr. Brown is standing at the center of the formation,

next to a hooded Sorrow in a billowing, light-amplifying cloak. That must be the new Followed. But why is Dr. Brown with her? Is she a prisoner? Or . . .

The glowing Sorrow's trijointed fingers push their hood back, revealing eyes covered by mirrored lenses that gleam silver in the floodlights.

Tarn lets out a startled cry.

Shock crashes over me, immediately followed by relief so intense my muscles feel like Jell-O. I don't know how he survived that blow from Pel's hammer, but Ord is alive. And, judging from the entourage, he's still Followed.

"Hello, Alice Watson," Ord says to Mom. "Welcome to my planet."

SIXTEEN

"What do you think they're talking about in there?" Leela says.

We're sitting with Jay at one of the fire pits in front of the mess hall, watching the double doors of Ground Control. A Taker stands at attention on either side of the entrance. Ord is in there, with Tarn and Dr. Brown and my parents. They've been behind closed doors in Mom's office for nearly two hours now.

"'We promise, we're only going to steal a third of your world. Half, tops,'" Jay jokes.

"We aren't stealing anything!" Leela protests. "I'm sure if the Sorrow want us to go, the commander will respect that."

Jay makes a dubious face. "*Sure* might be a strong word,"

he says, scratching at the nanobot-laced bandage wrapped around his clawed leg.

"I can't believe you didn't let Tarn heal your leg," Leela says. "It feels strange, but it doesn't hurt, and it itches way less than nanites."

"Tarn didn't offer," Jay says, "so I didn't bring it up. It seems like a really big deal to him. And I'm not dying or anything. Tiny, itchy robots will do me just fine."

"So sensitive for one so pessimistic," Leela says.

"Dubious," Jay says, "not pessimistic. There's a difference."

She snorts and tosses the gray-green grass stem she's playing with at his head. "I still think there's a sixty-forty chance we're going home."

"We aren't going home," I say. "We might not have known about the Sorrow, but the ISA did. They aren't suddenly going to grow a conscience about it now."

"We aren't talking about the ISA," Leela counters. "We're talking about the commander. No way she's just going to go along with this."

I don't know what to say to that, so I don't say anything. None of us know what my mother will do in the face of a possible human extinction. I'm not sure Mom does either.

"You sound like you're hoping we bail," Jay says.

Leela shrugs. "Not hoping, really. But we've already caused a civil war and nearly wrecked the ecosystem, and we haven't even finished constructing base camp. If the commander has the chance to undo this, then maybe she should."

For a moment, I'm profoundly jealous of Leela all over again. She has such absolute faith in my mother. I wish I still felt that way. I understand why Mom agreed to come to Tau, but that doesn't mean it was right. It doesn't mean she was wrong, either. We can't gamble the future of the human race on a fixer-upper planet like Proxima Centauri b. But does that make it okay to force our way onto Tau? I don't know. I don't think so, but it's all so complicated. I hate that.

"They're coming out!" Jay says, breaking me out of my inward spiral of misery. We all straighten as the doors from Ground Control swing open, but it's just Dr. Kao.

"How are things going in there?" Leela calls as he zips his float-chair across the square to us.

"Very well," Dr. Kao says. "So well that the Sorrow have agreed to join us for a late dinner. I need volunteers. You three will do nicely." With that he continues into the mess hall, not giving us the chance to make excuses.

"Well, we knew this was going to end in kitchen patrol eventually," Jay says, hauling himself to his feet.

"Speak for yourself," Leela grumbles. "We aren't all flyer-stealing delinquents." But she seems kind of relieved to have something to do. She follows Dr. Kao into the mess hall.

I hesitate, looking back at Ground Control.

Jay puts his arm around my shoulders and squeezes gently. "It'll come out okay."

"You think?"

"It has so far," he says. "Against all odds." He tugs me toward the mess. "Come on—I'm wounded here. Give me a shoulder to lean on."

I slip my arm around his waist to support his weight but he's hardly limping, much less leaning on me.

"That leg is really hurting, huh?" I say.

"Not particularly," he says. "You mind?"

"Not particularly," I say.

His face overflows with a grin so big I can feel it tugging at the corners of my own mouth. What is wrong with me? The future of the human race is in jeopardy, and I'm grinning like an idiot over a boy. A boy who's grinning like an idiot over me.

Why does it feel like nothing else matters?

The incongruous happiness doesn't last. While we soak beans and measure rice, Jay gets everyone talking about all the food we can't get here. He goes into excruciating detail about his favorite vat-grown double cheeseburger, which comes with onions and cheese and some kind of sauce he thinks is amazing. I can hear how much he misses the flavors and smells in the shading of his voice. I wish I couldn't. But being around the Sorrow seems to have changed how I listen.

I jump at the chance to go to the 3D shop and print extra platters. If I don't get out of here, I'll blurt out the truth about Earth and Tau and ruin everything for Jay and Leela, and I don't want to do that. Not yet.

The 3D shop is quiet, which is disconcerting. The huge 3D printers have been running twenty-two hours a day since Mom initiated Stage Two. But Dr. Ganeshalingam—I guess she's Chief Ganeshalingam now, since she was Chief Penny's second-in-command—has preempted all five of the 3Ds to print parts for the new shuttle. They're just waiting for the salvage crews to finish recycling the wreckage of the *Wagon*.

I set one of the smaller 3Ds to print a dozen serving platters and then I go down to the bathrooms to pee. While I'm washing my hands, I catch a glimpse of myself in the mirrors. My hair has frizzed out of its braid in a halo around my face, and my thermal is spattered with bean juice. I can't go back to the mess like this. Jay is there.

I guess I should stop pretending I don't care what he thinks.

I pull on a fresh ISA Ship *Pioneer* thermal and hoodie, and a pair of soft gray cargo pants. I wash my face too, and rebraid my hair. I should probably cut it. Long hair just isn't practical right now. It won't be for a long time.

I study myself in the mirror. Pale skin touched with pink sunburn despite my blockers. Brown eyes dusted with gold. Brown hair already escaping its braid in wisps that curl around my ears and neck. I look the same, but I don't. Even if I cut my hair again, I won't look like I used to. Joanna Watson, cadet pilot, is gone, and for the first time I don't regret it. She was smart, and quick, and happy in a way I'm not sure I ever will be again. But I don't know if she was strong enough to deal with what's coming.

Am I?

I guess I'm going to find out.

When I get back to the 3D shop, Chris is stacking my freshly printed platters.

"Hi," I say.

"Hi," he says.

"I looked for you," I say. "I . . . I should have looked for you sooner, but the Sorrow came, and Ord is—"

"Yeah," Chris says. "I saw Dr. Brown. She told me."

"Oh," I say. I try to sound normal, but every word feels like it has sharp edges. "Where did you . . . I mean, I thought Dr. Brown was with Ord and Mom? Is she, um, I guess she's not?"

Chris shrugs. "Guess not. I went out to the greenhouse and she was there."

"What was she doing out there?" I wonder.

"Dunno," he says. "She was sitting on the ground, staring at the seedlings. They're already starting to die, you know, without Stage Three."

"Beth said they would," I say.

He nods. "I asked Dr. Brown what she was doing in

there, and she said she was, 'meditating on consequences.'"

"In the greenhouse?"

He shrugs. "I guess. I don't know." He makes an embarrassed face. "She said it weird, but I think she was doing the same thing I was."

"What were you doing?" I say, cautiously.

"I was trying to understand." He shrugs again. "It's dumb, I know. Dying plants and dirt can't really explain anything. But we wouldn't have had to go into that nest if not for Stage Three. I wouldn't have . . ." He trails off, scuffing the toe of his boot against the floor tiles. "So stupid. All over some dirt."

"There's more to it than that," I say. "More even than we knew. This isn't just about Tau."

"Don't you think I know that?" he snaps. "I'm thirteen, but I'm not stupid. The ISA didn't break all its own rules just for kicks. Something is really wrong back home, isn't it?"

Funny that Leela and Jay haven't realized that yet. Or maybe they have on some level, and they don't want to know anymore than I want to tell them. But Chris's universe has already been shredded. He's got no reason to delude himself.

"Yes," I say. "Pretty much everything is really wrong."

His face crumples. "And you're about to tell me that since all the adults are screwing up and everything is terrible, what I did, Miguel dying, none of that is my fault," he says. His voice cracks, sounding like a little boy's one word and a man's the next.

"No," I say. "I wasn't going to say that. You screwed up. But so did I. So did everyone. This whole situation is just . . ."

"A mess," he says.

"Yeah," I say.

"So what do we do now?" he says.

"I have no freaking idea."

"Yeah," he says. "Me either."

"Are you chiseling those platters by hand?" The delicate moment evaporates as Leela hustles into the 3D shop. "The commander and the Sorrow are already out in the square." She snags the stack of platters from Chris and grabs his hand, towing him along as she reverses course. "C'mon," she says. "If we have to do KP, you have to do KP."

A Sorrow song buzzes over my skin as we approach the square. It's late, but no one is sleeping in the Landing tonight. Everyone, including the little kids, has gathered in the square to watch the Givers sing.

The fire pits are covered, and the lights have been turned out so that we can see the full effect of the Givers' lantern cloaks. They're arranged so that their colors fade from a pink-tinged gold on one end of the line to a vivid bluish scarlet on the other.

Ord is showing off.

I don't blame him. The Givers are beautiful, and their

song is intoxicating. At least, I imagine this is what being drunk feels like. I've only been drunk once. The night they told me about my medical discharge I crashed the first senior cadet party I could find and drank as much as I could stand. I don't actually remember what it felt like. But that was the point—to forget. This night is different. I want to remember every second.

"What does it feel like for you?"

I drag my eyes away to find Jay watching me watch the Givers.

"You know that feeling," I say, "when you're a little kid and you spin as long and as fast as you can, then you fall down and you lie on your back and stare at the sky?"

He nods.

"That's it. Sort of," I say. "It's hard to put into words."

"It reminds me of swimming," he says, turning to look at the Givers again. "My friend's great-grandma used to take us to the community pool and throw a bunch of coins to the bottom so we could dive for them. You know how it is, when you stay down a little too long and your head gets kind of full and light at the same time?"

"Like you're a balloon that's about to pop," I say.

He grins. "Exactly."

The song trails off then. The crowd of humans and Sorrow falls quiet.

Ord comes to stand in front of the Givers. His robes amplify his blue-violet bioluminescence so much that it washes out their delicate spectrum of pinks to white.

"Friends," he calls in English. I feel a corresponding flutter of Sorrow sonar and twist, looking for the source. It's Tarn. He's standing off to the side, translating his brother's words for the other Sorrow.

"Ever since Lucille came to live with the Sorrow, I have dreamed of this day," Ord says. "And now that it's here, it is greater than my dreams. We are each strong and unique species in our own right. Together, we will do marvelous things. It will not be easy. Great sacrifices have been made to get us this far, and they will not be the last."

Jay and I exchange an uneasy look, but no one else seems to find that sentiment creepy. The others are nodding along as Ord continues, absorbing every word.

"This world is not always a gentle one," he says. "But its potential is as vast as the stars that you crossed to come here. Together we will make the most of it. Together we will thrive."

The square erupts in heartfelt applause. That speech could have been included in the GFP publicity packet, it's so perfectly tuned to what they want to hear. Does Ord know that? Did Dr. Brown tell him what to say? Or does he just happen to want exactly the same thing we want?

That seems like too much to hope for, but I'm tired of feeling dubious and angry. Something extraordinary is happening, and for once I'm going to enjoy it.

"If we are to share this world, we must understand each

other," Ord says. "I hope that we can accomplish that this evening." He reaches out a hand to beckon my mother forward. She steps to his side.

"Thank you, Ord," she says. "We want nothing more than for our species to be friends. And my father always said that a good friendship starts with a good meal. So let's eat!"

It's amazing how quickly the party becomes ordinary after that. Doc has declared our usual rice-and-beans concoction safe for the Sorrow, and most of the Takers accept a plate of food once Ord and Tarn have eaten. When the meal is finished, Dr. Kao pulls out his guitar and gets people singing. Dad grabs Mom and pulls her into a fast reel. Soon, lots of people are dancing. I even catch one of the Takers bouncing a little to the music. The Givers are the only ones who don't seem to be enjoying themselves. They don't eat or drink. I haven't even seen them move since their performance. They just stand at the edge of the square, glowing impassively.

A few pioneers drift off to their cabins as the night wears on, but most stay up, dancing and singing along with Dr. Kao. There's a giddy edge to it all. After the stress and sadness of losing twelve pioneers on the *Wagon*, the excitement over the Sorrow's arrival feels almost manic.

I'm sitting with my back against the mess hall, watching. The solar pavement is still warm enough under my legs to make the night chill pleasant instead of biting. Dr. Kao switches from a fast song to something old and soft that Grandpa used to hum while we worked in his garden.

"It's something unpredictable, but in the end it's right. . . ."

"So what about this song?" Jay says, sliding down the wall to sit beside me. "What does it feel like to you?"

I look back at the people singing around the fire pits as I contemplate my answer. There's something about the bright clamor of slightly out-of-tune voices that makes the song fit into the moment like a key in a lock. This is exactly what the girl who created all those improbable planets in crayon thought being a pioneer would be like. I've spent so much time trying to understand the nightmares that I almost didn't recognize the dream. The realization is startling. I have no idea how to even start to explain it to Jay.

"What does it feel like to you?" I ask instead, turning to look at him.

"It feels like home."

The words steal my breath. He smiles, black eyes shining in the firelight. The world slows down. The music and the fire and the people all around us are reduced to individual sensations. Warmth. Light. Rhythm. Music.

I kiss Jay.

He kisses me back.

I'm not sure we would have ever stopped, but a low, pulsing harmony sloshes over my skin. Suddenly, hunger burns through my stomach, followed by a hard charge of outrage that makes me shove Jay away.

"Sorry," I say.

"No need." He grimaces. "I feel it, too. It's awful."

"What are the Givers doing?" I twist to look back at them. They haven't moved, but the horrible song is definitely coming from them. Why are they doing this? I feel itchy all over. Like I want to hide. Or punch someone.

"Whatever this is, I hope it's short," Jay says, rubbing his temples. "Instant headache."

My head is throbbing too. I try to ignore it and focus on the melody and the sensations behind it. There's something about the song that I recognize.

"Does it sound familiar to you?" I ask Jay.

"Not really," he says. "I think I'd remember if I'd felt something like that before."

"Yeah . . ." I trail off, listening. He's right. The melody is definitely familiar, but the shape of the sound is wrong. I've never felt this before.

"It could be the Mourning chant," Jay says. "Maybe it just feels weird because we're not in the caves and the acoustics are different out here."

"Maybe . . ." I shake my head. "I don't know."

The Givers pivot into a single file line and walk to the fire pits. They keep singing as they circle the flames. With each step, the melody gets slower. Denser. Like they're bending space-time around us with their voices. Then, abruptly, their tempo accelerates. They pivot again and walk straight outward from their circle, striding through the crowd of humans and Sorrow and out of the square in all directions.

A Giver walks right past Jay and me. The familiar strangeness of their song tugs at the corners of my mind, insisting that I know what's happening here even though I don't.

"I'll be right back," I whisper to Jay.

I follow the Giver.

They walk in a straight line, eyes forward, singing steadily. I follow them all the way down to the river. They slow as they pass under the floral canopy of fido trees, looking up at the brilliantly colored petals that shimmer in the lights from the recycling center. Then they keep walking, past the buildings to the riverbank. I think about calling out to warn them about the particle shield, which runs along the water's edge. Then I realize that I can see the trees on the other side of the river clearly. The warping effect of the force field is gone.

The particle shield is down.

Sour fear curdles my confusion. This doesn't make any sense. I know Mom brought the shield back online before she and Dad escorted Ord to Ground Control. I saw her do it. So why is it down again?

Holy crap.

I need to text Mom and warn her. But before I can, the

Giver turns and pushes back their hood, revealing a familiar scarred face.

"Hello, juvenile," Pel says, humming the words in a minor harmony that makes my guts clench, as though I'm standing on something high and wobbly. Or maybe that's just the shock.

"I thought when you challenged Ord, it was a fight to the death," I say.

Pel pulls her blindfold away. Her round black eyes shine with color in the artificial light, like oil slicked over water. "In his wisdom, the Followed decided that my life was best given to another purpose."

"What purpose?" I ask. "What are you doing here?"

Instead of answering, she pulls a wide, pronged knife from under her translucent cloak. "I tried to end this madness. I failed. Now we all pay the price."

I stumble-step backward, ready to run, as she raises the knife. But she doesn't attack me. She plunges the knife into her own stomach instead.

All the vague familiarity of the song slams together into something concrete and terrible. I know what they're doing. The only question left is . . .

"Why? Why are you doing this?"

"I am not Followed," she says. "Your question is for Ord. Not me."

She drags the knife across her belly. Pale blood and gore spill down the front of her robe. She starts to sing again as she collapses to her knees.

Pel isn't the only Giver out here dying right now—I'm sure of it. The sonar must feel different because we're surrounded by buildings instead of trees, but this is the hunting song. Pel and the other Givers are the bait. Ord is using them to lure phytoraptors into the Landing.

SEVENTEEN

There are phytoraptors in the Landing.

The thought burns through my brain, but there's no time to be shocked. I have to move. I have to do something. But what?

For three whole seconds, I consider trying to communicate with the phytoraptors. But even if they weren't crazed from the Sorrow's hunting ritual, we're way out of Bob's hunting range. These raptors can't possibly be from his nest. There's no reason to think they've learned any sign language. If I try to approach one, it will almost certainly kill me before I can sign *Hello*. I need to focus on warning the other pioneers. But will that do us any good? The phytoraptors are almost invisible when they're camouflaged. Knowing they're out there won't protect anyone. Unless . . .

I yank my flex off and shake it out into tablet form. I pull up the Settings menu for the Landing's wireless network and swipe frantically until I find the wall screen settings. Then I switch the default for every screen in the Landing to "celebration"—the same rainbow strobe light that Jay's flex was set to. Bob's camouflage never quite worked while he was wearing that flex. Hopefully the shifting lights will have the same effect on these raptors.

Hot-pink light blooms from every wall in the Landing. It fades and then swells blue and then red and then green.

A huge shape hurtles past me. That was a phytoraptor. It's working. I can see them. There's another one. And another.

I bolt for the nearest cabin and duck inside. It's a single-family unit. The floor of the common room is littered with tiny dolls woven from the gray-blue reeds that grow on the riverbank.

"Joanna?" Dr. Ito, one of our geologists, sticks her head out of the bedroom. Her two-year-old son, Kai, is perched on her hip, chewing on one of the reed dolls. "What's happening?"

"Predators," I say, tapping out a text to Mom that says pretty much the same thing I'm telling Dr. Ito. "The Landing is being attacked by pack predators."

I hit Send.

"That's impossible," Dr. Ito protests. "There aren't any . . ."

"I know the survey report says there aren't any large predators on this continent," I say, cutting her off. I don't have time to have this conversation again right now. "But trust me, they're out there."

She doesn't really believe me. I can see it in her face. No one else will either.

"Here," I say. "Read this." I pull up Dr. Brown's files, which I copied for myself before I gave her flex to Mom. I compress the *Chorulux phytoraptor* folder, attach it to a copy of the text I just sent, and forward it to the "All E&P Team" group. There's no more time for secrets now.

A shrill tearing sound rips down the outside of the cabin, sending adrenaline zinging through my bloodstream.

"What the hell was that?" Dr. Ito whispers.

"Claws," I say as the sound scrapes through the cabin again. There's a phytoraptor out there, trying to get in.

Kai whimpers, "Ma, ma, ma, ma," pointing in the direction of the clawing sounds as Dr. Ito swipes through the files I just sent out, wide-eyed in horror.

"Stay inside, okay?" I say, starting for the back door.

"No way," Dr. Ito says. "You're not going out there!"

Claws shriek over the walls again. She's right. I'm unarmed. I won't last long out there on my own. The truth is, I've probably done everything I can do to protect the others.

Dr. Ito rocks Kai soothingly. He clings to her.

I want my mom so badly right now.

Another sharp phytoraptor scream punches through the Landing. Why is Ord doing this? He can't possibly expect Mom to make an alliance with him now. Unless he's assuming that we won't realize the Sorrow lured the phyto-raptors here. But that seems naive of him. Even if I hadn't recognized the hunting chant, it would have been pretty obvious that someone sabotaged the shield. From there, it wouldn't have been hard to figure out that he and Dr. Brown were responsible.

"Don't worry, guys," Dr. Ito says, soothing herself as much as Kai and me. "It doesn't matter how big those things are, they won't last long against marines with rifles. They'll all be gone soon, and then we'll be safe."

Her words are like a light switch in my brain. I know why the Sorrow are doing this. Dr. Brown told Chris she was meditating on consequences when he saw her in the greenhouse. I assumed that she was talking about how we almost destroyed this planet by trying to make it our home. But Dr. Brown was already thinking about using Stage Three as a weapon when Beth told her about it, back in the caves. At the time, I thought we convinced her it was too dangerous. But now I'm pretty sure that's not true. I'm pretty sure she told Ord that we had a weapon that could wipe out the phytoraptors. And I'm pretty sure that they're using this attack as cover, so they can steal it.

I smack at my flex again. "Call Beth!"

"Please wait," my flex replies. It only takes a few seconds to connect the call, but each one feels like a year.

My sister picks up, audio only.

"What, Joanna?" She sounds irritated and slightly out of breath.

"Tell me that you've already destroyed Stage Three," I say.

"I've incinerated six of the ten petri dishes," she says. She sucks in breath through her teeth, like she's doing something really delicate. Then I hear the crackling hiss of a laser welder. "Make that seven."

My anxiety explodes into relief. I should have known that if I could figure this out, Beth would too.

Beth swears. Fear snaps back through my body.

"Beth! What's—"

"Sorrow Takers are outside the greenhouse," she says.

"Get out of there, Beth!" I plead. "They'll kill you!"

"Probably," she says. "But I have three more dishes to destroy. I'm not leaving."

"Beth! You have to—"

She hangs up.

I bolt for the door, ignoring Dr. Ito's protests.

I run through the Landing. It's chaos. Phytoraptors are everywhere. People are fighting back with whatever they have. I can hear gunfire in the distance. And screaming.

I take a left turn at the school, but I'm moving so fast that my feet skid out from under me and I go sprawling. Pain shreds through my knees and palms as they scrape over the solar pavement, but I ignore it and scramble back to my feet.

Gasping for breath, I look up and find myself face to fangs with a phytoraptor with a lopsided crown of thorns growing around its skull. It opens its mouth in a fanged mockery of a smile.

Then it attacks.

The milliseconds splinter into individual impressions. Swiping claws. A hissing roar. Vicious, serrated teeth. The flat crack of a gunshot. It all feels like it happens in the same heartbeat.

The phytoraptor collapses at my feet.

My frozen joints unlock so quickly that I stagger to keep from falling.

I look up to see that Jay and Leela are jogging toward me. They're both carrying rifles.

"You okay, Hotshot?" Jay calls.

"We have to get to the greenhouse!" I say, pushing my shaky legs back into a run.

"What the hell, Jo?" Leela calls as they scramble after me.

"This is all a distraction," I shout. "Ord and Dr. Brown are trying to steal Stage Three."

"What?" Leela says. "Why?"

"He wants to release it," Jay says, fitting the pieces together immediately. "He thinks he can use it as a weapon."

"We need to tell the commander, Jo," Leela says. "Right now. This is way, way over our heads."

"Beth is in there," I say. "I'm going."

Leela swears copiously, but she stays with me. Jay does

too. He's fighting to keep up on his injured leg, but I don't slow down. We don't have far to go now, but every step feels like a light-year. There are bodies all over the place. Some of them are still moving. Moaning. A lot of them aren't.

Finally, we reach the greenhouse. It looks like a bubble of sunlight floating in the night. A pair of Sorrow Takers are guarding the doors and I can see Ord inside, facing off with Beth. She's still alive. For now.

We creep closer, staying low and close to the buildings so the Takers won't see us. We're almost there when I see a lanky body with dark skin sprawled in the middle of the street.

I bite down hard on a shocked gasp. "Chris!"

"Is he dead?" Jay whispers.

"No," I say. I can see his chest rising and falling in the light spilling from the greenhouse.

"What was he doing out here?" Leela hisses.

"He saw Dr. Brown in the greenhouses earlier," I whisper back, "while Ord was negotiating with Mom. He told me about it. That's how I figured out Dr. Brown and Ord were planning to steal Stage Three. He must have figured it out too."

"And he tried to stop them," Jay says.

I curse under my breath.

"He looks bad," Leela says. "We have to get him out of here."

"We're going to have to split up," Jay says. "Whoever grabs him is going to need cover."

"It has to be me, doesn't it?" Leela says.

"I think so," I say. "Jay has a messed-up leg, and if someone has to talk Beth out of there . . ."

"It's you," Leela says, finishing my thought. "Fine. Okay. I'm going. But I'm coming back. I'll bring help."

"Hurry," Jay says. "I think we're going to need it."

"I hate this," Leela says.

"Me too," I say.

She grabs me close in a quick, rough hug. Then she pushes me away.

"Don't die," she says.

With that, Leela darts into the street, levers Chris's limp form over her shoulder—and runs.

One of the Takers bellows in Sorrow, pulls a triangular shard of crystal from their robe, and throws it with a sharp snap of their wrist. My whole body clenches as the shard spins past Leela's head and slices straight through the cabin behind her.

She doesn't stop.

The Taker snatches another gleaming shard from their robe, but Jay steps between them and Leela.

"Drop it!" he shouts, aiming his rifle at the Sorrow. "I don't want to hurt you."

The second Taker brandishes a huge staff bristling with crystal spikes and hiss-moans, spattering us with sonar like oil from a frying pan.

"I don't want to hurt either of you," Jay repeats. "I just want to get my friend out of there."

"Beth can leave anytime she wishes," Tarn calls from behind us.

I spin to find him striding up the street behind us. He's unarmed except for a plain wooden staff. He gestures to the two Takers to lower their weapons. "We also desire to do as little harm as possible."

"Except to the kid you left for dead in the middle of the street out there," Jay snaps.

Tarn covers his face with his hands for a moment, palms in. "Chris attacked a Taker with the knife my brother gave him. The Taker acted to defend her own life."

"Maybe so," I say. "But a lot of other people are dying who haven't done anything to the Sorrow."

"Except land your starships on our world and build a city without invitation or explanation," Tarn says. "Conflict cannot be completely unexpected."

Inside the greenhouse, Beth shrieks.

I lunge for the doors. One of the Takers gets in my way, but Tarn hum-hisses something decisive with sharp edges, and they step back.

I throw open the doors, and Jay and I charge inside.

Beth is standing with her back to her lab table, clutching a sealed dish of Stage Three bacteria in one hand and a laser welder in the other. Ord is pointing a huge, black rifle with a thick stock at her head. I didn't even know weapons like that were in the 3D fabrication library. I've only seen them in history vids.

"Lucille assures me that you are valuable to our future, which is the only reason I have not yet taken your life," Ord snarls at Beth. "But I will end you if you do not give me the Stage Three."

"Just give it to him, Beth," I say.

"Absolutely not," she says. "If he wants to stop me, he's going to have to shoot me."

"That would be a terrible waste," Dr. Brown says, emerging from the storage area at the back of the greenhouse, carrying a stun gun.

She fires.

Beth crumples, unconscious.

"Beth!" I lunge for my sister, but Ord steps between us, his enormous gun pointed at my belly. Jay grabs me, hauling me back.

"There's no need for that," he says to Ord, nodding to the huge weapon. "We're just here for Beth. We won't get in your way."

"No, you won't," Dr. Brown agrees, tucking the stun gun into her robe and pulling out an insulated steel canister.

But I can't help myself.

"Don't do this!" I plead as she takes the petri dish of Stage Three from Beth's limp fingers and seals it in the canister. "Please, Ord. It isn't worth it."

"That is for me to judge," he says. "I am Followed."

"Relax, Joanna," Dr. Brown says. "We're not just going to release Stage Three and hope for the best. We have a plan."

"Your sister will inoculate the solace trees and the Sorrow against the bacteria," Ord says, as though this were all a foregone conclusion. "And my Takers will seek out and destroy the infected Beasts. Everything that matters will be safe."

His words make me want to scream. To shake him. Doesn't he realize that *everything* matters? A planet is more than just the sum of its parts. You can't destroy pieces of it and expect the rest to keep going on like nothing happened.

"Seems pretty arrogant," Jay says behind me. "Thinking you can control random mutations in bacteria."

"Yes," Dr. Brown says calmly, "it is. Arrogance is a vice our species share. But your opinion wasn't requested, nor is it required. Humanity has taken far greater risks with Earth, for far less gain. This is Ord's world. This risk is his to take."

"It isn't just his world," I cry. "This planet belongs to all of the Sorrow, including Pel and the others you forced to commit suicide tonight. And it belongs to the phytoraptors and the solace trees and every other living thing on Tau. It's not up to you, who or what is important. Who lives and dies."

"Yes, it is," Ord says. "I am Followed. If sacrifices are

necessary to destroy the Beasts, so be it."

"Now, if you'll excuse us," Dr. Brown says.

"No," Beth says, groaning as she struggles to sit up. The shoulder of her uniform is charred from where the stun bolt hit her, and her left arm is hanging limp. "I won't let you use my work to commit genocide."

Ord stalks to my sister, looming over her. *"You* won't *let* me?" he rasps. His harmonic voice scrapes over my skin like sandpaper. "The Beasts took my father when I was still pouchborne. I should have died then. But I thrived. I grew. I became Followed. My leadership has since been challenged four times, by four great warriors. But I am still Followed. Powerful alien creatures from beyond the stars invaded my world. But I turned the Beasts into a weapon, and I defeated them. In this, the Sorrow's greatest enemy became my tool. And today, as the sun rises, I will force our enemy to destroy themselves. I do as I see fit. *You* cannot hope to stop me."

With that, he kicks Beth in the stomach, sending her flying into the plexiglass wall.

Beth gasps a scream as the air explodes from her lungs. I throw myself past Ord, no longer caring what he might do to me. I can feel Jay beside me. I can hear him telling Beth to hold still while he checks her ribs, but my brain is spinning too frantically to focus. As she pushes him away and staggers to her feet, pieces of information start to weave themselves together in a new pattern. I think I'm figuring something out. Something that could change everything.

The question is, What can I do about it?

Ord turns to Dr. Brown. "Are you ready to leave this place?"

"I am," she says. She's talking to him, but she's still looking at me. There's something in her face underneath the mask of serenity. What is it? Sadness? Resignation? Fear? Maybe all three?

Ord hums a triumphant chord and heads for the doors. Dr. Brown follows him.

I don't have much time.

I pull off my flex and press it against the transparent wall screen behind me. "Computer, access file Backup: *Chorulux phytoraptor*: Encounters: Sunflower. Play in three-sixty mode."

The transparent walls of the greenhouse flicker, then fill with the three-sixty of the sunny Diamond Range valley where the Rangers died.

Dr. Brown gasps as though in physical pain.

"No!"

"Yes. You deserve to know what really happened to your crew," I say. "You deserve to know what really happened to Pasha."

"I know what happened," she whispers, staring at Dr. Pasha as he steps into the three-sixty. The raw pain in her face makes her look more human than I've ever seen her. "I've watched this every day for five years."

"And somehow, you never saw it for what it is," I say as

her younger self's laughter burbles through the audio feed of the recording. The low thrum follows it. That's what I need Dr. Brown to hear. But she isn't listening. She's staring at Pasha's face. Soaking him in.

Abruptly, I realize that she isn't seeing or hearing anything else. Just him. That's why she never heard the truth, despite all the times she's watched this three-sixty in her empty cabin in the caves. All she ever sees is Pasha dying.

"Computer, cut picture," I say. "Isolate background noise and amplify."

The walls fade back to transparency, and Dr. Brown and Dr. Pasha's playful banter drops to a murmur. But the hum gets louder. It pulses through the greenhouse, rising and falling in a dense, itchy melody that makes my skin feel like it's too tight. The shape of the sound is there, as well as the melody, and at this volume you can really feel it. It's unmistakable.

Ord lunges forward and presses his gun to my head.

"Turn. It. Off."

I don't argue with him. I don't need to. I can see the truth in Dr. Brown's face.

"Computer. Cut feed."

The hum dies. Dr. Brown doesn't move.

"I heard the hunting song in the background when I watched this in your cabin in the caves," I say. "But I didn't know what it was then. I didn't put it together until Ord said he defeated invaders from the stars using the phytoraptors. He didn't just mean tonight. He's done this before."

Jay sucks in a sharp breath. "He did it to the Rangers, too."

"That's right," I say. "It wasn't Dr. Pasha's fault that the phytoraptors suddenly turned on them. It wasn't even the phytoraptors' fault. Ord is the one who attacked and killed the Rangers—the raptors were just his weapon of choice."

Ord keeps his gun pointed at me, but he looks to Dr. Brown. "Lucille. Please, you must understand—"

"Why?" Dr. Brown grabs the barrel of Ord's gun and pushes it aside as she steps between us. She reaches out and pulls off his mirrored sunglasses so she can look into his liquid black eyes. "Why did you do it?"

His violet biolight darkens nearly to red, but he doesn't look away.

"What else was I to do?" he says. "I did not know you then. All I knew was that you were not of this world and you were powerful. We watched you. We considered you. And then your people sought to communicate with the Beasts. I could not permit that." He strokes her cheek. "It was the only solution I could see."

She stares into his eyes for a long time. Then she nods.

"I understand."

My stomach drops into my boots.

"What?" I say. "You can't possibly—"

She spins to glare at me. "Don't tell me what I can or can't think, little girl. We all do what we must for our people."

"In this, we are all alike," Ord says, resting a hand possessively on her shoulder. "Lucille understands my determination better than any other."

"He's right," she says. "I do."

She's still standing between Ord and me. He doesn't see her press the canister of Stage Three into my hands. She looks me right in the eye and says, "Now it's time for you to do what must be done."

My heart stops. She wants me to take the Stage Three and run. I can see that. But what's going to happen to her?

Dr. Brown whispers, soundlessly: *Please.*

I squeeze her hand once.

Then I grab Beth and Jay and run.

Crack! Crack! Crack! Crack! Ord's gun spits fire as we blast through the doors to the greenhouse, but I don't look back. I don't stop.

"What just happened?" Jay shouts.

"She gave me the Stage Three," I shout back. "We have to destroy it."

A Taker throws themselves into my path. There's no time to dodge them, so I plow past their swinging knife and drive my shoulder into their torso. They go sprawling, but I manage to stay on my feet and keep running.

We make it another block before Jay shouts something behind me. There's a quick crackle of gunfire, a scuffle, then a wet thud.

I spin back just in time to see Jay collapsing to his knees, blood spreading across the front of his thermal.

Ord is standing behind him. Jay's blood is dripping from his pronged knife.

"Jay!" I shout.

"Keep going," he rasps.

Ord raises his knife to strike again, but Jay reaches up and grabs his arm, flipping Ord over his shoulder. Ord hangs on to Jay's wrist as he rolls to his feet, using his momentum to fling Jay across the street. Jay's body hits the pavement with a wet crack. He rolls, moaning.

Ord kicks him in the head. Jay collapses.

This time he doesn't get up.

A hollow roar fills my ears, blocking out all other sound. Beth is shouting at me, but I can't hear her. I can't breathe.

Jay still isn't moving.

I think he might be dead.

Beth grabs my elbow and shakes me, hard. This time, I hear her. "Joanna! Come on! Move!"

My feet feel like they're magnetized to the ground, but the urgency in her voice drags me back into the moment. I force myself into a run. The motion kick-starts my brain.

"The school!" I shout to Beth. "Get to the school! We can lock ourselves in there and call for help!"

We stumble around a corner and almost collide with Tarn.

I yank Beth backward, ready to reverse course, but Ord

and the Takers from the greenhouse are right behind us. We're trapped.

"Please give me the Stage Three," Tarn says quietly.

"No," Beth says.

Tarn spins his staff in a short arc across his body and smacks the end of it against Beth's head. She collapses without a sound.

I clench the canister tight as I face Tarn over my sister's unconscious body. "I'm not giving this to you. You're going to have to take it," I say.

"I understand," Tarn says. "But I will regret harming you."

"Then why are you doing this?"

"I follow Ord," he says.

"You don't have to," I say. "You've seen things that Ord hasn't. You understand things that Ord doesn't."

Tarn lost his blindfold somewhere in the race to catch up with us. His face is bare. His eyes squint against the dim light of the moons.

"Make your own choice," I plead. "Do what *you* believe is right, Tarn."

From behind me, I feel Ord barking orders at his brother in Sorrow. I know what he's saying without translation.

Kill her.

Tarn looks from his brother to me. He moans a soft Sorrow melody that makes me want to weep. "Following my pouch mate is the only way to help him make the right choices now. It's the only way to be sure that the Sorrow will survive."

He's made his decision.

"I'm sorry, Joanna," he says, lifting his staff.

I feint left and dodge right, around Tarn. I only make it a few more steps before the end of his staff connects with my spine and my legs go numb. I collapse.

Tarn rolls me over and pries the canister from my fingers.

We make eye contact.

"The juvenile is dead," he calls to his brother, lying in English. "I have the Stage Three. Let us leave this place."

He straightens, leaving my line of sight. I want to get up, or at least call for help on my flex, but if I try, Ord will know that Tarn lied. Then he'll kill me. Or Tarn will.

I have to play dead and wait.

I'm not aware of losing consciousness, but when I wake up, Leela is leaning over me. Her flex is draped over my throat.

"Don't move yet," she says. "You've been out for a while."

"Ord—"

"Gone," Leela says. "A flyer with *Vulcan* colors landed in the square thirty minutes ago. Took them all out of here. The raptors are gone too. They bolted pretty fast, once we got to our guns."

"Are the others okay?"

"Beth is okay. So is Chris," she assures me. "I got him to medical in time. Dr. Kruppa is working on him. I grabbed Dad and Sarge and came back for you guys as soon as I could. We found you like this."

"What about Jay?"

Leela swallows hard. "He's alive." She shakes her head. "But it's bad. He might . . ."

Die. Jay might die. The thought coils itself around me, crushing my bones.

"Dad is working on him," Leela adds, trying to sound optimistic. "That's why he had me check you out—you're . . ." She checks her flex and swears. "Have you been scanned since we got back?"

"No, I kept meaning to go to medical, but—"

"Jo," she says, looking up from her flex, wide-eyed, "your pacers are gone."

EIGHTEEN

"Don't move, okay?" She scrambles to her feet. "You need a real doctor."

She hurries off. I lie there, trying not to panic. Panic will make my heart beat faster, which might kill me without my pacers. Of course, that thought just makes me want to panic harder. How can my pacers be gone? Whatever happened to them, it must have been while I was passed out. I can't even sit up for long without them. Much less run, or climb cliffs, or fight.

Unless I don't need them anymore.

The thought strikes my brain and flares like a match. Tarn said, "When a Giver heals, the body is restored to its true state." The Givers healed my broken ankle and my burns. But if the Sorrow healing ritual restores a body to its true state, does that mean that they healed my heart and lungs as well?

I take a deep breath, focusing on the sensation of air rushing in through my nose, down my windpipe, and into my lungs. I can feel the breath inflating them against my rib cage, easily. I breathe out, pushing the air through my mouth and letting my lungs deflate.

It feels easy. Smooth. The way it did before the accident, when I never thought about what it felt like to breathe.

I sit up.

I don't see any sparks or get light-headed. My pulse doesn't jump.

I stand up.

I'm still fine. My heart is beating a little faster, but I'm not short of breath. I'm not feeling dizzy.

"Joanna!" Doc snaps from across the road, where he's still working on Jay. "Lie down right now."

"I can't," I say. "I don't need to. I need to . . ."

I need to go. Now. While there's still time.

I run.

If I'm wrong and my heart is still a mess, then I'm not going to make it very far. But if I'm right, that means I can fly. And if I can fly, I can go after Ord and Tarn. I can stop them before they infect the phytoraptors.

The flyers are parked side by side on the airfield, their black solar skin shimmering under the floodlights. I race to the closest one, open the rear doors, and bound up the ramp into the flyer.

I'm not even that out of breath.

Exhilaration sweeps through me, momentarily blasting away the grief and anxiety and terror that are crammed into my brain.

I don't need my pacers anymore.

I bring the flyer online and initiate the preflight sequence. The rotors roar to life as I drop into the pilot's seat and press the autoconnect button on my harness. A black webbing skims out from its straps and bonds with the chair.

I pull the navigation app up on the wall screen in front of me. I have green lights on all systems. The flyer is ready.

I plant my fingers on the piloting app and push up.

The flyer rises. The ground falls away below me. My heart thuds steadily in my chest.

I'm flying. I'm actually flying.

I feel invincible for the first seven minutes. Then I hit the choppy mountain air and my confidence evaporates. Unfamiliar Tau winds batter the flyer, tossing me dangerously close to the ragged peaks and cliff. To make matters worse, they've updated the nav app since the last time I flew, so the controls feel awkward and unfamiliar.

The rotors scream in protest as I inadvertently sideswipe a cliff.

I switch to autopilot.

The flyer slows immediately. I look to the east, where the sun is already peeking over the horizon. At this speed, I might not make it to the nest in time. But I haven't flown in almost two years, and crashing into a mountain and dying isn't going to help anyone.

What possessed me to I think I could do this?

A memory flickers through my head. My own voice whispering from another time, another impossible moment.

I can do this. We're going to make it. You believe me, right?

Teddy's voice whispers back . . .

Always.

I wish Teddy were here. He always believed in me.

Maybe he still does.

Einstein said that all points of time exist at once. It's only our limited human brains that need to think of the past, the present, and the future as different things. If that's true, then somewhere, some *when*, Teddy is still out there. Believing in me.

If I'm going to do this, I might as well do it right. I press my fingers into the nav app.

"Computer, switch to manual, please."

I can feel the flyer slide back into my control as the computer responds, "Yes, Joanna."

Always.

The word rings in my ears as I press my hands against the nav app and the flyer hurtles forward once more.

A few minutes later, I see a web of focused light arcing over the trees up ahead. It makes the air shimmer and shift, distorting my view of the phytoraptors planted in the ravine.

A flyer with *Vulcan* markings is perched on the cliffs. Sorrow Takers and Givers are buzzing around it.

I swing my flyer high around the rim of the ravine, putting the sun at my back, where light-sensitive Sorrow eyes won't look for me. As I try to figure out what to do next, nine pale-robed Givers arrange themselves in a line, facing the nest. They kneel. Ord's sunglasses spark and flare in the sunlight as he walks up the line, pressing something to each of their lips in turn.

It's the petri dish of Stage Three. It has to be.

They're going to sacrifice themselves in the nest. Once the phytoraptors feed on them, they'll be infected. Then Ord can tell his people that "the Beasts" destroyed themselves with their own voracious hunger.

This is going to make him a living legend. The Sorrow will follow him for the rest of his life.

Unless I stop him.

The Givers push to their feet as one. They about-face and slowly proceed along the edge of the cliff. They're heading for the same cascade of fallen rocks we used to get into the nest. There's no time for a plan. I have to do something now.

I push my hands forward, swinging the flyer out over the ravine. Ord's head snaps up as I start my descent. He makes a sweeping gesture to his Takers, and then he spins and hurries up the ramp into his flyer.

"Particle shield on high," I tell the computer as my flyer

dips into the web of light. The force field shimmers into place and the woven light explodes around me, scattering itself off the shields in a cascade of rainbows.

The phytoraptors begin to stir immediately.

Of course! The light is what puts them into a trance. Disrupting it wakes them up.

The web of light shimmers back into place above the flyer's shield as I drop below it. I quickly reverse the engine's thrust.

The flyer rises.

Rainbows bounce all around me as the carefully focused sunbeams shatter once more.

The phytoraptors start to move around, slowly. Too slowly. I rev the flyer's engines.

"Come on! Run!"

But the phytoraptors aren't afraid of the flyer. They're fascinated. Even worse, they're starting to notice the Givers, who are moving slowly and deliberately between them.

A flat *boom* rattles the flyer. I have to yank at the controls to keep it from slamming into a cliff.

Boom! Boom!

What is that? I can't take my hands off the navigation app, so I pull it across the wall screens with me as I pivot my chair to look behind me.

Ord is standing on the cliffs, shooting at me with his huge gun.

Boom!

The flyer jerks hard as another spray of bullets explodes against the shield. It's designed to protect the flyer from debris and radiation, not combat. It won't last long against that gun.

Boom!

I start to lift the flyer out of range, but just then a phytoraptor hurdles the cliff in front of me and races for the trees. Half a dozen more follow. I twist, looking down into the ravine where phytoraptors are fleeing in all directions. They're bounding up the cliffs and swimming upriver, totally ignoring the Givers.

Ord's gunfire is scaring the phytoraptors away. All I have to do is stay here and let him keep firing at me until the raptors get clear. I just hope I survive that long.

Boom!

He fires again, and again, and again. My hands fly over the navigation app, fighting to compensate for the shock waves that reverberate through the shields.

Boom!

The wall screens flash red.

"Shields at critical, Joanna," the computer says. "Brace for failure in five . . . four . . . three . . ."

Boom! The flyer shudders around me again as the computer keeps counting down. I need to get out of range. Now.

I slide both hands upward, ordering the flyer to rise. Ord follows it up, spraying bullets from his huge gun.

"Two . . . one . . ."

My shields fail.

Crack! Crack! Crack!

The flyer jumps and sags under my hands as a bullet shatters one of the rotors. I try to compensate, but the flyer is out of control. It spins, hurtling sideways. I yank upward on the controls and rev the engine, pouring on speed so that the flyer hits the edge of the cliff and bounces, skidding upside down into the thick tangle of solace trees on the other side of the ravine.

I hang from my harness for a moment, blood pounding in my temples, trying to catch my breath.

I can't believe that worked.

I twist in my seat, grabbing the armrest before I untether myself and let my legs swing down to what used to be the ceiling. Then I unlock the rear doors. The ramp only unfolds halfway before it gets stuck, but there's enough room to crawl out.

My head is pounding, and my neck is so stiff it feels brittle. I think I've got whiplash, and possibly a concussion. But I'm alive. I'm on solid ground. And the phytoraptors made it out of their nest.

I did what I came here to do.

A Sorrow roar crashes against my skin seconds before Ord's staff slams into the backs of my knees, sweeping my feet out from under me. My chin cracks against a tree root, pain exploding through my head as flashing white lights momentarily blind me.

My vision swims back into focus as I force my numb

legs to move. I make it to my hands and knees, but then Ord kicks me in the ribs. The impact knocks the air from my lungs and spins me onto my back.

He leans in and spits a series of harsh Sorrow words in my face, his sonar battering me with his fury.

"Foolish juvenile," he snarls, switching to English. "You have just given your life for nothing."

"No," I gasp. "I gave it to stop you."

"You didn't stop me." My heart sinks as he pulls the silver canister of Stage Three from his robe. "Perhaps not today, but soon the Beasts will crumble and rot. And I will live to see it."

I don't stop to think. I launch myself at him, grasping wildly for the canister. My fingers close around the cool metal oval, and I rip it from his hands.

I'm so surprised that I don't bother to try to check my forward momentum as I careen past him, stumble over the solace tree roots, and go sprawling.

Ord roars a furious sonar blast that feels like the burning cold of space. He charges me, knife out. I scramble forward, but he grabs my hips and yanks me back, spinning me under him as he drives his knife down toward my chest.

I grab his wrist and push up as hard as I can. It isn't enough. I scream, throwing everything left in my body into stopping the knife. He growls, filling the air with sonic vibrations that make me feel like his anger and hatred are drilling through my pores.

The knife's fang-like points press against the weave of

my utility harness, digging in. Pushing through.

Wham! Something big and green slams into Ord.

A high-pitched phytoraptor call shatters the air. I lurch up on one elbow to see Ord locked in combat with a raptor. Ord kicks into their chest, sending them sliding away. The phytoraptor rolls to their feet and shrieks again. The raptor's smooth, bald head shifts from brown to green to violet as they circle Ord through the trees.

Bob just saved my life.

The fight is brutal and fast. Ord and Bob attack and fall back in a violent tangle that is weirdly beautiful and terrifying at the same time.

Every cell of my body hurts, but I drag myself to my feet. I have to get the Stage Three away from Bob. But I only make it a few meters before Tarn and a trio of armed Takers race out of the woods, heading straight toward me. I try to move faster, but my head is swimming, and every step jolts pain through my neck.

In seconds, I'm surrounded.

"Please," I call to Tarn. "Just let me go."

"Give me the Stage Three," he counters. "I don't wish to hurt you."

"Then don't," I say. "Don't do this. Even if Beth can protect the Sorrow and the solace trees, there's no way to know what you'll lose. Tau will never be the same. It might seem like it's worth it, to destroy the phytoraptors, but it isn't. Trust me. We did this to our world. We changed stuff, and we destroyed stuff, so that we could have more of what we wanted. We kept doing it until it was too late. I never knew our home world the way it was, before we started ripping it apart in the name of improvement. And now . . ." I stop, gulping in air. "And now we have to leave Earth behind in order to save it. We'll never get back what we've lost."

"Neither will we, Joanna," Tarn says. "The world I knew is gone. It ended the moment Lucille landed her spacecraft on our soil. Your presence on this planet will change everything for us, no matter what we do. Ord is simply harnessing that transformation for our benefit. Now I'm going to take the Stage Three. Please don't resist."

I can't. Even if I wanted to, I'm too badly hurt to fight.

So maybe it's time to stop.

"What if we left?" I say.

Tarn rumbles something in Sorrow that feels like the stab of a hypodermic needle. Sharp and authoritative.

The Takers holding my arms step back.

"You would do this for the Beasts?" Tarn says. "You would give up a whole world for the sake of vicious preda-tors who have slaughtered your own people?"

"No," I say. "But I would do it for you. I would do it for Tau. I loved this planet before I saw it. I loved it before I even knew it existed. I was born too late to protect Earth, but it's not too late for Tau. I can't promise you my mother will listen to me, or that our people will listen to her. But I'll try. The Sorrow deserve a chance to do better than us. So if you let me take the Stage Three and destroy it, I will do my best to make my people leave Tau."

Before Tarn can react to the offer, a trijointed hand grabs my arm and yanks it upward. I feel the bone pop free of my shoulder socket. The canister slides from my suddenly numb fingers.

Ord hisses a blast of burning sonar as he drops me in a heap and sweeps up the canister.

"Stupid. Useless." He sputters, snarling at Tarn in Sorrow again before veering back into English. "You can't stop me." He throws his arms wide, pointing to where Bob is staggering toward us. "And neither can your Beast. This ends now!"

He starts toward Bob with the canister.

Tarn gets in his way.

"Wait, pouch mate. Consider the possibility that Joanna is right. Even if Stage Three can be controlled, there will be consequences. They may be grave. I know we can protect the Solace, but what of the rest of our world?"

"What of it?" Ord snarls. "If sacrifices must be made, so be it. I have chosen. And I am Followed!" He drops into his own language. Growling something cold and furious.

Tarn looks past his brother to meet my eyes. Then he turns back to Ord. "You've made the wrong choice, pouch mate. I can no longer follow you."

Ord roars in his brother's face and punches him hard in the chest. Tarn doubles over. Ord steps over him, snatching up Tarn's unadorned staff as he strides toward Bob.

Bob swipes at Ord, but the Sorrow ducks his claws and slams the end of the staff up into Bob's chest. Bob flies backward, thudding to the ground meters away. He rolls onto his side, keening in pain.

Ord unscrews the lid of the canister and pulls out the sealed petri dish.

He's going to infect Bob.

The thought burns through my veins like rocket fuel, propelling me forward. I throw myself at Ord, knocking the petri dish from his fingers. He shrieks in rage, tossing me away. I try to scramble for the Stage Three, but Ord leaps onto my back, driving me to the ground.

He grabs my bad shoulder and twists. Something tears deep inside the joint, and pain whites out my vision as he rolls me over.

When I can see again, Ord's pronged knife is in his hand. He swings it up, ready to drive it down into my chest. I try to twist away, but the whole side of my body is numb. I can't move.

I'm going to die.

The knife falls from Ord's suddenly nerveless fingers. Thick, silver blood bubbles from his transparent lips. He looks down in shock at the tip of Tarn's knife, protruding from his chest.

Tarn's wail scrapes over my skin and tears at my soul. He drops to one knee beside his brother, reaching out to catch Ord as he falls. Dead.

The Takers rush forward, knives out. For a moment, I think they're attacking, but instead they fall to their knees in front of Tarn. They flip their knives and hold them out, hilts first.

That's when I realize what Tarn has done. By killing his brother, he's just become the leader of the Sorrow.

Tarn rumbles something quiet that I can barely feel, and the Takers sheath their knives.

Tarn looks up at me.

"I did what I had to do to keep my promise. Now it's time for you to do the same."

With that, Tarn heaves his brother's body into his arms. He stands and calls the Takers. They fall into a single line behind him as he walks away.

I stare after them, numb with shock and pain.

What have I done?

I hear footsteps behind me.

I whirl to find Bob looming over me. His claws are still glistening with Ord's blood.

Fear skates up my spine, but Bob flexes his hands and the thick talons retract into his fingertips. He points one long finger at me and then forms a thumbs-up and circles it.

Okay?

My heart gives a single hard thud in my chest as relief hammers through me.

Bob repeats the gesture. *Okay?*

I manage to lift my good arm and squeeze my thumb

and index finger together. The okay sign. Then I press my fingers to my lips and lift them again.

Thank you.

With that, Bob lopes away into the trees. As he moves, his skin ripples into camouflage mode, and he fades from sight.

NINETEEN

I wake up in medical.

It's quiet. The ward is mostly empty. I see Chris sleeping a few beds down. The vitals monitor beside him glows with comfortingly green lights.

"Finally decided to join us, huh?"

I bolt upright in bed at the sound of Jay's voice. Then I groan a curse as an aftershock of pain ripples out from my shoulder.

"And so happy about it, too," Jay says, smirking at me from his scanner bed on the other side of the room.

"Listen, pal," I say. The ergofoam bed molds itself around me, supporting my weight as I gingerly ease to my feet. "I know someone told you that you were funny, once." I try standing up. My legs don't collapse under me, so I limp across the room to his bed. "But they lied."

Those are the last words I manage to get out before Jay grabs the front of my hospital gown and pulls me close. Then he's kissing me, and there are no more words. The pain and the grief and the worry all evaporate. There's nothing but the way his hands feel tangled in my hair. The way his lips feel, cracked and dry and warm and subtly doing something to my tongue that feels like fireworks charging through my nervous system.

He pulls back, letting himself collapse against the ergofoam of his scanner bed.

"Hey, where do you think you're going?"

His face splits in a goofy grin.

"Some of us need oxygen."

"Oxygen is overrated," I say, leaning in to kiss him again. He kisses me back, but he doesn't pull himself up off the bed. I can feel his heart pounding, and I don't think it's just because I'm such a good kisser.

"Are you okay?" I say, dropping into the visitor's chair beside him.

He shrugs, leaning back into the ergofoam. "I'm not dying or anything, but Ord nicked a few important nerve endings when he stabbed me in the back. Might be temporary. Might end up in braces or even a chair." He says it like it's no big deal, but there's doubt crawling under his voice as he adds, "You mind?"

"I always wanted a cybernetic boyfriend."

Oh. Shit. I just called Jay Lim my boyfriend.

That ridiculous grin explodes over his face again.

"I knew I was the man of your dreams."

After that, there's more kissing.

A series of melodramatic gagging noises breaks up the mood. Leela hurls herself onto the empty scanner bed next to Jay's. "You guys are the worst," she says, propping her boots up on the bed and folding her arms behind her head.

"I think it's sweet," Chris says, sitting up in his bed to make a face at me. "Gross, but in a romantic way."

I feel the heat of a blush washing over my face. I totally forgot that we were in a public place. With doctors and nurses in it. Oh no. "Please tell me your dad isn't here."

Leela bursts out laughing. "You're in luck. Dr. Kruppa is on duty, and she's debriding the wound on Chief Ganeshalingam's arm at the moment." She leans over to eye the readout on Jay's bed and smirks. "But Dad always supports a little cardiovascular exercise during recovery. I'm sure he wouldn't object."

"Nothing but comedians in here," Jay mutters. He's blushing, too.

Leela snorts. "As much as I enjoy mocking you two, I promised the commander I'd let her know as soon as you woke up, Jo. So . . ."

"Is she okay?" I say, realizing abruptly that I don't know.

"Yeah," Leela says. "She and your dad and Beth are all fine."

"What about Dr. Brown?" I say. "Ord shot her, I think. Is she dead?"

"We don't know," Leela says. "We haven't found any sign of a body, but it's possible she was brought to a triage station and she got mixed in with the other casualties."

"How many did we lose?" I ask, my stomach churning.

"Eighty-four," Chris says quietly.

"What? That's . . ." That's nearly half our team. Friends. People I've known since I was a child. Gone. "How?"

"A bunch of people were hiding in the 3D shop," Jay says. "Some phytoraptors got in and . . ." He shakes his head.

"That's awful," I say. The words feel shallow, compared to the sucking black hole of terribleness at the pit of my stomach. How is it even possible that so many people died last night? How can we go on without them?

We're quiet after that. Guess nobody else has words big enough for the grief either.

"I should text the commander," Leela says, deflating the suffocating silence. "You ready, Jo?"

Am I ready to tell Mom that I just promised our new home away? I'll never be ready for that. I nod anyway.

I take my time walking to Ground Control. Pioneer's Landing feels different today. Frayed, like the dead are threads yanked from the fabric of this place. The teams working to repair the damaged structures are full of injured people who look like they should still be in medical. The central square is empty, except for a few colorful insect analogs, fluttering around the fido trees we transplanted from the river.

I pull open the door to Ground Control, but before I can walk inside, Beth says, behind me, "I thought you were dead." I turn to see her sitting under one of the fido trees in the garden. "When you disappeared, and Mom figured out that the flyer was gone, I knew you'd gone after them."

"How?"

"You're my sister," she says. "I've known you since you were fourteen minutes old. I knew you'd try. I was afraid that they would kill you."

"I was pretty sure they were going to, for a while there," I say.

"This is the third time I've thought you were dead in the last week, Joanna," she says. "Don't do it again. Please. It's very distracting."

A week ago, that would have hurt my feelings. But I didn't know her at all then. Not really. That's one thing this planet has given me.

"I love you, Beth."

"I love you, too," she says. "Obviously. Which is why I need you to aspire to a less exciting lifestyle."

"We're pioneers," I say. "I'm not sure that's possible."

"You're good at impossible," she says. "Mom's expecting you. You shouldn't be late."

With that, she walks back up the street that leads to the greenhouse.

I watch her go.

When Teddy was alive, the three of us felt like a set. The Watson kids. Maybe Beth and I are finally finding a way to fit together without him between us.

I push through the door to Ground Control and walk back to Mom's office. My parents are both there, waiting.

I tell them what happened in the nest. I tell them about my promise to Tarn. They aren't happy. I didn't think they would be. But they aren't as furious as I expected.

"It kept you alive and saved a planet from environmental catastrophe," Mom says. "Ideal or not, that's a success."

"But was it a lie? Will we leave?"

Asking the question out loud rips a gaping, terrified hole through my resolve. I desperately hope, just for a few seconds, that she says no. We've given up so much to get here. I don't want to eke out an existence on the polar ice of Proxima Centauri b. I want to stay on Tau.

But if she says no, then Tarn killed his brother for a lie. My lie. And I don't want that, either.

I can hear the echoes of my internal dilemma in my mother's sigh. "I wish I could say yes."

"We need to consider it, Alice," Dad says. "I understand the urgency of the situation back home, but we have fifty years. There's a whole galaxy full of planets out there. We don't need to steal our place in the stars."

Their eyes meet for a long moment. Mom sighs. "You're right. Of course, you're right. But that doesn't mean I can convince Central Command."

Dad's lips twitch. If his eyes didn't look so sad, I'd call it a little grin. "I've always put my money on you. Haven't lost a bet yet."

Mom sucks in a shaky breath and nods. "You know, I wanted ballet lessons for my tenth birthday. My father talked me into learning to fly instead. I regret that sometimes."

Dad pulls her close. She rests her head on his chest.

Watching them, I feel my eyes get tight and hot. Tears prickle. I just put the future of this world and three species of intelligent beings on my mother's shoulders. I expected it to be a relief, knowing that she's finally going to stand up and take charge of this mess. But it makes me ache for her. I can imagine all too well how overwhelming it must be.

Dad catches the look on my face. He reaches out and tugs the end of my braid. "Think of it this way, Al," he says to Mom. "If you'd grown up to be a ballerina instead of a pilot commander, you'd probably have married someone else, and you'd have normal kids. That would be boring."

Mom snorts a laugh. "You're not as funny as you think you are, Nick."

"You married me," he says, smirking.

She rolls her eyes. "I know. I did it on purpose, too. Imagine."

She steps away from him, gathering herself once more.

"All right, no more feeling sorry for ourselves," she says. "We've got work to do."

Of course, we can't even report what's happened to Central Command with the *Pioneer*'s superluminal transponder down. We have to wait until the new shuttle is finished, so we can get up to the ship and see what's wrong.

In the meantime, Mom and Dad decide not to tell the others that we might have to bail. Mom keeps everyone busy building the new shuttle. Even the little kids are helping. It's a big, complicated job. And it keeps anyone from asking why we've stopped construction on the Landing.

Weeks pass.

We see the occasional phytoraptor lurking around the shields, but no one has seen the Sorrow since Tarn became Followed.

We hold memorial services for the people who died in the shuttle crash and the phytoraptor attack. Mom has Doc seal the bodies in inso crates instead of burying them, but we erect a memorial stone on the riverbank. I sit by it sometimes, after I finish recycling the dinner dishes. Sometimes I cry. Sometimes I don't. Sometimes Chris meets me there and we sit together.

I split my time between working on the new shuttle and helping Jay deal with the nanosurgical therapy on his back. In the evenings, he and I hang out with Beth and Leela and Chris in the greenhouse. Chris doesn't say much. He doesn't say much to anyone these days. I hope he told his dad and Dr. Kao everything he told me about what happened in the nest, but I don't feel like I can ask. Chris will tell me more if he wants to.

One morning, when the new shuttle is almost finished, Dad wakes Beth and me before dawn. He wants us to show him the nest.

"I have to see it at least once."

I expect Mom to be waiting at the flyer, but she isn't.

"Who's flying?" I ask.

"You are," Dad says.

The thought catches my breath.

"But I'm still not cleared," I say. My cardiovascular system is as good as new. Doc ran the scans twice. But nobody's had time to check me out on the flyer and re-instate my clearances.

"We're pioneers living on the farthest frontier in human history," Dad says. "I think that means we can skip some of the paperwork."

"Are you sure?"

"We're sure," Beth says. "And dawn is thirty-four min-utes away, so . . ."

Dad puts a hand on my shoulder. "You don't have to, if you don't feel like you're ready."

Am I? The last time I flew, it was just my own life on the line. But now, with Beth and Dad on board . . . I'm starting to understand why Leela finds being a pilot so terrifying.

But I've done a lot of scary stuff lately.

Dad and Beth settle in behind me as I run preflight

checks. They're all green. I press my hands to the nav app. The rotors bite into the air, pulling the flyer off the ground.

We hover over the Landing, looking down on the neat rows of cabins and labs that pinwheel out from the town square. With no warning at all, tears well in my eyes. How ridiculous of me, to long for something we haven't even lost yet.

"Joanna," Beth says.

"We're going, we're going."

With one last look down at the Landing, I swing my hands over the navigation app and push the flyer west toward the mountains.

I leave the autopilot off, soaring between the jagged peaks of the Diamond Range on manual control. The air currents coil around us, lofting us through the brightening sky. The first tendrils of morning light catch at the prismatic peaks of the mountains below, melting the light like rainbow syrup over the wells of green that twist through them.

When we reach the nest, the sky is blossoming with a thousand shades of blue. I set the flyer down in the clearing my crash chewed out of the forest after Ord shot me down. From here we can watch the nest without having to risk direct interaction. We're just in time. The rotors have barely stopped turning when we see the first phytoraptors swing down the cliffs on the other side of the ravine. Soon they're streaming around us, coming home for the morning light. Their skins molt through green into violet purples and browns and back again as they move.

Abruptly, a tall, skinny phytoraptor with a sharp ridge protruding from their forehead turns and stalks straight toward us. They smack their huge hands flat against the hull over and over again. Hard enough that the whole flyer shimmies under the impact.

My hands twitch to the controls, but Dad stops me. "Wait. I want to see what it does."

The phytoraptor smacks the flyer a few more times. Then they step back.

They raise their hand and sign.

Hello.

I see you.

Then they drop back to their knuckles and feet and gallop for the edge of the ridge, throwing themselves over and into the valley.

"Tell me I didn't imagine that," Dad whispers.

"If you did, so did I," I breathe.

"Why are we whispering?" Beth says. "They can't hear us."

Dad bursts into a breathless, awestruck laugh. "I don't know, Beth. I don't know."

But I do. The moment feels sacred. Terrifying. Wondrous. These creatures are teaching each other to communicate with us, and they're doing it all on their own. This is something no other human in the galaxy has ever seen. And we're watching it happen. Together.

We stay to watch the dawn light hit the nest. I watch Dad instead. He's practically got his nose pressed against the wall screens, taking it all in. The last few weeks have carved years into his face, but they're gone now. Scrubbed away by wonder and delight.

By the time we get back, it's almost midday. Chris is waiting for Beth and me in the greenhouse. He looks excited. And possibly terrified.

"Tarn is here," he says before we even have a chance to greet him. "He's in the office with your mom."

"What?" I say. "When did he—"

"Just after dawn," Chris says, answering my question before I finish it. "I was sitting by the memorial stone, and he just walked up to the shields on the other side of the river."

"Did he tell you why he's here?" Beth asks.

Chris shakes his head. "He asked to speak to the commander, so I took him to her office. Then I came here, but you guys were gone."

"Did he bring Takers?" I say.

Chris shakes his head again. "It was just him."

Tarn's approach is so humble in comparison with Ord's elaborate procession of armed Takers and glowing Givers. But it's more than humility. It's a demonstration of strength. Tarn isn't afraid of the light. And he isn't afraid of us.

"I have to go," I say. "I have to see him before he leaves."

I run all the way to the square. Mom's office door is still closed. Tarn must still be in there.

I sit under the fido trees by the doors into Ground Control and wait, trying to figure out exactly what I want to say to Tarn. I don't even know if he'll talk to me. He killed his own brother to keep our deal, a deal Mom may not be able to keep. I wouldn't blame him if he hated me.

Tarn emerges from Mom's office.

"Hello, Joanna," he says.

"It wasn't a lie." The words just pop out of their own volition.

Tarn pushes back his hood. In the midday light, I can see every detail of him through his skin. Bone. Muscle. The pale yellow light of the blood in his veins.

"I do not question that," he says. "I know you meant your words."

"I hope my people will honor our deal."

"So do I," he says. "I wish that circumstances were different. More than I can say. But the Sorrow are not ready to share our world, and they now follow me. Their needs are my needs."

"I understand that," I say.

"I believe your mother does as well," Tarn says. "But she tells me that the final decision is not hers."

"It isn't," I say. "She reports to other people back home, and it's . . ." I don't know how much Mom told him, or how much I should. Finally, I settle on "The situation is very complicated for us."

"For me, it is simple," Tarn says. "I have given the commander ten days to confirm that humanity will leave this world in peace. If she can't do that, I will be forced to take action."

Action. Stomach acid lurches into the back of my mouth at the word. When Ord decided to take action, he used the phytoraptors to kill eighty-four of our people. Tarn is smarter than Ord. What will he do if we don't live up to my promise?

"I hope . . ." Tarn trails off into a melodic Sorrow hum, like he can't find the words in English. The sonar whispers over my skin like a cool mist. "It has been a pleasure to know you, Joanna Watson. I wish I could continue to do so."

"Me too," I say. I have to force the words to grow larger than a whisper. "Me too."

He leaves without another word.

TWENTY

I can't sleep.

I get up when the sky starts to lighten and go to the mess hall. Jay is already there, helping Dr. Kao set up. He hasn't been sleeping well since he started wearing cybernetic braces on his legs. He hasn't said anything, but I think it hurts when he takes them off.

After I eat, Jay and I walk along the river. He's getting better at walking in the braces, but every step is still awkward and unsteady.

The morning is chilly. The fluorescent blossoms of the fido trees are fading. Going white. The seasons are changing.

"I wonder what winter is like here," I say.

Jay nods, his eyes wandering over the shining mountains. "You think we're going to be here to find out?"

I told him about my promise to Tarn and the ticking clock to relocate billions of humans before Earth's ecosystem collapses. I tell him everything these days.

"I guess I hope not," I say. "I wish . . ." I start to say that I wish things were different. But if things were different, I might not be standing here in the crisp chill next to him. And I can't bring myself to regret that.

He doesn't ask me to finish the thought. He just pulls me close. It isn't the first time, but it never fails to amaze me how well our bodies fit. I rest my head on his chest and watch the sunrise.

"Am I interrupting something?"

Mom's voice jars me out of the moment. She's less than a meter away, but I didn't hear her coming.

"Oh, ah, no," I stammer. I haven't told her what's happening between Jay and me, but she doesn't look surprised.

Jay, of course, isn't even flustered. "Morning, Commander."

"Good morning, Corporal," she says. "Mind if I steal my daughter?"

Mom promoted Jay last week. He tried to argue against it, because of his legs. She listened politely, and then promoted him anyway. I swear he's been walking easier since then. Like the fact that she believes in him makes him stronger.

"You're the boss," he says. "Catch you later, Hotshot."

I follow Mom back through the Landing. I'm surprised

when she walks right past Ground Control, through the square, and keeps going.

"Are we going to engineering?" I ask. It's the only public building on this side of the settlement. Everything else over here is houses. Ours is just behind Ground Control, but we've already passed it.

Mom shoots me a mischievous grin.

"Nope." She turns left at the next intersection. This road leads to the airfield. I can see our new shuttle from here. *Trailblazer* is stenciled on its side in green. The ramp is down, waiting to be boarded.

"You want me to come to the *Pioneer* with you?"

"Leela has requested a transfer back into the marine squadron," Mom says. "Since we're very short on marines, and I have another excellent cadet pilot available, I'd like to approve her request. But I need to clear you for orbital flight first. You game?"

I look up at the *Trailblazer*. Do I really want to be Cadet Pilot Joanna Watson again? Does it matter? We need Leela out there, protecting us. Which means Mom needs me to get back in the pilot seat. Actually, the whole human race is going to need me. If we have any hope of moving three billion people to another planet, we're going to need every space pilot we have, and then some. That's scary, but I'd be lying if I said it wasn't kind of exciting, too.

I walk through the airlock into the passenger cabin. I strap myself into the pilot's seat. I look up in time to catch the ghost of a smile darting across Mom's lips as she follows me and settles into the copilot's seat next to me.

"Preflight safety checks, please," I call to the computer.

"Of course, Joanna," it says. The navigation app appears on the wall screen in front of me. The list of safety checks starts turning green, one item at a time. I swipe through the important ones, manually confirming the tests. I don't look up at Mom, but I can feel her watching. Nervous sparks pop under my shoulder blades as I complete the checks and request a go for launch from Ground Control. Suddenly, I want to be airborne so badly I can hardly sit still.

Dad's voice replies. "*Trailblazer*, you are a go. Happy trails, ladies."

"Computer," I say, "begin ignition sequence, please."

"My pleasure, Joanna," the computer says. "Ignition in three . . . two . . . one . . . liftoff!"

The engine rumbles to life under us. My body gets heavier as the landing struts shove against the ground and the *Trailblazer* blasts upward.

The wall screens are still a blank gray. I almost forgot the best part.

"Display exterior cameras, computer. Please."

Tau Ceti e opens up below us in a single burst of light and color. It's so beautiful, it makes my throat ache all over again.

"Sometimes I wish I'd just stuck to construction duty," I

347

say as the turquoise sky starts to thin out above us and turn sparkling black.

"Me too," Mom says. "But the Sorrow would have meant trouble for us, eventually. And we would have been a disaster for them. It would have taken us a long time to admit it, if not for you. You always were braver than me."

"That's not true."

"Oh yeah?" She says. "Then why were you the one who figured out that one of you could get to the engine room and manually eject the core? I didn't even consider it."

"I didn't know better," I say. "I didn't think . . . I didn't realize what might happen to us. I think Teddy did. But I didn't."

"Would you have done it?" Mom asks. "If you'd known?"

I turn to look at her. She looks older than she did on Tau Day One, and younger too, somehow. She doesn't look like "Mom" anymore. Or the commander. She just looks like a person. It's weird. Alarming. But . . . I don't know, satisfying, I guess. Like an unfamiliar telemetry equation that I'm finally beginning to understand.

"I hope so," I say. "I hope I'm as brave as he was."

Pink and blue flames are starting to lick the hull now. We're breaking through the atmosphere.

"You are," she says. "You're so much more than we ever expected you to be." There are so many unspoken things layered in her words. Pride. Grief. Resignation. Maybe fear.

Before I can figure out what to do with all that, *Trailblazer* bursts free of Tau's atmosphere and we're in space.

The nav app projects a glowing line across the wall screens that swings out around the planet and ends in the *Pioneer*. I double-check the telemetry, but then I let the autopilot guide us into orbit.

I look out to deep space. Our future home is out there, somewhere. Is it Proxima Centauri b, or will we find another place with a warm blue sky and wide green land? I hope so. It won't be easy to find another world like Tau. There's a good chance I'll spend most of my life searching. But I think I'm okay with that.

We're approaching the *Pioneer*. I take manual control back from the computer. I could let autopilot bring us in, but this is my favorite part. Besides, there won't be a better time to test my rusty skills than right now, with Mom right next to me.

I pivot my fingers on the navigation app to put the *Trailblazer* into a spin, matching the *Pioneer*'s rotation. I don't know this shuttle yet, not the way I did the *Wagon*. It's the same design, but the thrum of metal and carbon is fundamentally different under my fingers. Still, I can feel it when we're lined up properly—it's like a tuning fork inside my head, letting me know the pitch is just right. There's barely a shimmy as our docking port connects with the *Pioneer*.

I can feel the grin on my face all over my body. The joy is still there. I wasn't sure it would be.

"Shall we?" Mom says, releasing her harness.

We cross into the *Pioneer* together. The ship sings quietly around us. She's been waiting. The exterior cameras are already on three-sixty mode in the bridge. Tau Ceti c and a are eclipsing Tau Ceti right now. They look tiny in the fiery embrace of the star.

Mom asks the computer to run a diagnostic of the superluminal transponder.

"All systems are functional, Commander," the computer replies, almost instantly.

"That's impossible," Mom says. "We haven't been able to send or receive data from Earth in fifty-two days. Something is wrong with the transponder."

"I do not detect a malfunction, Commander," the computer says.

"Then run the diagnostic again," Mom snaps.

My heart thuds against my ribs as the computer works. Once. Twice. Three times. Four.

"All systems are functioning within normal parameters, Commander," the computer says, calmly. Of course it's calm. It's a computer. It doesn't have a setting for panic.

"Fine," Mom says, pulling up the manual diagnostic panel as she speaks. "Send a ping to the Earth beacon. Request immediate response."

"Yes, Commander," the computer says.

I turn to look down at Tau Ceti e. The Southern Continent is below us now—vast and almost black-green in places, it's so rich with vegetation. Beyond it the ocean drapes the orbital horizon in a thousand shades of green-blue. That's when I see them. A cluster of brilliant lights rising behind the planet. They aren't stars. They're too close.

Anxiety prickles over my skin like a thousand tiny spiders.

"Is that a ship?"

Mom follows my gaze.

"What the f—"

"I have an incoming transmission, Commander," the computer says. "From the ISA *Prairie*."

"On-screen," Mom says. It's almost a whisper.

Grandpa's face flickers onto the wall screen in front of us. His head is still shaved and sticky with drying inso goo. "Alice, thank Christ."

"What are you doing here, Dad?" Mom says. "We aren't ready for a second wave. There have been complications—"

"It doesn't matter," he says, cutting her off. "The Earth . . ." He swallows hard, like he has to brace himself to say it out loud. "The Earth Restoration Project . . . things went wrong, Alice. Horribly, horribly wrong. Earth is uninhabitable. This is all that's left of humanity. Tau is our home now."

ACKNOWLEDGMENTS

It's possible that I am the luckiest woman on Earth. I was born to parents who love me and have always challenged me to follow my path wherever it leads. I've managed to collect a group of friends along the way who are there for me no matter how big or small the problem, no matter how far away we happen to be from each other at the time. I'm married to a wonderful man who makes me a better person, and together we have somehow managed to produce a tiny human who is better than either of us. And as if that wasn't enough, I have the supreme privilege of writing stories that other people get to read. I have so much gratitude for that, and for all the people in my life who make that possible.

A few of them have been particularly active in supporting

the creation of this book. First, *The Pioneer* would not exist without the impossible persistence of Petersen Harris. So . . .

Thanks, Pete.

I must also say a heartfelt thank-you to Wyck Godfrey for his inspiration and guidance in crafting this story. Also, Marty Bowen and Isaac Klausner at Temple Hill for helping *The Pioneer* find its way in the world. And, of course, many thanks to Emilia Rhodes and Alice Jerman at Harper-Teen, first for saying yes and then for helping me shape the world of *The Pioneer* into a novel. I'm also deeply grateful for Simon Lipskar and Genevieve Gagne-Hawes at Writer's House, who have tirelessly read my drafts and advocated for me and for this book.

But they aren't the only ones. A number of generous and talented people have contributed their thoughts, feelings, and time to help me make this book what it is. Without Alli Dyer, this book would not be nearly as cool. It would also have far too many commas. Menaka Chandukar has listened to me talk about the fictional planet of Tau Ceti e and its inhabitants far more than it's reasonable to ask of anyone. And Tom Brady has always offered his clear eyes and guidance through the wilderness of draft writing. Then there's Katie Lovejoy, Kaitlyn Wittig Menguc, Janice Kao, Nicola Monat-Jacobs, Jane Nelson, Amber Berdie, Dr. Kagan Tumer, Dr. Liney Arnadottir, First Officer Kevin Millard, and Dr. Manda Clair Jost. Thank you all for lending me your expertise to make this world, and this future, as authentic and accurate as possible.

And last, but certainly not least, my family: My parents, Connie and Kenneth Tyler, who have always given me their ears, their eyes, and their constant support. My husband, Dr. Geoff Hollinger, who provided both his scientific expertise and his imagination in helping me create the world of *The Pioneer* and hardly ever complained about me typing in bed until all hours of the night. And my daughter, Toni, for whom the adventure of life is just beginning.

BRIDGET TYLER

grew up in Berkeley, California. She went on to attend NYU, living in New York and London before completing her degree and moving to Los Angeles to work in the film and television industry as an executive and writer. She now lives in Oregon with her husband, a robotics professor at Oregon State University, and her daughter.

Visit her online at
www.bridgettyler.com.